NORTHWARD DREAMS

NORTHWARD DREAMS

a novel

MISSOURI BREAKS PRESS

Missouri Breaks Press
missouribreakspress@gmail.com

Missouri Breaks Press paperback ISBN-13: 979-8-9903324-2-3
Missouri Breaks Press e-book ISBN-13: 979-8-9903324-1-6

Visit the author's website at www.craig-lancaster.com

Printed in the United States of America

0 9 8 7 6 5 4 3 2 1

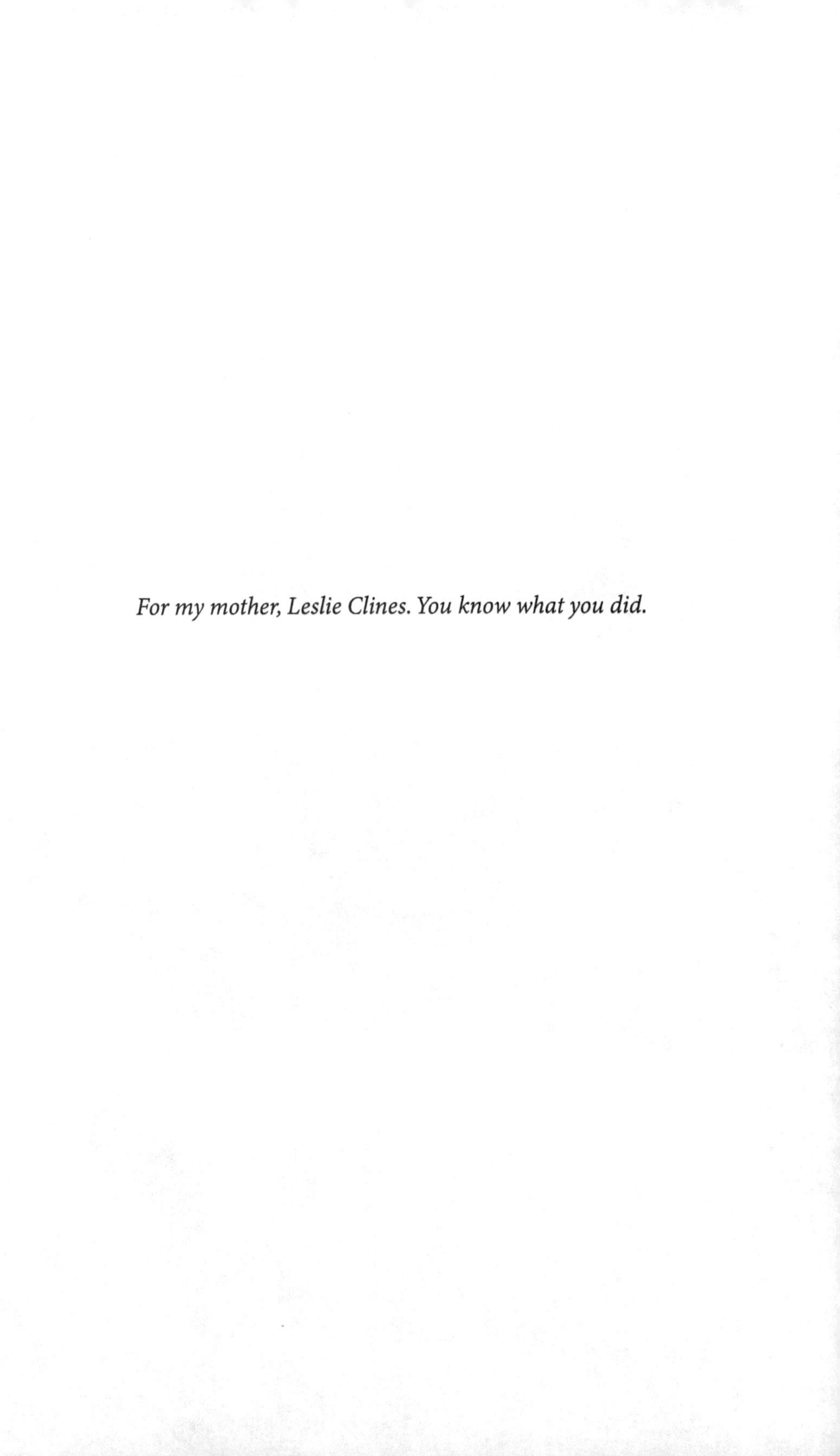

For my mother, Leslie Clines. You know what you did.

Opal Knudsen

1926-2002

You step out the back door and alight in the patchwork yard that's been beaten raw by winter and washed away by spring and is soon to be burned up by summer. You close your eyes and take a big snort of the June air. It's warm, warmer than it's been in some days, and you're thankful for it, for what it portends. These bones, especially, and your doggedly stubborn left side, still not back to full strength, are thankful for it. You open your eyes, and the sense of now that rests uneasily alongside your memories comes crashing in on you.

Another house going up on the last twenty acres you sold off. That'll be ten tidy little structures now, another twenty to come, arranged in pretty, curved rows that enfold each other, if the blueprint tacked to the inside wall of the construction shed over there is to be believed. You'd dropped by just last week, a fresh huckleberry pie and a round of reminiscence on offer, an old lady's take on the way things used to be around here, when you could move without getting your arms entangled with someone else's. A "thank you, ma'am" for the pastry, a bit of quiet indulgence for the rest as you shook out your memories for those young men, then back to work they went, mumbled thanks flung in your direction. It's their dirt now. Let them do with it as they will.

In your nearer vision, it's the same thing, what is now and what was before held uneasily together by memory and by old photographs you have inside the house somewhere. With just a bit of the money from the last land sale, you'd had the barn bulldozed at last and sold off for scrap lumber. Wasn't any living thing that needed it anymore, wasn't any reason for you to go wandering in— you'd steadfastly resisted it whenever you could, a sidestepping of the unwanted memories it held—and wasn't a place where anybody had any business. Many was the time back then that you'd stand outside it, yelling at your toddling daughter to get out of there and stick to the house. *I don't want you in there, you hear me?* And she'd come out, sheepish and scolded, and tell you she was just having fun, and you'd say, *yes, yes, I know, but there's rats and snakes in there, and you need to stay away from it.* It's been weeks now since the whole works got pushed over and tumbled down and trucked away, and still you come out to the yard and feel the pure astonishment that it's not there. Time, you've decided, works that way, puts certain expectations on you, then dares you to accept what changes may come. You can't resist, and if you give up your agency, you just get pulled along in the wake until it's done with you, or you're done with it.

You're not done with it, you've decided. They've been on you to come west, "assisted living" being the particularly nasty pile-up of words they've conjured, and you're not going to do it, so long as you have a voice to speak. You've fought for the ground under your feet. And if there have been losses along the way—and surely there have been, if you care to number them off, and you don't, not anymore— you've come by them honestly. A woman can live on that.

You kneel, the knees of your jeans in the mud, and you take the clipping shears from your apron pocket. You size up the job, and you pitch forward into the bush.

Two crows, languid on the telephone line above, bear witness. Across the way, the hammering goes on, beating out a rhythm, a simple song for the dead and gone.

1

August 2012 | Denton County, Texas

The jangle of the cellphone—unmistakable, jarring, relentless—enters the slipstream of a sunken reverie, a mishmash of now and then, of events known and impressionistic, of faces presented and obscured, of times endured and never breached. As the tone loops through for a second run-through, then a third, Nate Ray tumbles nearer consciousness. His hand emerges from under the sheet and cuts off the ringer, then slips back into the crumpled bedding left sticky and sour from night sweats.

The light comes in now, defying the inclination toward running down sleep again. Nate's eyelids flap. He's on his back, staring into the plastic molded ceiling, fixated on the AC unit that up and stopped whirring a week ago, more maintenance deferred until god knows when.

She's gone. Nate knows that sure enough even with his eyes closed. It was a jackpot the night before that she'd even come around, and there had been some unspoken—*thank Christ*—finality to it all, a let's-have-one-last-hurrah roll together through the night. He'd fallen asleep with his nose in her chest, that much he remembered, and here he is alone, as it should be, no memory of her eventual movement toward the door.

Nate folds himself up to sitting, halfway at least, elbows at his sides like hydraulic lifts, pushing him up. He's making an inventory now of every ache—the ones chronic, like the left knee Doctor Simmons at the VA says will need replacing, and the ones that come on without warning or an appointment.

Next, he swings his legs toward the floor, cupping the trouble knee with his hands to keep it stabilized. The problem, of course, is that Doctor Simmons, wise though he may be, isn't the authority on exactly when the knee will be dealt with and who'll be carrying the freight on it. It's the latter point on which Nate and Veterans Affairs find themselves at an unbalanced impasse, Nate's contention being that an unremarkable stint in the navy ought to be good for a new knee, at least, and the VA's contention being that, well, no. It's a staredown the bureaucrats can play into eternity—it's not their knee, after all—and the list of deferred maintenance grows ever longer.

The melodic ping comes, alerting him to a message, and Nate grabs the phone and flips it open to see what he's missed in the fitful night and early morning. The deliverer of the latest voice mail, Ronnie, can wait—*forever would be nice*, Nate thinks, *but fat chance of scoring that kind of luck this late into things*. Karen's message, dropped in at 6:23 a.m., no doubt soon after she granted her own release from the trailer, bears listening.

I tried to wake you. Figures. You know, I keep hoping you'll actually surprise me and show up. Guess I'll know in an hour and a half or so. Listen, Nate, if you don't, I'm gonna need you to hitch up and get off my property, OK? It's too hard.

"Too hard for the both of us," he says, and he deletes the message. It's a hell of a thing, he thinks not for the first time, to have these get-togethers be a point of such pain when daylight comes around again and reconsideration is put on the table. Everything he's taken, she's offered first. The job he never wanted. The pastureland he parked the trailer in two months ago, useful enough but also not as rare as gold. She's doing him a favor, sure, but it's not the last one he'll ever have a chance to call in. He's parked the rig in other places at other times, and he reckons he can find someplace new if it comes to that, if she's really had her fill, or if he's had his. It's gotten to the point that she wants something he's not prepared to give and she's not prepared to say, and this indistinct thing lies down between them at night, taking up most of the bed.

He moves into the living area of the trailer—he's seen this space called "the great room" in some of the newer models he's gawked at down at Camping World, but this isn't that in any configuration. It has a two-burner gas stove, the propone nearly drained, and a refrigerator that runs cold, praise be, but also cultivates mystery flora sprouting from foam boxes holding half-consumed takeout dinners. No microwave. No dishwasher. He's overdue for a black-water dump. A single basin aluminum sink ringed with gunk from who knows when. Sitting adjacent is a tattered couch, shedding foam like dandruff from the holes in the arms, and it lies aligned with the thirteen-inch color TV he's strapped into place with old speaker wire and which pulls in two over-the-air channels, and sometimes three if it's not raining, from the antenna he's rigged up on the roof. *Home.*

Nate takes a swig from the open bottle of Canadian Club that sits on the countertop. He cringes and squints and he smacks his lips and savors the washaway of morning tacky mouth, and he takes another for good measure, hair of the dog and all that.

The realizations and lines of thought that come to Nate these days don't lay out in parallels or even perpendiculars. They're at odd angles, lying crosswise against each other, overlapping, one thought the ignition source for some other bleak firing of the synapses that, sometimes, improves his position but mostly leaves him befuddled and behind the flow of things. The whisky has set his mind on spirits, which oddly, or maybe even predictably, brings into his head the voice of his learned son, the word pusher, who told him once about how whisky, no "e," refers to the Scottish and Canadian and even Japanese grain spirits but that whiskey, full-on "e," is for the grain spirits distilled here and in Ireland, and anyway, you shouldn't drink so much of it, Dad, because you know how you get. "Well," Nate had said, in another loosing of the tongue that he's regretted far longer than it ever took him to say the words, "that's fascinating and all, but I ain't interested in the vowels. Just the dollar signs and not too damn many of those, thank you very much."

He needs to call Brandon, he knows, but he needs to call Ronnie first, because that's the more loathsome chore and the one that might divert him directly back to that bottle and the identical one under the sink, if memory serves right.

Nate flips the phone open again and sets it on the countertop for easy dialing. He roots through the fridge and brings out a couple of eggs, turns on the burner and hopes for enough flame to get them scrambled, and when the works are all up and running, he patches through the number to the old man, who answers on the second ring with "You listen to my message?"

"No."

"Why the hell not?"

"I've missed you, Pop. Couldn't wait to talk to you." Nate reaches for the bottle, has it by the neck like a pullet, then lets it go.

"Sure."

"What do you need?"

"I need you to come over and spring me from this mortuary, which you'd know if you'd listened to me in the first place."

"Oh. Well, why didn't you say so?"

Nate says it only because he knows it'll bind the old man up something fierce, and the sputtering "I goddamn did" comes back as validation. Nate again toys with the bottle of whisky.

"OK, where we going?" A summons from Ronnie isn't new or notable. The place he calls "this mortuary" is, in fact, a perfectly respectable assisted-living center just north of Fort Worth, which has taken in Nate's father for the low, low price of his monthly Social Security check, his retirement disbursement, and the keys to a single-wide trailer house that's long since been liquidated and picked over for cash. When Ronnie gets restless, he calls for a ride, and Nate can usually settle him down with a middling beer or two and a plate of decent barbecue.

"Montana," Ronnie says.

"No, really."

"Really."

"I'm not going to Montana."

"You damn sure are. Gonna pick me up first, though."

"Why?"

"Because I said so."

The eggs, neglected, run hot, headed for hardness and, eventually, carbon, and Nate splashes them with the whisky. The liquid hisses and bubbles, and Nate scrapes at the mess with a spatula. "Gotta go," he says.

"No," Ronnie says. "Wait. I really need your help with this."

Nate turns off the gas, lifts the pan with a crusted rag, slaps it against the rim of the sink and splatters the contents.

"Why?"

"Your aunt died."

Nate blinks. "Linda?"

"Yeah."

"Your sister, you mean."

"Yeah," Ronnie says.

"I didn't know her. Not my business."

"Look, look," Ronnie says, and it's almost plaintive, almost vulnerable, a damn rarity from him. "I need a ride. Come on. Don't make me beg."

"I can't afford to make that trip." Nate looks around him at the squalor he's managed to ignore until the moment it all falls over onto him. "Ride the bus if it's so important to you."

"I'll pay."

"Right."

"I have some cash squirreled away."

"How much?"

"Enough. You coming?"

Nate rather doubts his story. A room, Ronnie has. Three squares, ditto. Somebody to clean his linens and buck out his trash, certainly. Even some old coots for games of penny ante, and who knows, maybe he's taken down a modest fortune there. But he's cash-poor. They've been through this, a year and a half ago after the third heart attack, liquidating everything they could before Ronnie went in. But whatever. If he can't put the first tank of gas in the truck, it'll be a short trip. Nothing better to do.

"Yeah, in a bit," Nate says.

Nate packs for brevity, not comfort. It had been a chore to pull even the slightest of details out of the old man. Where we going? *Montana, I told you.* Yeah, but where? *Billings.* How long we gonna be there? *A day or two. Not long. What's it to you? Got something better to do?*

Nate supposes he doesn't, which explains the duffel that's filling with underwear and socks and two pairs of jeans and enough T-shirts to scoot through a week if he can put them to double duty. Because why the hell not, in terms hypothetical (Brandon and his vocabulary in his head again) and promissory. Nate wonders how much the rascal has stashed away, how long he's had it, whether he had it in January, when Nate called him from the drunk tank, looking for bail, and Ronnie had said, "Sounds like you'll have time to think about some stuff, boy." At last, he pulls the flask from his hip and tosses it atop the clothes, thinking maybe he'll leave it alone en route. Maybe.

Even the light task of packing leaves him lightheaded and sweaty, the trailer an oven as August throttles up the heat, last night's drinks coming through his pores. Would thirteen hundred miles northward bring some respite from that? Nate surely hopes so.

He's nearly ready when Brandon lands in his thoughts yet again, the phone call he's still to make, the favor he'll ask for with no decent odds that the answer he wants will be coming. What then? Well, another dance with Karen, another negotiation, another fractional gain, or maybe just a loss put off until it can be better absorbed.

Nate sends out the call.

"Not a good day" comes the response upon pickup.

"Just as well," Nate says. "I need you tomorrow."

"What?"

"Can you come get this trailer, tow it back to your place?"

"My place?"

"Yeah," Nate says. "Big request, I know. Wouldn't make it if . . . well, I wouldn't make it."

"No. I can't stash it here."

"Just for a couple of days, that's all."

"Your truck get repo'd?"

"No. But nice you'd assume so."

"Educated guess."

"I'm taking your grandpa up to Montana."

"Lucky you."

Nate draws a hand, stinky with cheap Canadian, across his nose and mouth. "Nothing you're thinking that I haven't already thought. Nothing smart you're gonna say that hasn't already flapped out of my gums. Can you help me?"

"I guess," Brandon says. "Kelly's not gonna like it."

"Well," Nate says, "add it to my tab."

"I'll take 'Things That Will Never Be Paid' for $600, Alex."

"Huh?"

"Nothing," Brandon says. "Never mind. I'll get your rig. But don't leave me hanging on this or I'll sell it for scrap. I'm serious."

It's not an idle threat, Nate knows. The squaring away of Ronnie's affairs had put a fright into him, and between benders, he'd made sure his own son's name was on everything so there wouldn't be any undue burdens if, someday, they found Nate's abandoned carcass down in Corsicana cozied up to some nice piece of ass. Not a bad way to go, all things considered.

"I hear you," Nate says. "Thanks."

There's no avoiding Karen in the leaving, and Nate has concluded that avoidance is already well played out as a relationship strategy, if *relationship* is even the word for what the two of them have been playing at. It's more like a friendship rooted in another time and place—high school, *Jesus Christ*—that has somehow endured, changing both broadly and imperceptibly through the decades and the weaving in and out of each other's sphere, until they were left with what they have: an employer-employee setup where the former is forever frustrated at the latter's chronic absenteeism, a personal rapport that finds communion in a bottle, and enough comfort and shamelessness with one another to get naked and have a go from time to time. Nate sees now, in hindsight, that it's the reintroduction of sex into matters that's fooling with them, more so, perhaps, than even the not showing up for work and the booze. She's been hinting that it portends something more for them, something deeper and more meaningful, and all the while he's been hoping for nothing more than another hard-on with the next spin of the rock. Time's coming fast when a guy won't even be able to count on that.

Whatever she's got in mind can't work like that. Nothing can, he thinks.

He stops off at her store on his way to the interstate, peels back the automatic window on the passenger side. She comes out and frames herself there in the gap, elbows poking across the boundary line.

"This is my answer, I guess," she says. She looks tired, no doubt because she *is* tired. She's built something here—more than a farm stand, more than a feed store, a place with knickknacks and baked goods and wooden spoons and all kinds of other stuff the interloping suburbanites from down around Dallas and Fort Worth find irresistible—and it siphons off her life in chunks. She really could have used his help, and that he never had any intention of giving it to her takes him only halfway to regret.

"Going north," he says. "The old man wants to see Montana."

A laugh squirts out of her. "The two of you, together, all the way up there?"

"Yup."

"Well, I'm grateful I'm not the cops in Colorado or Wyoming when you guys have your blowout. I'm grateful for that, at least."

He leans across the distance. "You've been real good to me, Karen. Better than I have coming."

"You're goddamned right. So what?"

"Brandon will get the trailer out of here tomorrow. He promised me he will."

"*His* word I can trust."

"All right, then," Nate says. "Be seeing you."

He engages the window, then she smacks the rising glass with an open hand, and he lowers it again. She leans farther in this time. He holds his spot.

"Take care of yourself out there, Nate," she says. "I probably won't be pissed at you forever, but I'm sure gonna try."

He nods, smiles, gives her a dorky salute that brings another sputtering laugh. "Forever's a long time, though."

2

October 1972 | Mills, Wyoming

It's the best part of the evening, on the nights when Electra can have it, and there haven't been nearly enough of those, she's come to find out in just a few months of wanting them. When Ronnie is on some highway somewhere—to Omaha and Des Moines and back again on this run, but it could be anywhere—and her boy is in bed and Charley's voice is coming over the line like in the Glen Campbell song, she can run the extension from the kitchen to the bedroom, fall back onto her own pillow, close her eyes, and imagine something else. Something better.

Something not this, anyway.

"You're all set?" Charley asks. The words come out tender and loving, even if they never invoke that word, *love*, when they talk, and yet the question is also fixed with a bailout she can hear, should her answer not be what he's hoping to receive. She gets the feeling he's been holding back, just a little, just in case she can't manage this thing she proposes to do. *Well, Charley Stidham, you beautiful man, prepare to be pleasantly surprised.*

"All set. Car is packed," she says. "I'm gone at first light."

"I'm glad," he says. "I've been waiting."

"Me, too." She laughs behind the words and gets a quizzical "what?" in response, and she knows it wasn't funny at all—it was entirely serious and entirely terrifying, actually, getting to this fraught point—but it's just how the remembrance of things strikes her now.

"I loaded the car in about three hundred trips Nathan never saw," she says. "He's down for a nap, and I run out with a suitcase. He's in the backyard, and I put the cooler in there. He's eating his macaroni, and I slip out with my purse. Didn't dare touch his toys or he'd know, so I'll grab those in the morning. I was dodging him all day. Like a spy."

"You haven't told him?"

"No," she says, "not yet. I think he knows, somehow. Not much gets by him. But I figure it's better to fess up when we're on our way and any fussing he does will be within the car doors."

"Perspicacious," Charley says.

"What's that?"

"Nathan. You said not much gets by him. He's perspicacious."

The rhythmic tumble of the syllables in Electra's ears pleases her in a way that she wouldn't be able to explain and wouldn't want to share with anyone else anyway. Charley has been doing that to her for going on four months now, across long-distance phone calls that always originate with him in Texas, lest they be found out, and always find her in Wyoming and must be putting a terrible dent in his check register. They're nothing, really, and yet also everything, his little asides, the crumbles of conversation he pulls out and examines, the way he tells her without saying so explicitly that he's heard her, that she has something to say and something he ought to acknowledge. Been a long time since she's felt that from someone else. He's closer to her now, at two days of hard driving, than Ronnie has been in years. When she realized that, there was no backing away from what it meant.

"You're so funny," she says. "This is why, you know."

"I know."

"You know how I feel."

"I know," he says. "Me, too."

She sits up, reaches into the end table drawer and withdraws the little satchel she's been hiding around the house, moving it daily in an abundance of caution or a surplus of paranoia. It's been in the pantry, where Ronnie would never look, and even in a spare tire in the garage, where he well might, a prospect that spooked her so thoroughly that she snuck out in the night and moved it into Nathan's closet. She opens the satchel and fingers the cash she's gathered, enough to get where they're going and then some. She checks to make sure her driver's license is there, the Social Security cards, the birth certificates. All is in order, same as it was an hour earlier, and an hour before that, and will be in the hours yet to come, when she'll surely keep checking.

She closes the satchel and flips it to the backside, where the tiny hashmarks she's cut with her fingernail sit stealthily, not even noticeable unless you know what you are looking for. One for every phone call, twenty-two now, and she uses her brightly painted forefinger to make another. *Twenty-three.* Twenty-three phone calls with Charley and one night in person that she holds close like something holy, and collectively those are the fulcrum by which she's going to wrench open the now and make a faithful leap toward whatever tomorrows may come.

"No chance he'll—" Charley starts, and she cuts him off with a terse "no, none."

"OK."

"He left a few hours ago," she says, softer now. "Probably not even in Nebraska yet."

"OK, good."

Electra looks at the clock. "Late where you are," she says.

"I guess. I'm not going to be able to sleep, I don't think."

"Me, either."

"But you need to," he says.

"Yes."

"I'm gonna let you go now," he says. "Tomorrow night. You call me collect. Let me know you're OK."

"I'll be OK when it's done."

"But in the interim," he says, and she smiles and assures him, saying, "I'll call. You can count on it."

"You know how I feel," he says.

"You know how *I* feel."

Electra douses the hall light, lest the spray spill into the bedroom when she cracks the door and slips inside to check on the boy, as she does nightly.

As the leaving has drawn near, it's been the hardest part for her, this dogged attention to doing normal things while waiting for the coming changes. Slinging her husband's—soon to be *former* husband's, and without too awful much thrashing about when it comes to that, she hopes—favorite meals when he's there. Letting him crawl atop her and have a go when she will never want it again, because denying him that would surely send up the reddest of flags. Quiet acquiescence in almost all things, punctuated by the occasional and outsized fight from her, usually about something measly and small, so he knows she's still possessed of at least some her own brain and pigheadedness. The last row, she remembers well. His eggs were not suitably runny, a fact he pointed out with what was, by any measure, a reasonable amount of tact. She pulled the plate from under his chin, smashed it to shards in the sink, told him where the pans were, said to make his own if hers were so damned deficient. That was Wednesday, and it's Monday now, and he'd moved silently and deferentially around her these past few days. Praise be for respites. Ever since she made her mind up, she's been carrying fear about the decision, and the bulk of it resides within rather than without. Not once, not ever, has he raised a hand to her or to the boy, even in frayed times when she thought for sure he would. She thinks that if she told him, look, I'm leaving you, he'd plead with her some but he wouldn't take any unreasonable measures in stopping her. She doesn't say it because she can't put sufficient words to her reasons even as they compel her to no other choice. She doesn't want what she has, not one minute longer, and she doesn't want it for Nathan, and that's everything. And nothing. She thinks sometimes maybe she's crazy. If she is, it's incurable.

She thinks about all of that, as she stands on Nathan's side of the door, and it grates on her in the recollect. It wasn't entirely calculated, her rant about the eggs, even if it had served her purposes. This is who she is these days, in large measure, a defensive and disproportionate woman with a hair trigger on her temper now that her mind is made up. And though she is well certain Ronnie has had his own role in breaking her will along the way—their years together have been a long while just in the abstract, let alone in the way she marks time, mostly alone—she figures she'd lain it out there to be fractured, and damned if she can pinpoint when. She thinks of what Amy, her lawyer, had said when she had asked if she was crazy for wanting what she wants. "No, you're not crazy. You're just determined to have it. *That's* the difference."

"Mommy?"

Her throat catches. *Damn.* She'd hoped for slumber.

"Yes?"

"Where are we going?"

Double damn.

"Going?"

"I know we are."

She crosses the room and nudges him, and he scoots over. She lies down next to her boy, same as she did a couple of hours earlier, when she'd read him a little bit of *Ghost Town Treasure* and he'd murmured along with the words, five years old and already in chapter books, the best of signs. His precocity is also a full signal of why these recent decisions are so vital. They're not just for her, though it's the selfish things that inform the way she's overtaken by fluttering when Charley calls. They're for Nathan, too. In the long run, she would say, they're mostly for him.

"We're going somewhere you'll like," she says.

"Daddy's not coming?"

"No, not this time." She bites off further words that might be coming up behind to bring a comforting context to things. On some day—one not too far off, she imagines—he'll have to be told the truth of the thing, that he lives in Texas now and Daddy doesn't and Mommy and Daddy don't live together anymore. She doesn't want to have to backtrack on promises she can't keep. That will be a hard day, one that might well set Nathan to bucking the new circumstances he'll be in. He loves his Daddy, as a boy should. A few hours earlier, he was standing in the front yard, waving goodbye as the truck and its load headed out to Poison Spider Road and then the highway, toward distant destinations. "I'll see you when you get home," Nathan shouted after the truck, a blared horn coming back to him in acknowledgment.

No, kid, you won't.

"Where?" Nathan presses.

"I'll tell you soon," she says, and she rotates toward him, blinking, letting in the light so she can see the lovely outlines of him. She runs fingers through the thicket of hair that matches his father's, coarse and dense and black as the room they're in. "For now, why don't you just close your eyes"—now she dots the eyelids with an index finger—"and imagine all the places we can go and all the things we can see."

"Africa," he says. *He knows what Africa is. What a kid.*

"Maybe. Someday, maybe."

"I want to see a zebra."

His eyes come open, seeking approval, and she touches them closed again.

"We could maybe do that," she says. "What fun we'll have if we do."

Nathan wriggles with joy and nestles into her, and the gravity of it drops atop her. She's known straight along that it's going to be hard, but the degree is only now coming to her, when there's nothing left to plan and only the scariest of it to do. She wishes she could get Charley on the line for one last pep talk, but unless he intuits this desire and makes the call, she'll have to ride this one out alone.

"Will you stay here with me?" he asks.

"*Shhh.* Sleep now. I'll stay for a bit. But you have to sleep."

"I will," he whispers.

She sets her head back on the pillow. He burrows into the covers.

She listens. She waits. She doesn't close her own eyes, leaden as they feel in her head. Too much to do. Such scant time to do it in. It's all so close now, and all so immeasurably far.

When Electra is certain he's down to stay, she disentangles herself from the boy and leaves the mattress by inches, careful to keep the shifts from being too abrupt and rousing him. She's standing by the bed when he flops onto his stomach, his left arm dangling at an angle possible only in unconsciousness, and she catches her breath and waits for his rhythmic inhales and exhales to return. When they do, she takes her leave.

In the kitchen, she piles lunchmeat on bread dotted with yellow mustard and mayonnaise, and these she wraps in wax paper and deposits into a plain brown paper sack. Lunch for the coming tomorrow, and maybe even the one beyond that, if her attitude toward eating is the same as it's been for a week now. She's barely kept anything down, scurrying when she can to the backyard and yakking in the unraked leaves. Tomorrow night, in Trinidad,

Colorado, if the timeline she's charted holds, she'll get Nathan some of that infernal fast food he clamors for, a McDonald's hamburger or a bucket of chicken. He'll like that, and though she abhors the stuff, it'll serve as recompense for the patience she'll be asking him to exercise.

Next, she brews a pot of coffee, and she stands near the percolator and lets the steamy tendrils of the deep roast swirl through her system. When it's done, she transfers it to a battered metal thermos, the only thing she's taking that's Ronnie's alone. He can fight her for it in the divorce if he wants it back. That paperwork will be hitting his table soon enough.

When she's done with all that, she washes the soiled dishes and utensils, dries them, puts them away. She sweeps the kitchen, dusts the furniture, straightens the family photos, the play acting they did in happier times, on the wood-paneled wall. She figures she owes him two things, and only those two: a fair brokering when they get to the legalities, and a clean house when he returns to find the rupture. She aims to deliver on both.

All of that finished, Electra realizes that she needn't have worried about sleep at all, that she's dead tired and—she checks the clock on the kitchen wall—just shy of five hours away from getting gone. She goes into the bedroom, hips aching, and she takes the alarm clock from the bedside table and carries it to the couch and sets it. She'll sleep here. Her last rest in that bed, *his* bed, has come and gone, and good riddance to it.

She lies back at an angle, right arm folded over and behind her head, and she almost gets out a full remembrance of Charley's first words to her before exhaustion wins.

"Yours is the reddest hair I've ever seen."

"Yeah, well, I didn't choose it."

"Why not? It's the prettiest color there is."

3

July 2002 | Billings, Montana

They're in the thick of the city, Cherie and her mom, and it's coming together—what Cherie recognizes, what's changed, the fuzziness of memory about how long it's been. A while, for sure.

"When'd we last come out this way? Together?" Cherie asks, face still tilted toward the passenger-side glass and the warehouses of the industrial district sliding past.

Anna clears her throat but doesn't say anything. Cherie spins herself a quarter-turn, granting attention.

"Mom?"

"I'm trying to think," Anna says now. "I guess if I have to think about it, it's been too long, huh?"

"I guess." Cherie considers her hands, clenched in her lap and squeezing blood from the knuckles. She relaxes the grip. She makes a hitch in her seating position, toward Anna.

Her mother has gotten old, and fast. Old to begin with in their journey together, at least by society's convention, a thirty-one-year-old first-time mother, only-time mother as it'll turn out, unless she's got a whale of a surprise lurking out there in the future. She's forty-nine now, and Cherie is cognizant of how every annum has etched itself into the weary face and the bony hands and the loosening skin of her arms and the hair that's thinning out, not noticeable in the day to day but certainly so in the longer view she's been afforded.

Anna snaps her fingers.

"Two years ago, come Thanksgiving," she says. "That's when it was, I'm pretty sure."

"No. That long?"

"Yep."

Cherie sure enough remembers that. Her grandma wasn't like the stereotype, certainly wasn't like the kindly, matronly, pillowy-soft grandmas some of her friends have. So it had been a surprise that year when she had called them and said, "I don't feel like makin' the drive this year. You come to me, how about?" Opal Knudsen's taking a pass on drinking downtown at night and skiing the Lick Creek Loop by day should have been all the signal they needed that something wasn't quite right, but they'd simply loaded up and driven into Billings from Bozeman, a couple of hours, shared the only other bedroom in Opal's house and made their way through a Thanksgiving dinner, such as it was, three Hungry-Man trays nuked into dryness. They then watched Randy Moss and the Vikings burn the Cowboys on Opal's snowy TV screen. All around, something short of satisfying.

"We should have come more often," Cherie says, and in the next moment she regrets the words, because she knows her mother will calcify them in her heart. "But, you know, life and stuff."

"Life and stuff," Anna repeats. "It gets in the way."

Cherie grins, big and encouraging, and she juts it out there until her mother makes eye contact and ponies up her own, grimmer smile. Surely Anna has regrets; piling those up comes with the mere act of living, which Cherie knows to be true enough even from the vantage point of her mere eighteen years. Just as Anna wanted to pull away from Opal, wanted to find the distance that gave her both sovereignty and some easy means of getting back to her mother in a time of need, so does Cherie want to cut loose and fling herself toward the horizons. She could have had Annapolis and all that follows, clear paths to wherever she imagines she might want to go. Instead, she'll be taking day classes at Montana State, at home in Bozeman. It's just the two of them now, has been for a long time, and with Opal gone, this is no time to be bailing, she has decided.

"We should have," Anna says. "It just—"

"I know," Cherie says. It just went by quick, and endings have a tendency toward the sudden and the unexpected. Opal, waking up on a fine June day, doggedly and insistently independent even after the stroke in the winter of 2001. Opal, pitching over in the hydrangea soon after, found there by a neighbor in the falling dusk. *Here, gone.*

The same effect holds in the smaller life cycles. One day you're a sophomore and you can't imagine a bigger thrill than receiving the attentions of Brett Tomashek. The next, after seemingly a rushed in-between time, you're wearing a mortarboard and being handed a diploma and Brett Tomashek and every other boy—you know what they want, and you will not give it up—can go pound sand. You have things to do.

Anna cuts left at the fairgrounds and the car heads up the rise into the Billings Heights, disconnected from and almost a distant cousin of the city in the bowl, the one hemmed in by rimrocks to the north and the Yellowstone River to the south. Traffic grows thicker, like a stew left on the range. Cherie recognizes the contours but is baffled by the particulars and the transience of strip malls, of chain fast food, of nail salons and dog groomers. She settles back. It'll be a just a bit yet before it all thins out and they come to the turnoff toward Opal's place.

"How you feeling?" Anna asks.

"Antsy."

"Me, too."

"A little sad."

Anna murmurs something indistinct, and then, "Me, too."

Cherie fidgets. The larger truth of the matter is that she didn't want to come but also didn't see any way to pass on it. Life's obligations, she is finding out, don't fit into just one box. There are those you take onto yourself, like a mortgage or, more particular to her, a student loan. There are those thrust upon you, homework and job duties and the like, or the way her mother rallied out here for a week after Opal's stroke. And then there are those that are handed out the moment you draw breath and are fully revealed to you over time. Here's your family. You don't know them, you might not even come to like them, but they're yours, and you're now a carrier of the story they've given you. You can expand it, write the next turns in a different color of ink, turn slapstick into sorrow or prosperity into horror, but you have a responsibility to the underpinnings.

So here you are. And here comes Opal's little white house on a little piece of land that was once something grander until she sold it off, chunk by chunk, as she bowed to age and the need of money. Her land once grew sugar beets and alfalfa. Now, it sprouts subdivisions.

And here comes that prickle on the skin, that feeling beyond all rationality that Opal is still there somehow, that the atoms have scattered but the spirit persists, and Cherie is going to have to go in there and do what needs to be done, to close this thing out and to hold her splintering mother together, and that all seemed so much more possible when it was just a concept and not an in-your-face reality.

Anna parks the car and sets the brake, and she goes to pieces. Cherie loosens her seat belt and leans in across the console, arms around the older woman, head on her shoulder, words and warm breath on her ear. "It's OK, Mom. Really, it's OK."

Inside, it's a gut shot of just how much has to be done yet. "How can one woman have so much . . ." Cherie stretches her arms and oscillates her head, taking it all in again, the sheer magnitude of a lifetime's piling up. "So much shit. Let's call it what it is."

Anna, across the living room, clucks her tongue at the profanity even as she's equally awed by the size of the chore before them. Cherie can see it in her mother's face. They knew, but they didn't know, and now here's the realization.

"Don't say *shit*," Anna says. "Say *opportunity*."

"Opportunity for what? Eventual back surgery?"

"Honey."

Cherie walks the circumference, shaking her head. It really is remarkable how the tonnage didn't register when Opal was a living, breathing creature, responsible for it all and free to choose whether to have it or not. You're not thinking of yourself in a time like that, not imagining a day when she won't be here and what's hers will now be yours, and the onus for dealing with it will be on you alone. Cherie thinks now that if she had been able to project this out, she might have said, "Hey, grandma, when'd you become such a packrat?" and maybe tease her into some sort of action. She can also well imagine the rejoinder that would have been volleyed back.

"And anyway," Anna says, "it's not one person. It's her. It's me. It's my grandparents before us. It's you, too. I'll bet you find some of your dolls and picture books somewhere."

"Hooray," Cherie says. "An archeological dig."

"Oh, stop."

"Seriously. Have you been down to the basement? Photo albums piled to the ceiling. Boxes. More boxes after those. So many boxes."

"I want those albums," Anna says.

"Sure."

"And the dishes."

"Why?"

"Because I do."

"OK," Cherie says.

They've talked about this, what they'll salvage and what they'll scrap, and there's one thing only that Cherie wants, a 1930s Thorens powder puff music box, given to Opal by her own mother after a trip to New York, a little painting of three women on the canister top. It plays "I Kiss Your Hand, Madame" and "Button Up Your Overcoat," and the plinking notes—and the hardier ones Opal was given to idly humming—run through Cherie's memories. First thing she did, upon arrival, was flit inside, take it from the mantelpiece, and carry it back to the car.

But Anna wants more, understandable because there's more of her here, and that's fine, but they had not discussed the dishes. They're nothing special—there had been no wedding, and thus there was no fine china pattern—and Cherie fears that her mother's grief will move ever more items from the "junk it" pile to the "take it" group, and she'll be faced with this same problem again, down the road, when another generation falls away and its tidal wave of crap lands on someone else. On her.

Anna is gone again inside the pain, and she slumps into Opal's TV-watching chair and covers her eyes and tries to smother the heaves, but there's nothing to shroud what's happening to her. It's been like this since they got the word, unpredictable spasms of grief, not so much that they've rendered Anna nonfunctional, but also unrelenting when they come on. When Cherie yields to her own crying, it's not so much for Opal, whom she surely misses but also just as surely knew would be leaving eventually and who squeezed more than the actuarial projection from this life. No, she cries for her own mother and the burdens she carries that can't be relieved.

Cherie kneels to her mom and says, "Come on, now." Anna gamely wipes her face clear and smiles and says, "I know."

Cherie stands. "Let's start tomorrow. I saw a restaurant up on Main Street, looked good. Let's eat, then let's start fresh on this stuff in the morning."

"No," Anna says, "I'd like to get started now."

"One load," Cherie says. "One trailer load, so we can start in the morning with a dump run. Then dinner. Compromise?"

"Compromise."

Cherie stretches a hand to her mother, who takes it and comes up from the chair.

"I'll start in here," Anna says, waving a hand across the overstuffed living room.

"Good enough. I'll start sorting out the back."

Cherie leaves her there and cuts through the hallway, to the two bedrooms that parallel each other. On the wall, black-and-white still lifes Opal took as a younger woman, and a portrait that catches Cherie's attention, a sour-faced old woman she's looked at many, many times before, but now, with the dying-light shadows crossing the woman's jowls, she sees deeper into the visage. Hannah Knudsen, Opal's mother, foretold her daughter's old-lady features back in the 1940s, as her time was drawing nigh, and she also zooms forward a half-century and has something to say about how time is sanding away at Anna. It frightens Cherie. *Is this what I have to look forward to?*

She touches the frame, tilts it upward to get it on the level. She then moves a finger across Hannah's face and darkens the light. By the time the photograph was taken, there had been loss, a lot of it, principally Alvin, Hannah's husband and Opal's father, and Hannah's biggest loss, her own passing, was edging into view. This was a woman who'd earned her right to be grim as she sat for a portrait. This was also a woman who saw and presumably heard a delicate, lovely music box while visiting a great American city and brought it home, in essence, to a girl who would be born in 1984, far beyond Hannah's own reach. That's something, isn't it?

"Smile, great-grandma," Cherie whispers. "It's not all bad."

4

September 1952 | Three Forks, Montana

Dusk has come up and bowed quickly to darkness in the river valley, and the boy is running late. A morning of fence-mending stretched on to an afternoon and then an early evening—it got so as Berta drove out in the truck at lunchtime, bringing sandwiches and lemonade when he and Tom didn't show—and now he's hunched over in the chicken coop, laying into the last of his chores, his arena lit up by a single lightbulb.

"Ronnie?" Berta's voice comes to him from outside.

He backhands the sweat off his brow. "Just finishing up."

"Ronnie, come eat. This'll wait. I'll help you after supper."

"Rather just get it done, thanks."

He hears the patter of her clogged feet to the door, and this is no damn good. Where's he going to put her when she comes in? Tom Foley built this coop for eight laying hens and one confident rooster, Ol' Jeff, and one person, and not so much room for the last of those.

She breaches the door and pushes herself into the jamb. She's a small woman, maybe just a smidge under five feet, strong with her hands and wide of berth and soft in the eyes. Ronnie can't look at her without remembering the first time he saw her and Tom, as he stood there on their front stoop, trying to puff himself up bigger than he was. Once he saw her take the measure of him, he had a hope that they'd say yes, and they did.

"Tom's antsy to eat," she says.

"I don't mean to keep him. I'll be done soon."

He sets back to his work, but her presence has changed the space, two people breathing in it, two sets of eyes, two hands working and two wringing. He feels her gaze on his back, and he turns to her.

"What?"

"Nothing," she says. The cold air has made its way in and turns her breath to vapor.

"OK."

"It's just—" She starts and stops in the same breath, then she starts again. "You've been inside yourself lately."

"Have I?"

"You have. It's all right. I don't want to pry."

Ronnie thinks that's true enough, she doesn't want to be nosy, but she also surely knows she has a talent for drawing him into saying things he doesn't necessarily want to part with. She's warm and kindly, and in conversation she shuts up and listens, a rarity in his sixteen years of experience. What she and Tom know about him, not even the half of it and yet more than Ronnie ever expected to tell, is on account of her not prying and not flapping her mouth when her ears are open.

He sets down a cup of feed.

"You know I owe you and Tom more than I could repay, right?"

"Ronnie, it's us what owes you."

He backhands another line of sweat off his brow, feels the sandy grit. He knows the stink hangs heavy on him.

"Even so," he says, "I'm grateful. I want you to know that."

She nods and smiles, and this is how she does it, the not butting into business that isn't hers. Sure enough, he keeps going.

"I've been thinking I'd like to find my dad. Been on my mind."

"Your—"

"My dad," he says. "I ain't talked about him, I don't think."

"Where is he?"

Yes, well, that's the puzzler, Ronnie thinks. "I don't know. Might still be up Great Falls way. I heard him talk about Butte, I think. Once. I was just a kid. I don't really know anything about him."

"Bozeman, maybe?" she asks, and he hears the hope in her voice. Bozeman is just down the valley, same county. Bozeman would be easy, if he were there.

"I don't know. Maybe."

"I see."

"I got a name," he says. "Not much else. Nothing else, truthfully."

"A name's a start."

"I guess."

A shrill whistle, a single note coming from the porch, slices the night and penetrates the walls of the coop.

"Come on," she says, holding out a hand for him, beckoning. "Let's eat. Tom'll have some ideas about this, I imagine."

It's harder in the telling the second time around, different as the audience is. Ronnie figures they don't make them better than Tom Foley—he minds his business, he does what's right without having to debate himself, he doesn't say much and doesn't have to, because the doing leaves no mystery about where he stands. It's that last part, the leading silence, that makes finding the words a harder task than it was with Berta.

Still, Ronnie chokes it out, the broad strokes of it anyway. There's a man he knew when he was a little tyke, his dad, and thirteen years have gone by since then and he'd like to see him again, if he's out there for the seeing. Tom takes this in, his dinner plate pushed away, having been relieved of its beefsteak and scalloped potatoes and green beans.

"We've never asked you much about things up there," Tom says, pointing northward, the general direction from which Ronnie came to them.

"I appreciate that, sir."

"But gotta ask you this: Would you be safe around this fella?"

Safe, now there's a word not exactly precise in its meanings. Ronnie can't rightly say safe is a luxury he's known. He flashes on his first weeks with Tom and Berta, springtime, when the night terrors would chase him out of bed and into the barn and he'd hide under straw until daybreak, then come slinking back to the house for breakfast. Those acts would have been irrational if not for his direct knowledge of occasions when hiding himself away would have spared him a beating, or deferred one, anyway. Tom put a stop to it with a simple, terse "ain't nothing going to happen to you here, boy" when they'd taken a break from back-furrowing the south field. Ever since, Ronnie has stuck to his bed, a stretch going on a year and a half now.

"I think so," Ronnie says. "He never raised a hand to me."

"From what you're saying, he never saw you get more'n knee high to a grasshopper."

"That's true."

"What I'm saying is," Tom says, "you don't think so, but you don't know for sure."

"No," Ronnie says. "But still, I'd like to find him."

"I see."

Here, Berta steps in to shore up the give-and-take inadequacies of her husband. "We understand. We'll do what we can for you."

"Thank you," Ronnie says.

"We'll help," Tom says. "Going to have to be delicate in the looking around. You say he might be in Great Falls?"

"The Fairfield Bench."

"So around there, anyway," Tom says.

"Might be. That's where I saw him last."

"Well, OK. I'll ask around a little bit, see if I can get a line on him. Don't want anything too public up there, though."

"No," Ronnie says.

"We'll find him," Tom says. "Meantime, you stay on what needs doing around here, OK?"

"Sure."

"This could take a bit, and you're not gone yet."

Ronnie looks to Berta, who's welling up.

"Yes, sir," he says.

Ronnie Ray

1936-

You sit in the single-wide that you'd asked for—no, *demanded*—as the absolute minimum for even considering coming back. Set off from the house, it's two hundred and thirty-eight square feet for you and for her and for every dream you'd packed up back at Fort Ord and deferred until later. All against your better judgment. All because of a letter from your sister asking, begging, you to come and help set the farm right. *Bob and I can't*, she'd written, *and they're going to lose it*, and the implication was that you could, that you didn't have any better prospects. And you didn't—stuck at E-3, best marksman in the outfit but too headstrong to get promoted up the chain, and forget NCO, buddy boy, because that was never going to happen. Dead end. New wife. No prospects on the horizon. Nineteen hundred and sixty-three staring you in the face. Your thirtieth year, just a few turns away.

Yeah, OK, you'd said, and here you are. And now you're stuck.

If you're being honest—and why not?—it is different now. The first time he went to manhandle you, you headlocked him there in the milking parlor—he couldn't move, could barely breathe—and you told him, "The next time, I kill you. And there won't be a third." The message had gone through clear enough, and he'd backed off. The crop had come in, you'd found a way to move around each other wordlessly to get it done. The farm, tottering, had been stabilized.

So what are you doing? Why are you still here?

The same questions come from Electra when she brings your coffee, before you head out into the maw of another day. You have no good answers. You came back—you knew you shouldn't have, people you trust as much as told you, long ago, that you should never come back—because . . . well, because of Ma. That's it. Dick could die at the bottom of a lake for all you care. But Ma, she was stuck here, stuck with him, his failures also her failures, and you couldn't bear that. You thought you could help. You thought, maybe, you could get on the right side with her at last, if you could sweep the rest away.

You can't. You see that now.

So you tell Electra that you've had your fill, that it's not working, that you want to go, and you know she's happy with that, because she wants to go, too. The occasional night out in Great Falls, some dancing and too much drink, just isn't cutting it. And here, on this lonely bench, she knows both too much and not enough. She's restless. She wants a baby, and you can't even begin to picture that, but she tells you there's a time coming when it'll happen and it'll be right, and that time won't come as long as the two of you are here. More than that, she's worried for you. You can feel it when you lie down with her at night, the tension that infuses everything.

"Where do you want to go?" she asks, and you tell her you don't know, that there's not much money for the going anyway.

"I could ask my folks."

No.

"I could," she says. "It's important."

Yeah.

"Where do you want to go?" she asks again.

So you tell her what's been on your head, bring up the name of Mike Ferguson, Fergie, your old pal, and you ask if she remembers him. "Vaguely," she says.

Fergie went home to Wyoming after leaving the Army. He's down there now, you say, driving a truck. Maybe you could catch on.

"Wyoming?"

It's just a thought, you say.

"A truck?"

You get with the right outfit, you say, and it could be a good living.

"What about California?" she asks.

No.

"OK."

It's played out, you say.

"OK. Well, let's go now. Tonight. Let's get out of here. I'll call Daddy."

OK, you say.

"OK," she says. "Wyoming."

You drain the last of the coffee. Hike up your pants and belt them tight. Put the cup in the sink and give her a kiss. He's out there, waiting for you, another day of chores and silent seething. You might or might not see Ma, depending. Either way, you're gone, and if it wouldn't hurt her so bad, you'd light the curtains on this place and watch it burn as you drive away.

5

October 1972 | Cheyenne, Wyoming

Electra waits while the young man outside her window pumps the gas. Freezing, sideways rain pelts him, soaking the flannel shirt he wears, and she wonders if he has a mother—of course he has a mother, everyone does, that's silly—but specifically she wonders if his mother saw him wearing that and heading out into this muck and just let him go. She imagines Nathan at a similar age, eighteen or nineteen at most, and sees herself with gray hair where the red is now, glasses perched on her nose, sitting on the couch with a blanket in her lap, as big, strapping, beautiful Future Nathan ducks his head through the doorway. Future Electra stops him with a gentle command: "Put on your slicker. It's raining."

They're in Cheyenne now, ten miles to the state line, if that, and thank god for it. The bottom half of Wyoming has been in their path like a rock, not just standing in the way of Colorado and below it New Mexico and Texas but also obscuring her ability to access the vision that has compelled her to where she now sits. What she imagines on the other end and holds like a security blanket is of little comfort now, when everything is a test of will and each slow-peeling mile is a hurdle. Every possession she cares to move forward with is packed up in her Firebird, her boy asleep in the white bucket seat beside her. He has scarcely moved since she carried him out in the early-morning darkness—so heavy he's getting—and set him into the seat and kissed him. A little stirring around Douglas, fifty miles into it, a fluttering of the eyes, words that followed: "We're on our adventure?" To that, she'd not been committed to full speech, just a guttural *mmm hmm* and silent pleas that he stay down in his slumber. He did. He has. He is. She's grateful.

The gas attendant, finished, goes to rap her window, and Electra throws up a hand to stop him, signals that she's getting out. She grabs her pocket purse from the console, opens the door and eases herself out. The attendant backs up. "Boy's sleeping," she says, soft as the morning. She pushes the door gently shut.

"Two-eighty-eight, ma'am."

Electra digs into her stash. "Heard anything about the weather south of here?" she asks. She looks at him with expectation, her face pinched tight, feeling the slap of the rain.

"Nothing special," he says.

"OK, then." She passes the three singles to him and waits for the change, which makes him grumbly as he digs through his cash box. *Pound sand, kid*, she thinks. *And put on your raincoat.*

The transaction done, she's now thinking coffee, the other fuel for what lies beyond. Denver is half again as far as she's already come, and tonight's landing spot, Trinidad, is twice again as far as that. Five hours, maybe a little more, most of them probably not as blessedly quiet as these first few have been.

Sure enough, as she crosses over to the passenger side, ready to retrieve the thermos that's on the floorboard below Nathan, he's awake and chipper and staring at her, a fully living boy yanked from the depths of sleep. She smiles big and waves to him from beyond the rain-dotted glass, and he presses his nose and fingers against the window and closes his eyes and she falls in love again and again.

She opens the door. "Hi there, Sport."

"I'm awake."

"Yes, you are." She leans in and kisses him on the cheek, and he wipes it off. "Are you hungry?" she asks.

"A little."

"Let me get it." The food and drink, such as it is, also sit below his feet, the most accessible part of the car given how thoroughly packed the back of it is. For the first time, she finds herself wishing for a station wagon, not the zippy Firebird that Ronnie bought for her in '66, a peace offering in her first season of deep discontent with him and the life pockmarked by absenteeism that they were only just holding together. In the ensuing years, she's metastasized the hurt, the loneliness, and when she's been tempted to think she should have driven toward the horizon long ago, she thinks of Nathan, who joined them a year later and remained the reason to stay, until even he and the shaming power of the nuclear ideal wasn't enough. No amount of disharmony she'd give back if it meant giving him over, too. No way. And anyway, the Firebird has the requisite capability now, when she's at last ready to run.

She hands the boy a plastic bag, tucked into itself for closure. It's filled with Cheerios. "This OK?"

He plucks it from her fingers. "Yes."

"You need anything to drink?"

"No."

"OK," she says.

In her vision, over the hardtop of the car and across the parking lot, she sees the butt end of a man disappear into a Freightliner cabover, and she wonders why she didn't notice the rig before. It's a telltale deep red tractor, and it's pulling a yellow cargo trailer, and that's a truck from Ronnie's employer, unmistakable if you've seen it as often as Electra has. *It can't be him, can it?* Ronnie should be in the gaping in-between of Nebraska or Iowa now, not sitting at a truck stop in Cheyenne. Her mind makes tracks across the possibilities: *It's not him at all* and *don't be silly, it might be him because plans change and you've seen it before and so what if it's not him when it might be one of his buddies* and *might be one of his buddies who's been in your house and has sat at your kitchen table and knows your car and, oh boy, wouldn't it be something if you didn't even make it to Colorado without being found out?*

"Mommy, are you OK?"

"Yes." *No.*

"We need to go," she says.

She closes the door and lopes around to the driver's side on legs gone to rubber. Forget the coffee; she's in the middle of every sense she possesses. She guns the car and sets the transmission and whips around in a right-hand U-turn, nearly clipping a Dodge pickup coming up behind. There's a honk and an "I'm sorry" the pickup driver can't hear and a "Mommy!" she can and an "OK, OK, it's OK," and she drives around back of the restaurant, speeding, defying her desire for control. She zips behind the big rigs parked parallel in diagonal lines.

"Why are you going so fast, Mommy?"

"It's OK, it's OK," she says, to herself, mostly, but she knows he hears it, too.

The crossing traffic at the highway juncture has grown thick, the good people of Cheyenne getting on with their day, and she repeatedly raps the steering wheel while looking for an opening, and her left foot pounds up and down, rapid fire, on the floorboard.

"Come on," she says.

"Where are we going?" Nathan asks.

She looks to him, frantic, then back at the traffic so he doesn't catch the panic. "I'll tell you soon."

"You already said that."

"Well, there you go."

"Mommy!"

"Just shut up, OK?" The words are out of her like a rifle volley, unstoppable once they start, and the boy, in a single fluid motion, slumps in his seat, pouts, then collapses into sobs.

She looks to him, and he wads himself up like a closed fist, no way in for her. Traffic still coming, she looks in her rearview mirror and sees the snub nose of the Freightliner riding up on her. *Shit.* She looks again to the traffic, and an opening comes. She punches the gas, a rubber-burning whip into the flow, and two cars later, the Freightliner makes its lumbering turn in the same direction.

"Shit, shit," she says. She looks at Nathan, who burrows deeper into his pout.

Her right hand reaches for him while the left wobbles on the wheel, jittery and anemic. She checks the mirror and the truck looms, rising above the line of traffic. The crossroads approach— keep on south to Denver and points below or veer right, toward Utah and Nevada and California. In two instants, the ancient pangs come and go, like a clamor of hunger. She thinks of that most westward of destinations, home once but no more, where she met Ronnie and from where he pulled her away, and in the next beat, she's back to the moment and fixated on the days that will play out elsewhere. *Maybe.*

She summons what the Firebird can offer her and gains some distance. Again, she checks the mirror. Behind her, the two-car buffer falls away, headed west. The Freightliner has opened the throttle and bears down.

"You told me to shut up." Nathan sits, arms crossing his chest, hugging himself, still brooding and cross.

"I didn't mean it." Her eyes move from the road to him and back to the road and then to the mirror. The gap closes.

"Shit," she says again.

"Mommy, no."

"Sorry."

If she's not maxing out the speed, she's hitting the top of her comfort with it, and she's no match for the horsepower behind her now that the truck has an open straightaway. The last exit for Wyoming comes and goes, and the gap shrinks, and she mashes the accelerator again and grants herself a few feet more.

"Slow down, Mommy."

Ahead, she sees the big welcome sign coming into view, Wyoming this side of it, Colorado on the other, and as she gets there, she veers from the highway at too great a speed. The slight fall in asphalt elevation jostles them and scrambles their things in the backseat, and she stands on the brake to calm the overstimulated car.

Above them, directly out the windshield: WELCOME TO COLORFUL COLORADO.

To their left, the Freightliner barrels past and keeps going, and she watches the yellow trailer grow ever smaller against the gray horizon. Her heart, pumping double, rings in her ears. The air smells of rain and engine oil. She tastes blood in her mouth. She feels wetness in her underwear, her bladder having revolted.

"Mommy," Nathan says. "Where are we going?"

Electra drops her face into her hands and she weeps.

Much later, Electra calls Charley from a phone booth in the motel parking lot, after finally loosening her tongue and leveling with the boy, after answering his initial questions even as he promised more, after Colorado largely cooperates, after packing out some of the car and setting up camp in their room, after a bag of McDonald's that he mostly devoured and she yakked into the toilet, after she put him to bed and made sure he was out. Darkness enfolds her outside the glass; inside, the single light flickers and threatens to go out. She props herself up in the box so she can see the room—twelve steps away, she counted—and can be there should he awaken.

She tells Charley of her day, but only the boring parts, only the parts where she got on the road on time and made good progress and endured Nathan's fussiness—"He has a right, you know, this is all new to him"—and got to where she was going, and checked into this flashing neon sign flanked by a dozen tidy rooms, color TV a prominent selling point if they wanted it, which Nathan did for a mercifully short time.

After they cover all that, it's tomorrow on their lips, the day they've been oriented toward.

"Did you ever imagine it would come to this?" Charley asks, and she thinks it an odd question. Does he not know that she's imagined it almost since that first moment, when they sat together at Sally Briggs' party—a *soiree*, Sally called it—and disappeared into their conversation as the booze and the finger foods and the revelry swirled around them? Does he not know that she walked home that night, half a block, thinking that she'd just experienced a moment when life shows you other avenues? Does he not know how her heart plummeted when he told her he'd be headed back to Texas the next morning?

He must know.

"I did," she says, her answer.

"I did, too," he says.

"You know how I feel," she says.

"Right back at you, lady," he says, and she giggles. "If you just come on over here, I'll tell you how much."

She shivers, from the words or the anticipation or the world outside. The night has gone clear and cold and dark.

"Be there soon," she says.

"You'd better."

Electra wiggles the key in the lockset and turns the knob gone wobbly with use. Light creases into the opening and she slips through, then cuts it off. In the darkness, she sheds jeans, socks, blouse, bra, then she shimmies into the nightgown she left on the edge of the bed.

The stench of past travelers' cigarettes hangs in the air. Nathan's pants and Mountain View Elementary T-shirt and fresh underwear and socks lie on the table, ready for him come morning. She has a momentary, unwelcome thought, a memory pulling her back as she tries to break away. She's tried to do it cleanly, but there's always debris. The people she didn't tell, who'll be finding out in waves. Not even Sally, her best friend and, more immediately, Charley's sister. Not yet. It's not safe. She could still turn around, in fear or an absence of gumption. She could still be weak.

Electra sets herself down and drifts away, bonded to her boy in the double bed, three men sharing space in her head. The one whose light is fading, the one whose glow can be seen in the distance, the one still to grow and to become and to discover. She thinks a prayer. She doesn't dare say it for fear of waking Nathan up.

God, please, let him grow in this ground I'm taking him to.

6

August 2012 | Pueblo, Colorado

Nate holds the cellphone to his ear and shuffles through the parking lot of the La Quinta Inn, kicking pebbles down the asphalt as he goes. They skitter and jump and roll to new destinations, where they'll be stilled quarry for the next restless foot. At last, the cell towers find harmony and patch through the call, and Brandon gives him a muffled hello.

"You get it?" Nate asks.

"Get what?"

"My trailer."

"It's friggin' eight a.m."

Nate, prompted, checks his watch, a redundancy given the phone, and sure enough. Seven where he stands, eight where he'd rather be.

"I told you I'd get it," Brandon says. "I'm gonna get it."

"Appreciate it."

Nate turns the other way and walks another line, more heel

scraping, more stones unsettled. He stares off at the truck, at his father, standing there, faking patience. Morning has come too early, but only because night went on too late. Ronnie had pushed things farther than Nate had wanted to go. Given the hour of their departure, Nate had suggested Amarillo as a stopping point and then Raton and then Trinidad, on the other side of the pass, and Ronnie had been *no* straight down the line, *we gotta get farther up there so it's two days and not three.* Pueblo it had been, and Nate had picked out a La Quinta, a better brand of room, and silently dared Ronnie to dig deep and pay for it, which he did with cash. After that, Ronnie had watched the tube and the late news and Nate had sulked and refused to douse the light and had gone on pulling draws from the flask and getting deeper inside himself, the way one does, while Ronnie had sawed away, asleep on the opposite double bed.

"Where are you?" Brandon says now, having come the rest of the way out of sleep.

"Colorado."

"OK."

"Also known as hell," Nate says.

"Well, yeah, I suspect so, given the company you're keeping."

Nate is drawing close to the truck, and Ronnie slaps the side of it as he might a recalcitrant horse. *Come on, let's go.* Nate unfurls his arm and points at the old man, threatening, then turns away and walks the parking lot again.

"I do appreciate it," he says. "For real."

"OK," Brandon says.

"She pissed?"

Over the connection, he hears the rustle of bedsheets, a few grunts, the sound of footfalls from walking away, the beat of downward steps.

"She's not happy," Brandon says.

"Tell her I'm sorry. For this and for the other."

"Tell her yourself."

"Yeah, OK."

"Gotta go," Brandon says.

"Yeah, me, too."

Nate folds up the phone, puts it in his shirt pocket. He thirsts for the flask, now tucked into his luggage, and that is squared away at the truck with an old man who's chopping the thick air with his gripes. Ronnie cups his hands around his mouth for amplification: "Ain't got enough tomorrows for you to be wasting today."

They're up the highway a piece when Nate blurts it, having tried and failed to conjure a more nuanced way in. "What'd Linda die of?" Even straight out like that, the banality of it is apparent, and he's certain Ronnie knows he's faking interest in a ghost—a literal one now, he supposes, if one buys the popular view of the afterlife. But it's a question and a bid, and that's a damn sight better than anything they had yesterday.

"Diabetes? I don't know," Ronnie says. "Bob didn't say."

"So you assume diabetes? Why?"

"Well, she was always a blimp."

Nate laughs, unfunny as the response is. It's a buffer between all the things he wants to leave behind and those other things he still wishes to talk about.

"Bob's my uncle?"

"Yeah."

"Bob's your uncle," Nate says again, no longer a question. He speaks it with a cockney bent, as Paul McCartney might. He trails the line with a chuckle.

"Huh?"

"Nothing."

Nate chokes the steering wheel, bracing himself against traffic and tide. *It's as bad here as it is back home*, he thinks. Half the cars in the state clog one north-south artery, Interstate 25 here rather than Interstate 35 back there, but otherwise no difference. He feels nervy and shot, robbed of sleep by an inside job, by a thirst he can't slake, by something he can't stop once he gets started.

"Would have been nice to know my relatives," he says now.

"I guess." Ronnie eyeballs him. The older man is good with the surface, less so with the depth, and any halting advances in this area have previously gone skipping away like a flat rock side-armed into a lake.

"The relation is pretty thin, kid," Ronnie says after a bit.

"Nonexistent, you mean."

"I didn't say that."

"You didn't have to," Nate says. "I didn't know her. Says it all, doesn't it? Thicker than water, my ass."

"When it's storming out," Ronnie says, "there ain't nothing but water. You hear what I'm saying?"

"Yeah," Nate says. "You sure we're not driving into the storm?"

It's a good off-the-cuff line, he thinks, one that meets metaphor with metaphor, but he's mystified. It's an exchange unlike any he can remember their having—Charley Stidham, that was another thing, another time, another man, one who could talk and write all the livelong day without ever using a word in its precise, concrete meaning and yet still be perfectly clear in his intent. With Ronnie, Nate has forever braced for blunt force, and here he got poetry of a kind. *Well, I'll be damned.*

"No," Ronnie says. "I guess I'm not." He torques himself in the seat, presses his mottled forehead to the window glass, and watches it all go by.

I'll be double damned.

Nate gives a terse shake of his head, intent on clearing the thoughts but instead scattering them and agitating the hangover that's staying down only begrudgingly. Charley, that was an unexpected and interloping thought, some half-fired memory that inserted itself into the now, the way regrets and recriminations and reconsiderations sometimes do. A curious thing, how the happiest, most fulfilling moments can't be reheated for consumption but the ones you'd like to take back or redo are a buffet that moves with you and pushes onto your plate even when you've had your fill.

God, I need a drink.

"How's your boy?" Ronnie barrels back in.

"Fine. Good."

"Don't ever see much of him."

"Neither do I. Busy. They're having a baby," Nate says.

"No shit?" Ronnie slaps his knee, tickled. "Know what it is yet?"

"They haven't said."

Ronnie ruminates a bit. "Probably a boy," he says. "We run thick with them."

"I guess. Linda excepted."

Ronnie murmurs and clams up. Colorado Springs rushes by on both sides.

"He's angry with me," Nate says, regret chomping on the trailing syllables, but now he's said it, for what reason he cannot possibly conjure. Annette would tell him, were she still speaking in his direction, that he surely had one, else he wouldn't have let the words fly. We say what we say, we mean it or we don't, but there's always a reason for sending thoughts into the air. She said it a hundred times if she said it once, before she decided it best to say nothing to him ever again.

"What's he mad about?" Ronnie asks.

Nate is grim-lipped, nodding in tight ups and downs. "I did something stupid."

"What?"

"Rather not say."

"You brought it up, kid."

"I did. Now I'm bringing it down." The feeling of foolishness is a power wash, drenching and pummeling him. *Goddammit anyway. Six-some hundred miles to go and this thing now riding shotgun, all because you had a thought you couldn't button.*

"Suit yourself," Ronnie says.

The crossover into Wyoming brings a tightness to Nate's gut and an unease that spreads out inside him. He raps the center of his chest a couple of times, scaring up a belch that smells of what he poured into himself.

"Sorry."

"You got a problem, kid," Ronnie says, waving at the air.

Several, Nate thinks, *a good number of them close enough to punch*. Truth is, he'd been dreading this part, this entry into the state of his birth, a place with no mooring for any of the ways in which he identifies now. It doesn't help that they'll be driving across damn near four hundred miles of the state, meaning he'll get to wrestle for hours with something he can't even name. He remembers his mother telling him, there at the end when every word was a gift, that it was "the state in my way," Wyoming. He can feel the weight of those words now.

None of it made much sense, now or in the looking back, how a woman from the central coast of California and a man from some vague, not-talked-about origins in Montana ended up trying to make a go of it with Wyoming doing its damnedest to blow them around like tumbleweeds. Didn't make sense and didn't take, as it all turned out. She lived out her scant remaining days in Texas, the old man came down after she was gone and will surely die there, too, and if Nate can call the shot, he'll be planted in that same soil. Wyoming is a lonesome poem whispering through the past.

Ronnie has gone back to staring out the window, and though Nate has generally found it best to steer clear of whatever's in the old man's head, he'd be willing to take the nickel tour now. Nate's own thoughts, against his will, drift toward those buried northward dreams, those first days in Texas when he'd wake up thinking he'd be in his old bed back in Wyoming, only to realize his mother had moved them without his consultation, and he'd come out of bed sour and carry his anger down to breakfast. Then, later, he would stare out the window of his top-floor bedroom, fixating on the eastern horizon, where a squat blue water tower sat, hydrating the next town over. It was reminiscent, in his child's eye, of the one back in their little bedroom town outside Casper. It rose up and shadowed their old house, and he'd imagine there in Texas that he was looking at Wyoming, that maybe if he squinted hard enough he could see his dad, but he never could.

It's all a cloudburst of long-ago pining now. Nate shakes it off. It didn't last long, didn't take long for Texas and his new life there to get inside him, and for him to get inside it, for his new school to fit comfortably the way the old one did, for his friends he made to be the best buddies he'd ever have. It didn't take long for Nate to prefer it there to any other place he could think of. The losses in Wyoming were temporary, easily recovered from. The ones that hurt and persist in hurting happened in the place he calls home.

They're in Cheyenne now, and an untrammeled memory comes loose when he sees the standing, decommissioned missiles at the air base that sits astride the highway. He's seen them before, a flash of memory, their tips appearing to lean slantways, obscured through foggy glass, rain drumming outside, his mother in the opposite seat, driving the other way from where he and his father are headed now. He'd caught a glimpse and then closed his eyes and faked sleep. He remembers that and not much else, except that she'd been crying.

"I've been here before," Nate says.

"When?"

"Think about it."

It addles the old man when he catches the reference, as Nate knew and hoped it would. Ronnie fidgets and blinks and chews on his lip, and Nate overplays what he thinks he holds.

"Best day of my life, last time I was here," he says, and Ronnie, stricken, stares at him. "Best day of my life," Nate repeats. He digs it in. "Pretty bad day for you, though."

"You didn't always think so," Ronnie says. "Seem to remember a time when you thought it was a pretty bad day for you, too."

"I was a boy." The words come out of him hot. "I didn't know better. Later, I did, but you fixed that, didn't you?"

"Don't pretend we didn't have some good times."

"Fine. You don't pretend you were God's gift to fatherhood." He fixes his father in a side glance, alternately wishes for him to open it up so they can have the timeless fight again and hopes he won't. Ronnie shrugs. Nate can see that he's stung. *Good.*

"What do you hear from ol' Charley, anyway?" Ronnie asks.

Nate shrinks up inside. He shouldn't have jabbed the old man with his guard so perilously down. He's a crafty guy who still has some haymakers he can throw and land flush.

"Never mind."

"Let's talk about this if you want to talk so bad," Ronnie says.

"Never mind, I said."

"Suit yourself, kid." He curls a finger toward the windshield. "Get off up here. I gotta take a squirt."

Nate guides the truck off the highway to a parking spot at a gas station. Ronnie heads in on choppy steps, trying to stay ahead of his bladder. Nate slips out, roots around in the extended cab, unzips his duffel and finds it. He checks the front door, slinks down below the window and takes two quick slugs, then puts the flask back and zips up again. To the main cab now, he finds a plastic box of orange Tic-Tacs, tips his head and shakes them into his mouth, then chomps away. They break like chalk between his teeth.

When Ronnie comes back, Nate is in his seat, hands at eleven and two, sunglasses on. He stares into a day already intractable, with the greater part of it still ahead.

"We good?" Nate asks.

"We're good," Ronnie says.

7

September 1952 | Three Forks, Montana

Ronnie, on his knees, gets down low to the patch and eyeballs the delicate fruit, the second and last batch of the everbearing strawberries before they trim up the plants and cover them with straw for the winter. Beside him, Berta works with precise hands, pulling the berries at double his rate and dropping them into the metal pail between them.

Tom had cleared out that morning, headed north, a man to see about some pigs and a spoken message to let go into the human grapevine. It's the latter that has Ronnie balancing anticipation and dread. He's never far from that cold February night when he left the dairy farm. He just brought the cows in and skedaddled, walking low, carrying the suitcase he'd packed a week before and hidden in the rafters, shielded by the barn till he got to the fence line, then over the wire and down into the irrigation ditch, breathing easier, making frost in the air. He didn't think Dick and Ma would necessarily come straight after him—hell, he had counted on their not noticing until at least a few hours later, assuming he'd be in the barn working on this or that, and by then he'd be far off the bench and in somebody's car headed any old place. But he also figures, now, that if they catch wind of his whereabouts, they'll come for him, cheap child labor being preferable to any alternative they might have. Tom had promised discretion in his inquiries up there. Ronnie hadn't seen any choice but to trust him.

"We'll have this done in a jiffy," Berta says, holding a runt berry to her face for a better look. She pops it in her mouth and grins at him, caught in the act. "Can't help myself."

"Sorry I'm so poky," he says.

"Oh, don't be. I have years of practice on you. You cleaned that carburetor lickety-split. I couldn't have done that."

"I guess."

"Tom'll be glad of it."

Ronnie preens under the promise of appreciation. He figures he's wanted only one thing more than Tom Foley's approval, and that's the thing the old rancher has gone off to try to find for him. Tom is quick neither with a word nor with praise, so Ronnie has learned to listen and to obey, and especially to appreciate any kind words that come his way.

Berta, she's different. Warmer, more talkative, but also in line with her husband in a unified cause, and not in a subservient way. She has as much say as Tom does, just in different parts of their life together and in different ways.

"All of this for canning?" he asks her, a hopeful lilt in the words.

"Not all of it."

"Pie?" That upward pitch of the voice again.

"Maybe." She says it coyly, and he laughs.

"A pie would be just about right, wouldn't it?" she says now. "Getting cold at night. Dinner and pie and off to bed."

"Can't beat it," Ronnie says, grinning.

It's a normal moment between them, one he's thankful for, in a time that's gotten a little choppy with anticipation, his, and steeling for a permanent change that now can't be imagined, theirs. He's tried to be mindful of Tom's admonitions to keep his head in the work, that nobody knows how any of this is going to come out, so keep the expectations from running over the riverbanks. Problem is, expectations and imaginations can't be brooked, and even if his father can't be pulled up from wherever he is—*if* he is, Ronnie keeps reminding himself, as that's well in the possibility of what little he knows about the man—nothing will be the same again after the looking. That's scary for him and for the Foleys. He can feel it ever more ominously.

"I think that's it," Berta says, standing up and wiping her fingers down her apron, deep red streaks trailing them. "You see any more?"

"Nope." He stands, too.

"Well, then," she says, bending for the pail, grabbing it, and handing it to him. "A job done well, I'd say. Carry them in for me?"

"You bet."

He wants to hug her, a first-time impulse that he squelches. He wants to do it for a dozen things he can think of that she's done for him and for a dozen more he couldn't name but feels acutely. The morning after he told her and Tom what he wanted, she had him sit with her at the kitchen table after breakfast—Tom had squawked about the chores, and she'd told him, "You can manage them just fine for a few minutes"—and she'd asked Ronnie's help in writing out a newspaper ad.

Ronnie had balked, sensitive about the schooling that had petered out around the fourth grade, after Dick and Ma decided he could get more done if he didn't have to climb on that bus every morning. "I can't write much," he'd told her, and she'd cooed at him and said, "I'll do the writing. You help me come up with the words." The result was mostly her composition, with Ronnie supplying only the name.

*Sought: Oscar Ray, by Mrs. Thomas Foley of Three
Forks, who has important news regarding the
missing man's son.*

She'd told him they'd put it in the paper in Bozeman—"You never know"—and Butte first, since Ronnie had mentioned it, and they'd run it for a week and see what comes, if anything. If nobody responds, they'd try another two cities, maybe Helena and Missoula. Then Billings and Kalispell. Miles City and Glendive, if it came to that.

"We'll find him," she'd said, more hopeful than certain, he'd reckoned, but he'd sure been grateful.

Back at the house, she washes the berries in the basin sink and subdivides them, some for cooking and canning, some for baking. He's already done the chores Tom had left for him, the tractor repair and the sending out of the cows, so she asks him to help with the dusting, "just this once," she says, and he does so happily. The stink that's usually on him before lunchtime hasn't landed yet. It's a respite. The sun has come up into full climb, a late-season scorcher, and he's grateful to be out of the glare.

Later, when she's making the dough, he comes into the kitchen and asks her to show him how it's done.

"Really?" she asks.

"I'd like to know."

So she goes through it, what she's learned and what she's taken from her own mother, and her mother's mother before that. The butter that's as cold as can be before it's cut in, made so by being put in the icebox a half-hour earlier. Once the cutting in starts, it's pea size, not pebbles, that you should be aiming for, she says. The butter melts into the crust in the cooking, forming air pockets, and that's a good chunk of the taste right there.

Good pie crust, she says, is a matter of extremes. Ice-cold butter and water. Super-hot oven. Cool dough, made with lard. Don't work anything with a tool that can be done with your hands, she says. It'll taste better that way.

She lets him in there, lets him feel the dough, touch it, shape it. She watches, hovering, as she guides him through pouring in of the filling she's made. Together, they make the lattice top. He brushes the top with egg yolk and cream, under her direction. The pie goes into the oven, and soon the fragrance drifts through the living room, where they play gin rummy, and his stomach grumbles. Midday casts golden light through the windows and forms sunshine splotches on the floor. It's the laziest, best day he's had in who knows how long.

When the pie is done—no timer, no need for that, Berta has it all down by feel—she has him take the potholders and bring it out, then set it gently on a cooling rack. It's one of the most beautiful things he thinks he's ever seen.

"I want a slice now," he says, and she slaps his reaching hand lightly and laughs.

"It'll be better if you wait," she says. "Anticipation always makes it tastier."

Ronnie is lying in bed, not even partway down, when Tom comes home. The headlights from the pickup cut the night and penetrate the room he's in, putting contrast on the walls, and he's fully awake now, covers pulled to his chin, staring, waiting. Boots on the gravel outside, the shrill complaint of the front door's hinges as Berta opens it, waiting for him. The porch groans under Tom's weight, then he's in the house.

"I thought you'd stay the night," Ronnie hears Berta say, an indistinct negative grumble coming at her in return. Ronnie closes his eyes, clenches the lids, forces it. It's not going to work or fool anybody, least of all himself. He hears the clomping down the hall, feels Tom's presence in the doorway, senses the change in the quality of the light coming through.

"You awake?"

Ronnie opens his eyes, looks. Berta stands behind her husband. "Yes, sir."

"Well, come on in here and talk with me."

Ronnie clambers out of bed, pulls his jeans back on, trades his flannel nightshirt for a white cotton tee fresh from the drawer. The Foleys have been real good to him, a whole set of underwear and socks and tees last Christmas so he could rid himself of the tattered underlayers he brought with him. When he emerges, he finds the couple in the kitchen, Tom grinding his hands on the tabletop in front of him, Berta standing near.

"Sit down," Tom says, and Ronnie takes the chair opposite him. Now, to Berta, he says, "I'd like a slice of that pie."

"Your blood will be running high come morning," she says.

"Nonetheless."

She's at the icebox now, fetching it, a rattling around, and Tom dumps his first load.

"Your father is long gone from up there," he says, and at this, Berta's industry comes to a quieted halt. He says to her, "Honey, I'm hungry," and she's back at it again.

"He is?" Ronnie asks.

"Yeah." Tom waits for her, and after she sets the plate in front of him and hands him the fork, he cuts an angular corner, loads it up, takes it in his mouth, smacks appreciatively. "It's a good one, hon."

He chews and swallows and cuts again, and as the second bite goes in, Berta says, "Well, we'll just—" and Tom raises a hand, stopping her. He chews and he swallows again, and he stands up and goes to the cabinet by the sink and he gets a squat glass. Now to the fridge he goes and pulls a bottle of milk and fills the glass. He returns the milk, then comes back to the table and sits.

"There's more," he says.

Ronnie leans forward. "Yes, sir?"

"They know him, the people I talked to." He tips the glass to his lips, drinks it in, wipes his mouth with the back of his hand. He sets the glass down again. "Hasn't been around in years, they say."

"I see." Ronnie looks down, then up again at Berta's kind face, drawn up in sympathy. She's in her nightgown, brown hair gone mostly gray down on her shoulders in ringlets.

"They know you, too," Tom says.

Before Ronnie can get the words out—the objections rising up, the "you weren't going to talk about me" pregnant on his lips— Tom says, "There ain't no way to get into it without telling them *something*, and I can trust this guy. He'll keep it quiet."

"Who?" Ronnie puts little power behind the word.

"Fella by the name of Brenner. Pig farmer. Know him?"

Ronnie nods.

"He knows you, too. Knows what went on up there. Knows you're better off here with us." Berta comes around, holds tight Ronnie's shoulders, kneads the muscles shot through with tension.

"Yes, sir," he says, ashamed by what isn't said.

Tom pushes on. "Brenner says your dad is a decent enough guy, a little hard to take sometimes. 'Mischievous,' that was his word. But generally well-liked, he said. Said he'd keep an ear to the ground, but I expect we won't hear anything. 'If I was to see Oscar Ray, it'd be like seeing the dog do arithmetic,' he said. 'A little hard to believe.'" He chuckled, then squashed it. "I'm sorry, Ronnie."

"It's OK. Thank you for trying."

"We'll keep at it," Berta says.

"Yes," Tom says. "The ads might turn him up. Unless . . ." He pauses, considering. "Unless you want to forget about it."

"No, sir."

"No, I didn't imagine so." Tom lifts the glass he's been pushing around the table with a finger, finishes off the milk. He hands it to Berta along with the plate and fork. "Well, lights out," he says. "Tomorrow ain't gonna wait on us."

In the darkness, sleep fending him off, Ronnie finds restless purchase, the things he ran from stirred up again, whatever he's running to formless in his mind's eye. He's stymied by the endlessness of possibilities beyond him and the smallness of the world that holds him back. How is it that Tom Foley, a man whose porch he once stood on only because there wasn't a gate on the road like at the next place over, somehow knows Davey Brenner clear up there? It boggles him, this Montana, a high and wide place that's vast and cozy at once, a place where a boy can disappear but never quite get away.

He knows Tom is right about Brenner, that he's a kind and good man. He remembers the shock on Brenner's face at what he'd seen, when Ronnie had banged on his door for no better reason than it wasn't his own, when Brenner had finally coaxed Ronnie to lift his shirt and had seen the damage done. He remembers Mary Brenner's crying as she patched him up. He remembers their little girl showing him her doll while he stood still for the repair job, gritty mouthed and ashamed and trying not to let the girl know.

In the eyes-closed remembering, he doesn't sense that Tom is in the room with him until the man speaks in a whisper.

"Ronnie?"

"Yes, sir?"

The farmer drops onto the edge of the bed, and Ronnie scooches over to give him room, and this is by far their oddest juxtaposition yet. "There are things I don't want Berta to ever know," Tom whispers. "I waited till she was asleep. You know what I'm talking about, don't you?"

A whisper in return. "Yes, sir."

"I went up to see Dick Littler."

Meeker now, the terror pushing on him, Ronnie says, "Yes, sir."

"I made like I was lost, turned around. I drove up to the house. Your mom was in the yard there. He came out of the pole barn to see what was what."

The scene as it must have been blossoms in Ronnie's mind, verdant and smelly and awful.

"I told him I was up from Bozeman, that I'd driven the wrong way and gotten lost, asked him for directions back to the highway. I just wanted to put eyes on him. See him for myself. So I'm pointing where I came in from, where I think I might have gone wrong, and he's following the line of it with the good eye, and the dead one's just staring at me. He told me how to get back, and I thanked him."

"Yes, sir," Ronnie says again. His stomach feels swamped, as if he's chugged cement.

"It hurt me to thank him," Tom says. "I wanted to kill him, truth to be told. Ain't never felt that way about another man before."

He leans in close, near enough that Ronnie can feel the heat of Tom's breath on his cheeks. "You listen to me now," he says. "I know you'll be leaving us. Whatever happens or doesn't with your dad, you'll be leaving. You've set your mind to it, and that's a hard thing to unwind once it's done. Berta, she hopes you'll stay, but I know you're going."

"Yes, sir."

"You just make me one promise."

"Yes, sir?"

"You stay away from those people up there. Whatever you do, wherever it is you're going, you don't go back ever, you understand?"

"Yes."

"Nothing up there for you but misery. The cruelty lives on the outside of that man. I could feel it. And you're free of it now, the most important thing. You stay that way." Tom retracts himself now, sits up, ramrod straight, and the words come softly now. "A little girl, she come out of the chicken coop right before I got back in the pickup. Plump little girl. She smiled at me. Who's that?"

"Linda. My sister."

"Pretty girl."

"Yeah," Ronnie says.

"I wanted to pluck her up, put her in the pickup, make a run for it," Tom says, and Ronnie lets go the wish that he'd done it, a wish the farmer seems to sense. "But that wouldn't have worked out too well, I don't think."

"No, sir."

Tom stands, and he heads to the doorway and fills it. He turns back. "Get some rest now. Tomorrow's going to be a hard one, and I expect I just made it harder by cutting into our sleep. Good night."

"Good night, sir."

In the procession of night, the wind picks up, sifted by the trees, the notes of an elegy scratching out against the window glass. After a time, Ronnie tumbles headlong into the darkness, his mind at first unsettled by unbound memory and chaos, until he gets control of his breathing and wills himself to stay in the moment, and then the next one, and then the one after that, until his thoughts, at last, are tamped down and smoothed over by the unexpected kindnesses that have bloomed along the trail. His eyes flutter and close, and he's adrift in a place where there are no memories or monsters or regrets, all of that held in abeyance until he awakes again, and that will be another day down. You get comfort and quarter where you can. Finally and at last, there is just sleep.

8

July 2002 | Billings, Montana

The server comes by, through the stolid haze and the heavy thump of the twin amplifiers perched on either side of the small stage, while a mile of rough country road—Marilee, they called her, a regular apparently—makes an absolute mockery of Skid Row's "I'll Remember You." The server balances the drinks on a small tray that sits atop her fingertips and moves as she moves, ducks and dodges through the scrum, and, at last, arrives at their table. She sets the drinks down, a second cherry Coke for Cherie and a fourth beer for Anna, and shouts "anything else?" and Cherie says, no, no, just the check, please.

The server leaves, and Anna leans in, overly loud given the shrunken distance. "We don't have to go yet. This is fun, isn't it?"

Was fun, Cherie thinks, but that's long past. She taps her wrist where a watch might be and says, just as loudly, "Tomorrow, remember?" Anna, her mouth near the glass now, nods. She drinks, and the foam drops below the line.

Cherie can see what's coming, how she'll have to put herself between her mother and a fresh run at the server, how she'll have to be the blockade against just one more for the road, how she'll have to move Anna steadily to the door, gentle and yet insistent, pushing against the assorted bodies, against the desire to go the other way, back to the table, back to sitting there and having another beer. How she'll have to be the bad cop, again.

It's everything she loves and everything she resents, right here in the multitudes of a single human. Cherie knows it's a simple binary to Anna's way of thinking, to the extent that she's even aware of what she thinks about this anymore: There are good times in the drink and pain, unspoken and undefined and yet surely present, beyond it. (And didn't they have a good time, Anna would say if asked, up there together, warbling through "Summer Nights," Anna taking the Travolta parts, Cherie handling the Olivia Newton John?) For Cherie, though, every pixel of the proposition exists in technicolor, save for the one element that's black and white: *You want sobriety? OK. Stop drinking.*

Anna doesn't want sobriety, and thus Cherie reconciles herself again to loving the woman and despising the affliction.

The server returns, sets the paper check on the table. "I'll be your cashier when you're ready," she says, the words too loud by half now that Marilee has left the stage and the DJ has announced a short break. "Take your time."

"No, I have it," Cherie says, pushing the bill and two twenties back across the table. "Keep the change."

"Just one more," Anna says, not even halfway into the one she has in front of her.

"We're done," Cherie says.

"Another?" asks the server.

"Yes, please," Anna says, and Cherie trumps it with a flat "no."

The server shrugs and leaves, and Anna makes a pouty face and says, "You're no fun."

"I know I'm not. Drink your beer."

"Oh, yes," Anna says, effecting a voice of childlike discovery. "Yummy beer."

It's getting worse. Cherie knows this. In intermittent moments of despair, she's worn out the online searches for alcoholism, how to deal with alcoholism, an exploration of how alcoholism runs through families. It's the condition she suspects but has never been diagnosed, and she knows enough now to understand it's not the frequency but the inertia, that once Anna starts it becomes something she cannot regulate, and so it goes, the starts and the stumbles and the bottoming out, the promises to do better, even the occasional long stretch of abstinence, of seeming progress, but always, always a reunion with the glass. It's taking diminishingly fewer ounces to light her up, tonight's flotilla of PBRs, not the strongest stuff around, standing as the latest example of how quickly Anna can begin to lose herself.

"Come on now." Cherie stands, grabs Anna's purse with one hand and her elbow with the other, and she moves them toward the door.

"Don't handle me!"

"I'm not," Cherie says. "Come on."

Anna twists herself, breaking free, and she shoves Cherie in the chest, and the younger woman loses her balance backward and tumbles into a high top. Its patrons scramble, the table totters over, the glasses it carries shatters on the concrete floor, and Cherie lies, bewildered, in a pool of beer.

It's two beats—startled silence and then the rushing clamor of assistance—and Cherie is helped to her feet, her shirt drenched through, her jeans carrying the grime of the floor.

A couple of guys from the table adjacent to theirs hold Anna by the arms in support, not apprehension. Cherie looks to her mother, sees the horror on the face. She's seen it before. She will, no doubt, see it again.

"Are you all right?" someone asks Cherie.

"Yes. I'm sorry. I'm sorry for the mess."

"It's OK."

She looks again to Anna. "Come on, Mom."

The men let go of Anna, and she walks toward Cherie, obedient, downcast, like a dog fully aware of the transgression and anticipating a scolding. Through the glass doors they go, into the parking lot, a view to Main Street, lit up and simmering in the night. To the car. Cherie unlocks the passenger-side door, offers a hand that Anna accepts, helps her mother ease into the seat. Cherie goes around the back, stops at the hatch, opens it, finds a T-shirt on the floor, over the spare tire, and she uses it to mop her hair, her face. Up in front, Anna sobs. Cherie closes the hatch.

She goes to the driver's side door and lets herself in. She drops into the seat. The hoppy stink radiates off her. Anna's head is in her hands. Her shoulders heave. Cherie starts the car and lets it sit, idling. She sets her hands in her lap.

"I'm so stupid," Anna says.

"You're not stupid."

"So stupid."

"You're not stupid, you're a drunk," Cherie says, matter of fact, the only way she knows how to deliver it, and Anna renews her crying. "You don't have to be, but you are."

"It was just a mistake," Anna says.

"No."

"Just a mistake."

It's the same old impasse, one for which Cherie has lost patience. Her mother overcharges herself or misses the point altogether, Cherie tries for unvarnished truth, then Anna pleads down to a misdemeanor. The whole thing will look less grim to her mother in the morning, or at least she'll be able to slap a braver face on it. How many times has daylight arrived and with it some declaration that a turning point has been reached, that it'll be better now. That *Anna* will be better now. It's not, and she isn't.

"Put on your seat belt," Cherie says.

Come first light, Cherie gets up and sneaks across the hall to Opal's room and checks on her mother. Entirely predictably, Anna is on the far side of consciousness—she might well be out to sea till after lunch—but her breathing is unimpeded, and that's the relief point. So many times Cherie has come upon her closed door, fingers working before they touch the knob, a fear to go in and find what she dreads, a woman far too young for the cosmos but bound for there nonetheless.

She checks the curtains again, fastened in haste the night before as Anna burrowed in, well into another crying jag, Cherie telling her "just sleep, just sleep," which she finally did. She finds them secure, bringing on a tide of relief that she will have to come around on her own, without the intrusion of daybreak.

Cherie blames herself, as she often does, a failure of the boundaries prescribed by the Al-Anon books she's read. As she lay staring into the ceiling, she'd gone over it again, how what she'd seen from the road and thought was your basic American bistro was, rather, a karaoke bar—*bar* being the problematic term, even with talent the likes of Marilee—with nothing of greater sustenance than rubberized chicken fingers and overcooked fries. Problem was, Anna saw it, too, and she flitted inside and bade her daughter sit and warbled happily about their luck in finding such a place, and Cherie gave in. She thought she could manage it, and she can't, if she ever could.

In the kitchen, already upended by the work they got done before heading into town, Cherie pulls a Gatorade from the fridge and a chocolate chip granola bar from the box on the countertop, not the most complementary of flavor profiles, but they'll both do. She then sets them down again, remembering. From the calendar pinned to the wall—still on June, the last of Opal's months, the handwritten reminders of things she'll never do scrawled in the squares—Cherie rips out a misshapen piece of paper. She then goes to the junk drawer and finds a pen and makes quick work of it.

> *Mom, gone to the dump. Back soon. Hope you feel*
> *better. Love, C*

Cherie gets gone. Already, she feels the day leaning hard into her, how they'll be racing time to get everything squared—by tomorrow, she hopes, or by the next day at the outside—and get back home to Bozeman, a distant beacon now. She just won't know until her mother comes around what condition she'll be in or how helpful she'll be, and so Cherie figures twice the responsibility for herself in the calculation. For today, at least. Tonight, she'll keep them close to the house, maybe a Subway sandwich for dinner. It's a snarling dog, this thing that has her mother in its teeth, and Cherie has learned occasionally successful strategies for keeping one bad night from doubling into two.

Morning traffic flows toward town, the pitiable commuters and the retirees chasing summer in their RVs and the schoolkids turned loose from obligation in their older-model sedans. Cherie finds her place in the stream, eyes darting from one mirror to the next to the next, watching the trailer load she pulls, minding the tie-down straps, accounting for distance and the unpredictability of fellow motorists. She circumnavigates the fairgrounds and the wide loop that squares her up with downtown. Then, in time, it's under the train trestle, to the literal other side of the tracks, the worn-down and hardscrabble Billings. She knows the route well, having followed it with Opal more than once, pulling this very trailer and ridding the farm of this or that. She knows how Billings doesn't show its best face to those who see it only from the interstate, who get an eyeful of refineries and single-wide trailers and car lots. It's the looking beyond that brings the more delicate features into sharper relief. A view straight south, where she's headed, offers something of a *plein-air* canvas, each layer building on the previous for a depth of field that could take all your attentions if you let it. Cherie appreciates it for what it is—subtler than the sky-scraping peaks where she lives, if lesser in grandeur—and moves on.

On the scale at the dump, she's asked "city or county?" and she says "county." The guy fixes her with a stare that lingers in the places it shouldn't and says, "Gallatin County plates, though."

"Check the one on the trailer," she says. "It's my grandmother's stuff. She lives here. Lived here."

"If you say so."

"Well, can I go?"

"Sure you can handle that trailer, a little girl like you?"

"Yes, sir. I'm sure."

"I could help you. If you want."

"I doubt it," Cherie says, her patience gone like flash paper. "Can I go now, or would you like to stare at my tits a little longer?" She says it loudly, intentionally, with enough sauce to catch the attention of the coworker she sees on the other side of the shed, working away at a computer. He says, "Stop fucking around, Jeff, and let her go."

Jeff waves her through. Before her window is up, he says, "Bitch."

"Asshole," she sends back at him.

It's on the drive back that the foretold sadness settles over her, like a mesmerizing storm she's watched come down the mountain without bothering to take cover. They've had a hard year, she and her mom, with no suggestion that something easier is coming up behind it. Cherie figures, on some level, that these inexplicable moods are just the parts people are talking about when they tell you to just get over it. It's the stuff you must step through to get to something else.

She's less than a month out from standing there with Mr. Vickers as he put the diploma in her hand and thanked her, they're twelve days out from Opal's pitch-over in the yard, and somewhere in the intervening time, she let her commitment go. Told Annapolis she wasn't coming. Made inquiries about ROTC at Montana State. Started thinking of other ways she can actualize a job with the FBI, out there beyond another graduation or two. The future still seems pregnant with possibilities but... but the field of vision has narrowed, no doubt about that. Might as well have used those florid letters of recommendation from both Montana senators—the Republican *and* the Democrat, a true and rare instance of bipartisanship—and started a fire for all the good they're going to do her now. God help her, when they got the phone call about Opal, that was maybe Cherie's third thought: *I wonder what else is going to die.*

The instant, deflating answer: *The one thing you want right now.*

Even now, when she remembers telling her mother about her decision—saving the reveal until everything had been unwound, so she could pass it off as volition and not preemption, so Anna could say "oh, honey, are you sure?" with credibility even as she surged with relief—Cherie throbs with resentment for the why of the thing. Fear on her mother's behalf. An unwillingness to be two thousand miles away when the unraveling comes.

Memory and assumption are unbound now, knocking against each other in the swirl. The night they heard about Opal, Anna wailed into the deep evening over the loss, the compounded nature of it, that Larry Teasdale, the bearer of half her DNA, had been plucked from the earth over in Korea when she was little more than an electrical impulse in Opal's womb, and now here Opal was gone, too, nearly fifty years on, and what did she have to show for all of those losses?

How angry Cherie had been when she heard that. How hurt. *You have me,* she'd wanted to say, *same as I have you, and you had Opal, and Opal had you, and we've done all right, haven't we? Three generations of women, each of us with tenuous connections to our fathers. Yours a picture clipped from a high school yearbook. Mine in town but mostly out of my life, by his choice. Opal's on the wall of her farmhouse, the only one of them to come to a natural end of his obligation to his daughter. I'm sorry, Mom,* she remembers thinking, *but the hour is far too late to be crying over unreliable men.*

Back at the house, Cherie lines things up for a clean backing in of the trailer. She does it like a champ, a single, fluid run that puts the empty trailer's wheels squarely on the driveway gravel. She straightens up and pushes back, readying the flatbed for the next coming load.

She heads inside. The day promises to broil, so she lifts the windows in the living room and the kitchen, checks the screens for pest-sized holes and pronounces them good. Down the hallway she goes next, her feet finding the edges of the hardwood, where it's less squeaky. She presses an ear to Opal's bedroom door, Anna on the other side, and she closes her eyes and concentrates. A grumbling snore, then recession, then another, in rhythm.

Cherie goes back to the kitchen and puts the coffee on.

Charley Stidham

1939-

Once you see it—the way the tavern in Sundance Square is decked out and how the snapshots from all eras of your career have been blown up and put on the walls, and how people are lined up and standing outside, waiting to see you—you're knocked back even though it's been coming for weeks and has been preceded by months when you were fairly certain you were on the verge of doing it, of finally retiring. Once you made it official, your bosses at the newspaper went back and counted up every column you've ever written and trumpeted that number—8,813, holy shit, that's a lot of opining, at around 1,200 words a pop. Let's face it: You've written a damn library that's lined a lot of damn bird cages. And then came the series of house ads saying goodbye and inviting your readers to come around Saturday—this Saturday, today—and send you off properly. And now you're here, and now the folks are here, which still amazes you, and this is how you put the period at the end of that final sentence.

So you pose for pictures, and you indulge remembrances—the Cowboys fans and the Rangers fans and the Mavericks fans, the college football fanatics and the occasional person who wants to talk about the Cowtown Marathon or some boxing match when Fort Worth had a few pugilistic champions—and you're amazed by what people remember when they've taken it to heart, when they've transferred a piece of their own identities to these teams and these athletes. They remember things you long ago forgot. But you indulge them, because they're good people, and you have a few drinks, nothing you'd have ever done in a press box while on duty, but who's going to stop you now? Your boss—about your twentieth, you figure, and you'd say you've lost count, but you never bothered to keep track—stands up and says some nice words, as if he actually knows you. You get a plaque. It's all so very nice and so very unnecessary.

Thank god for Gwen. She sits beside you, keeps you company, holds your hand when you fidget, and you fidget a lot. You wouldn't be here if it were up to you. A career ought to end like it began, you think, quietly and without fanfare. But you're Charley Stidham, Mr. Fort Worth, everybody's favorite sports columnist, and there was no way you were just going to go home for good and mow the lawn into eternity.

It isn't until one guy approaches the table and slides a photostat copy across to you that you recognize he's any different from the other folks who've come over toting commemorative sections and footballs and helmets and asking for your signature, which is just the wildest concept ever. Your John Hancock was barely good for the last mortgage you signed.

"Remember this?" he asks. You pick it up, examine it, the haphazard layout of it a dead giveaway to the early seventies—hell, you haven't run that horrible sans serif type since 1980, if not earlier. You look at the headline, just the first three words, and you know it, and you can't believe it.

Nathan?

"Yes, sir."

You take in the vision of him. How can you account for the years gone by—good god, twenty-nine of them—just by looking a man in the face? How can you catch up to the years between, the way he's filled out, the way his hair has come in and gone away in the same pattern just about any man of his age would experience? And what is his age now? You do some quick math while memories spill into your head. It's now twenty-aught-five, as you like to say, so that makes him—you reach for the birthday; you used to know it by heart, goddamn it, what is it now, come on, come on, oh, right: February ninth—thirty-eight now. *Thirty-eight years old.* Was a time you might have thought you'd see those years right alongside him, guiding him and shaping him, but that time went into the ground with his mother.

I remember it, you say. Do you?

"You and me, Cowboys game? Of course I do," he says. "Will you sign it for me?"

He's not going to get away that easy, you think, not this time.

No, you say. Not yet. You stand. You reach for him. Gwen is looking at you, she's crying, she knows, and you can't let your eyes linger on her or you'll lose it, too. Come in here. Give me a hug, kid.

He sits with you and Gwen, a couple of hours later, a quieter place in a lonelier corner of downtown. He came here because you asked him to, asked him to wait, asked him for a bit of his time, and he said yes, and for that your gratitude spills over. And moment by moment spent, you find your comfort in his presence, see the boy you knew behind the man in front of you now, hear the familiar speech patterns, have a few shared laughs. You tell him about you and Gwen—she's right there with you, after all—and the girls the two of you had together, women now, one of them a *mother* now, the other too rangy to be kept close, tramping across Europe. He tells you about his son, eighteen, graduating from high school this year, and when you get hung up on the young father he must have been, he says, "High school sweetheart. Went into the navy. Didn't take. The sweetheart or the navy."

You're struck by something. You can still hear *her* when his mouth flies open, can see her inside his eyes and the small of his mouth, remember the way she would sometimes throw herself between the two of you in a fraught moment, until she learned to trust, and until you made your own way with him and all of you became a three-legged family and learned how to lope along together. And then . . .

You've always had her since she's been gone, as much as you can have anyone you've lost to stardust. But you haven't had him. It hurts again, right now, front and center of your chest. You only thought you'd packed it away.

He sips water. You offer him a beer. He says no thanks, not today, trying to cut back. You respect that.

Gwen, bless her, breaks the harder ice. "You're the surprise of the day, Nathan."

"Nate, ma'am."

Nate?

"Yes, sir. Felt more, I don't know, adult. Came a time that Nathan just didn't fit anymore."

"Well," she says. "You're the surprise of the day."

The best surprise, you tell him. You tell him you're flabbergasted. All this time. Where did it go?

Nathan—*Nate*—shrugs. "Just thought I'd come out and say hi."

You're glad he did. You think of the times you could have gone to him, wanted to, and didn't because Nathan's—*Nate's*—father drew an unmistakably clear boundary line, and you had to wrestle with your best idea of what was right for the boy inside the pile of possibilities that weren't what you'd have preferred. With Electra gone, you would have wanted to partner up with Ronnie, find a way to give the boy the best parts of two men who loved him. You suggested as much, pleaded as much, threatened to sue for as much, though you had no legal standing, just a moral one. And when the final no came down—"He's *my* son, and *my* responsibility, so stay away from him," Ronnie had said, and that was the second-worst breaking of your heart—you said what you could say to a nine-year-old boy, in words he could understand. You told him you loved him—that you'd always love him—but that you'd have to be leaving, that his daddy had it now. He cried, lord how he cried, and at the worst moment of it, you took him in and you set his face into the fleshiness of your shoulder so he couldn't see you coming apart. You set him in there and you wished for good things for the man who'd done this, hard as it was to have a charitable thought. You needed Ronnie to be OK so his son would be OK, too.

You ask him if he's had a good life.

Nate smiles. "Parts of it," he says. "Here's hoping."

You wish you'd have known this day was coming. You could have held on to the anticipation of it. You could have looked forward, instead of all those times the sadness crashed into you as you looked back.

You come damn close to breaking. Gwen squeezes your hand under the table. You sniffle and swallow and choke.

"I didn't mean to upset you," Nate says.

You tell him he didn't upset you. He couldn't upset you. You tell him you've thought of him often, that when he graduated from high school, you found his name in the small type in the newspaper—"the agate," he says, and you almost weep again—and you sent him every wish that was inside you to conjure. You put those wishes on the wind and hoped they'd scatter out and find him.

"I better be going," he says after a bit longer, and he stands, and you and Gwen stand, and you say you wish he didn't have to. Can you call him sometime? Can we do this again sometime? And he says, "I'll call you, OK?" And you tell him that'll be just fine, that you hope he will. You're retired after all. You're both flush with time and almost out of it.

9

August 2012 | Billings, Montana

Nate sits with Ronnie in the truck and watches what's going on down the hill. The road they're on follows the contours of a rise in the cemetery, with the action happening below them, a small cluster of people under a canopy, others scurrying around the line of cars, still others finding their seats, a hearse backed in for easy offloading of the casket to the platform.

They had come early, just a few hours of sleep after getting into Billings late, found this spot, watched for the procession, and after it had finally arrived and Nate had waited for the last car to clear and had started the engine, Ronnie had said, "No, hold up just a sec."

Still, they wait.

"It's about to start," Nate says. "Better get down there."

"OK, let's go."

They step out of the truck. Nate checks his shirt line (tucked) and his fly (engaged). He cups both hands over his mouth, expels a breath, then sucks it back in. He smells peppermint, and that will work fine.

They crunch gravel as they walk down to where everybody else is. The day has broken hot and bright, and a late-morning glare beats down, relentless. Nate catches the shape of the headstone arrangements, how they hug the hill in swoopy lines. The air here is pleasantly and surprisingly light for all the death and decay below their feet, for the Central Avenue bustle just beyond the fence, for all the passing cars belching up exhaust. The slight rise of the city skyline shimmers in the heat.

Once at the canopy, they head for the back row, where they stand, and Nate makes a quick inventory. Linda Penney's benediction has brought out maybe two dozen people. There's family, people better known to her than Nate and Ronnie, many of them dressed in black and sitting up front. Others came as they are, jeans and scuffed boots and everyday blouses and feed store gimme caps. One guy in shorts. *You do you, brother.*

The casket is lugged into place by five wide men, and the good pastor from Trinity Lutheran—he flings the multisyllabic name, but Nate doesn't catch it—commences and makes workmanlike brevity of it. *Linda Littler Penney loved. She was loved. She was of this earth and now she is of heaven and to receive her reward, for she loved the Lord Our God. She will be missed, but be not sad for her, for she has gone to glory. The good book says this and that and some other things, and let us take comfort in those words. Amen.*

When it's over and all that remains is to lower the casket into the hole, Ronnie takes a few steps forward, halting and uncertain. Nate hangs back, watching. There's a picture of her, on a little table beside the lectern. The face is squarish, almost, and soft and pillowy, the smiling mouth and the small nose and the eyes recessed into the corpulence. Ronnie picks the framed picture up, holds it close for the benefit of his failing eyes, then sets it down again. Nate moves up beside him and sets a hand on his shoulder. Ronnie lets it be.

On the other side, the man Nate sussed out as his uncle sidles up. He's a rockslide of a fellow, short and squat, almost as wide as he is tall, with everything below the breastbone cascading south at an acute angle.

"Glad you came."

Ronnie turns and faces him and offers a handshake that's accepted. "Bob. Thanks for calling and letting me know." Bob sniffs, wriggles, hikes up his belt, looks now beyond Ronnie.

"You must be Nathan."

"Nate. Yes, sir." Another handshake.

"Growed a bit since I saw you last."

"I don't recall," Nate says.

"Well, you were just a little guy." Bob laughs, his vigor not commensurate with their shared moment. "Doesn't mean it didn't happen, though."

"You bearing up?" Ronnie asks him.

"Oh, yeah, sure," Bob says. "It got there at the end where it was a relief to us both, I think. A lot of pain." Bob considers his shoes.

"Yeah," Ronnie says.

The rest of the congregants have filtered out to their cars, a few with pats on Bob's arm, leaving as they came. Cemetery workers arrive and begin folding and stacking chairs, preparing the canopy for decommission, shoveling dirt. The man in shorts, standing at a small pickup, shouts over: "Pop, come on."

"You guys coming to the house?" Bob asks. "Be nice to have a chance to talk."

"I don't know, Bob—" Ronnie starts.

"Cousins are coming down from Great Falls. Couldn't make it earlier. They'd love to see you."

"We'll be there," Nate says.

"Yeah, OK," Ronnie says.

"Great. You remember where we are?"

"We'll find it," Ronnie says.

They walk back up the hill, into the dust kicked up by Bob's truck. Nate slips a hand onto the back of his own neck to squeegee it down.

"Don't know what you did that for," Ronnie says. "I'd rather just rest up and get out of here." He's huffing hard on the incline, which serves him right for leaving his oxygen tank in the car, the vain old goat. He'll sure enough take a big hit of it once he gets there. *If he gets there.* Nate has a flash of a thought that almost sets him to uncontrollable giggling. *If you gotta go, go in a cemetery. That way, I can just roll you down the hill and into that hole they haven't filled yet.*

"You don't want to see everybody?" Nate asks.

"Not particularly."

"Well, maybe I do."

There's a stone bench in front of the resting place of Elmira Louise Hays, 1923-2007, who must have been well loved for the grandeur of her gravesite, and Ronnie takes the chance to sit, hands and ramrod arms first, his butt then gently laid in. "Need a minute here," he says.

"Take your time."

Ronnie sucks air, prodigiously to begin with and then steadily less so as his lungs fill and his breathing becomes less labored. Nate puts his hands in his front pockets and rocks on his feet, heels to the balls under his toes, then back again.

"It's nice here," Ronnie says. "Good spot."

"Yeah. You can see the golf course."

"I think I'd like me a hill like this," Ronnie says. "A view of something. When the time comes."

"I figured I'd just put you in a Folger's can. Let the wind have you."

Ronnie looks horrified. "You wouldn't."

"What difference does it make? You won't know."

"I sure as shit don't want to be burned up. You understand me?"

"Yeah, I got you. I was just making a joke. I haven't given it a thought." Nate chuckles. "Not entirely convinced that you'll die."

"Yeah, well, I might not." Ronnie is still hot. It comes out in the tenor of the words.

"OK. Jeez."

Ronnie stands again, then wordlessly renews the climb. Nate jogs a bit to catch up. They crest the hill to where the pickup sits. Nate unlocks it and holds the passenger door open for Ronnie, then closes it once he's lifted himself in there. On the other side, he slips into his own seat. Ronnie has the oxygen hose dangling from his nostrils, and the shots of sustenance click off.

"You ready?" Nate asks him.

"Yeah."

Nate guns the pickup. The AC vents blow warm air that turns quickly cold. He feels the sweat drying on his face. He puts the shifter in drive, pulls forward to the turnaround, does a U-turn, and heads for the street.

"Turn right up here," Ronnie says.

"Got it."

They're in the flow of traffic now, headed downhill, into the bowl that holds Billings proper. The Penney house lies beyond, Ronnie says, up on the bench, beyond the fairgrounds, a nice spot overlooking the river. At least it was, a long time ago. "The whole damn town has grown," he complains.

They drive a bit, silently. Downtown misaligns like a crooked smile, passes by, falls into the rearview. Warehouses and flophouses move in. Nate looks north at the rimrocks, which seem to float in the haze above it all.

"It was a nice service."

"It was." Ronnie chews on a thought. "Can I ask you a question?"

"Sure," Nate says. "Shoot."

"What'd you do with your mom?"

"When—"

"When she passed," Ronnie says.

Nate doesn't see it coming, and the first thought is that he'd never really considered that the old man didn't know, that he wasn't there, that he hadn't shown for his ex-wife's funeral because there hadn't been one, and even before that, he hadn't shown much interest when she was sick and still fighting it. Which, of course, put the two of them in different universes on the whole thing, because Nate wasn't anything but interested—obsessed, truthfully—back when he and Charley were keeping vigil and hoping against futile hope that there might be some narrow path to the other side, that she might find it and stay.

No, Ronnie Ray's interests—his alone—came only in the aftermath, selfishly and destructively, and Nate doesn't much want this to be something they'll talk about now, cool and detached and matter of fact. Fuck no. Nate stomps on it, to kill the notion dead wherever Ronnie sprung it from and for whatever reason.

"We burned her up."

Come evening, Nate is gloriously blistered—not belligerent, not morose, not inside the rage that had dropped on him earlier, but just terrifically and thoroughly lit up and ready to be friends with the world as it comes to him. However many people came out to say goodbye to Linda in the daylight, the number doubled and tripled through the afternoon and deep into the evening, so many of them making a pilgrimage to the little Penney house, offering regrets and partaking of the cheese tray and pouring a drink and sitting around and having a time of it, then leaving. It's been a churn of people in and people out. Nate has met them all, aided by introductions from Uncle Bob—"Bobberoo," Nate has taken to calling him aloud, now that he's lit up, to the older man's seeming delight.

Ronnie, too, has raised his sail into the prevailing wind and basks in the attentions of three matronly cousins down from Great Falls, as Bob foretold, all a decade or more younger than he is from the looks of them. They're daughters of his mother's brother, Pike. They coo over Ronnie and remind him of times past, filling in the corners of memory, and they speak reverently of the pompadour he had back in the day, how he came home from the Army looking like Elvis, his hair smeared with pomade and sculpted with a just-so flourish. Nate wishes he could have seen that.

Peg, the eldest of the three cousins, finds Nate and teases his hair with her fingers and says, "Ronnie, why didn't you bring this boy around more often?"

"Yeah, Ronnie," says Nate, who keeps hearing about a single visit—"had to be '69 or '70," Bobberoo says—for which he has no memory. "Why didn't you?"

Nate's father sits heavily in the loveseat across the living room. He carries a hard look as a first answer to the question. It changes the room, that look, the way he holds it on Nate and others pick up on the aggression. It's just family now, such as the family is. Bob and Jimmy, his son, and the cousins and two husbands, and Rhonda, Jimmy's ex, who's been keeping to the kitchen area and slinging the drinks.

"Time got away from me, I guess," Ronnie says.

Peg casts an arm around Nate's shoulders and pulls him in. "Well, you're here now, Nathan. That's what's important." She kisses him on the cheek, and he glows, and Ronnie stares them down.

"I guess," Ronnie says, "there was other things to do after your mother run off with that guy she was fucking up on Casper Mountain and—"

Nate rises to his feet, shucking his cousin's affections, and throws his glass—five ice cubes and two fingers of good Scotch. The thick bottom of it catches the coffee table without shattering. Its contents spray the carpet, and the glass glances off the table and clips the old man's forehead as he's standing up, trying to dodge it. A small cut opens, and Ronnie, standing there, touches the wound, then examines the blood on his hand as the rest of them scatter. Jimmy moves in and takes Nate by the arms, holding him, while Bob tries to make peace with "come on, now, don't do that."

"You're an asshole," Nate says. He strains against Jimmy's arm lock, unable to break it, then says, "Just let me go, man." Jimmy grudgingly relents.

The cousins—Peg and Wanda and Lorene—scurry to Ronnie and try to soothe him, but he's having none of that. He flings his hands, chasing them.

"And what do you care anyway?" Ronnie says, beating them into hastier retreat. He drops back into his seat. The cut has opened up, and blood streams toward his right eye.

Bob and his son move in. "You're bleeding, Ronnie," Bob says. "Come on, let's get you cleaned up."

Nate steps toward them, ready to object, ready to tell them he isn't worth the trouble, to spend their kindness elsewhere, when Rhonda cuts off his path and sets a gentle hand on his chest.

"How about we take a walk?" she says. Nate just looks at her. "Seriously," she says. "Let's walk it off."

Nighttime hangs heavy and acrid. Nate smells petroleum. He casts around from the sidewalk out front, working himself into a circle until he sees the source, the flare from the refinery just beyond the river. He pulls a deep breath in. Sobriety remains a far cry, but it's coming on now that he's in the open air.

"Can you walk?" Rhonda asks.

"Yeah."

"Little store up a few blocks," she says. "Let's get you some coffee."

They walk side by side on a sidewalk at first, till that peters out, then it's shoes on the ground, baked hard in the late-summer sun. Broken glass glitters under streetlamps.

"That was dumb of me," Nate says.

"It was. But understandable, too." She nudges him. "Nobody wants to hear that about their mom. I'd guess Bob is telling him that right now. He and Linda thought the world of Electra."

"You know her?"

"I know the name."

Nate decides right there that he likes her. He takes her for maybe fifty, strong hands, wide shoulders, trim. Her blonde hair is pulled back in a ponytail that reaches the middle of her shoulder blades. After they'd been introduced and Bobberoo had sorted out the relationships and Nate had said "*ex*-wife, huh?" and she'd said, "Welcome to the Penney family, where we keep it weird," she'd handed him a drink and clinked the glass with her own: "To the prodigal cousin." When he'd asked for a second, she'd said, "Not the savoring type, huh?" On the fourth, it was "slow down, sailor." That's all he remembers, except the last of it, when she saved him from further stupidity.

He stops. She does, too.

"What do you know about me?" he asks. "Because I don't know shit about you. Any of you."

She points ahead. "Almost there," she says. "Let's not get into it."

"Yeah, OK," Nate says. "I'll just come back in another forty-five years and we'll talk about it then."

She crosses her arms and looks at him. "OK," she says. "Don't ask me specifics, because I don't have any. I know Linda and your dad had a hard life up there in Great Falls, and that it was much harder for him than it was for her. She talked about it sometimes, not often, when she was feeling particularly blue. Nobody misses Dick Littler, I know that. I don't know about your grandma, but she stayed with him, cried about him after he was gone, a real basket case, I'm told, so, you know, draw your conclusions. I know your dad ran off—it kind of made him a family legend, I think, that he got away, which is why the cousins were all moony about him—and I know he and Linda reconnected at some point, but . . ."

"What?" Nate asks.

"It's just hard. That's all. I don't know a lot of details. Nobody talks about it, and I don't pry, but I think everybody understood that your dad, he just wasn't going to be coming around, you know?"

"I didn't know any of this," Nate says.

"Wish I could tell you more."

"Also," Nate says, "he's *not* a fucking legend."

"OK."

They walk on. Nate works his thoughts over awhile before turning them loose. "So where do you come in?"

"Ha," she says. "By marriage. Shouldn't have, but did, and, well, the bad isn't bad enough to make me give up the good."

"Meaning?"

"My daughter."

"I didn't meet her, I don't think," Nate says.

"Would have been a good trick. Emily. She's in Italy. She's trying to be a writer. Having an adventure, anyway."

"She'd probably enjoy talking with my son, the English teacher," Nate says. "Brandon."

"Well," Rhonda says, "aren't we just the creators of genius?"

Nate laughs.

"Anyway," she says, "I couldn't stay married to Jimmy. Twenty years was enough. But I loved Linda like a mother, whether by marriage or not. I know that. I was there with her at the end, with Bob. I love them. Period. So, I'm always on the outer edge, like tonight, part of them but not of them, not anymore."

Nate sees what she means. He can't reconcile her and the cousin he's only just met, not in a this-girl-for-this-boy sense. He wonders how something like that happens, and then he thinks of Annette and how she must feel about their long-ago getting together, after all that's happened in between. She and Rhonda could probably compare notes on the unfortunate exes to whom they owe their greatest happiness, in the form of another human.

"That Jimmy, he is—" Nate starts and doesn't finish, because he doesn't have any real knowledge from which proceed.

"Jimmy is a child."

"You'd know."

"I do," she says. "Come on, now. Let's get some coffee."

10

October 1972 | Trinidad, Colorado

Electra pulls back the curtain and sets a hand against the cold glass, smearing a frosty arc across the window. She presses forward, nearly kissing it. She looks out, and she curses herself for her recklessness. Snow, on the ground in drifts, stacked up on the car outside, and falling still. She hadn't seen it coming, hadn't watched the news, hadn't read the paper, was too lost in the hopes she was projecting a day ahead, and she didn't know. A mistake, a big one.

She moves along the wall to the doorway, finds the light switch, and flips it on. Nathan comes hard and fast out of sleep, groans and grumbles and rubs his eyes with knuckled fingers. "What?" he asks. "I'm sleeping."

"Yeah, well, time to get up," she says, and when that doesn't move him, she sharpens the words. "Nathan, now! Get up!" He kicks the covers, his legs flying like windmill blades, and scrambles from the bed.

"I have to pee," he says.

"So do it."

He goes into the bathroom and closes the door, his complaints a garble from behind the barrier. She isn't listening, anyway. She digs through their things, finds another sandwich bag filled with dry cereal, and sets it on the bed for him. His mittens come out of her suitcase, his heavier coat out of his. At some point, in planning to run, she'd foreseen inclement weather, and yet she'd missed its imminence. *Stupid.* These things she sets on the end table along with the clothes she'd laid out for him last night.

Nathan emerges. "It's snowing," he says, pointing toward the window.

"Yes, it is."

He identifies her bedside stash with another indicating finger. "I'm not eating that."

"Yes, you are."

"No!"

Here we go, Electra thinks. *He's fussy and sleepy and confused, and he's going to kick up a bigger fight than this has coming. Not today, Sport.*

She goes to him, gets down on a knee, takes him by the shoulders, and holds him with gentleness. She wets two fingers with her tongue and uses them to pat down a cowlick. He smells of chocolate bars and fryer grease, but she's not going to engage another battlefront by insisting on a bath. No time, anyway. Too damn cold, too.

"I know, I told you pancakes," she says. "You'll get them. But I need you to eat this for now, OK?"

"You said blueberry pancakes," he says.

Yes, OK, blueberry pancakes, if they're out there to be found on the precise route will be on—I hope—then yes.

"Of course," she says. "But this first, OK?"

"OK."

She stands again. "Good," she says. "Thank you. Now, eat and get dressed. Turn on the TV, if you want. Mommy has to go talk to someone, but she'll be right back, OK?"

"Can I come?"

"No," she says. "You stay here and watch our things. I'll be back in a couple of minutes, OK? Watch the TV."

"OK."

Electra waits until he has the TV set on and has cranked the dial nearly a full turn. He tunes in to a kids' show out of Denver, the screen pelted with pixels that look like snowfall, but in color, much more interesting than the black-and-white TV they left behind. Nathan sits on the edge of the bed, feet dangling, and eats his cereal with grubby hands.

She slips outside, pulls her coat tight around her, sets her feet toward the gas station next to the motel. Then she stops and raps the window, and when Nathan looks her way, she opens her mouth wide, presses her lips against the glass, making a seal, and blows her cheeks out and sends her eyes rolling wildly.

She pulls back and watches her son collapse into giggles, then he's off the bed and at the glass, and he mimics her, and she laughs, then points beyond him. "Stay here, OK?" she says, and he nods.

The parking lot is a slushy skating rink—rain that came first, now frozen, the snow dropping down atop it—and twice her feet slide in divergent directions, nearly forcing her into the splits. The second time, she puts a hand to the ground to stay upright and the snow melts and bleeds into her knit glove. Inch by hard-fought inch, she gets there, clearing the waist-high berm between the motel lot and the gas station, where the asphalt has been plowed and salted. Snow dusts her jeans.

When she finds the mechanic on duty—Rex, the tag on his shirt says—and makes her inquiry, he delivers news that keeps making everything worse.

"Gonna come down all day, I hear. If I was you, I'd just wait it out. Better tomorrow, and it'll be plowed."

"But you're not me," Electra says.

"Clearly."

"So," she says, "if I have to get down that hill—"

"Oh, sure," he says. "Make it down the hill without cracking yourself up, you're in the clear. Smooth sailing after that."

"So how do I do that?"

"Fly? Maybe you can do one of them *Star Trek* things. *I Dream of Jeannie*, maybe. Blink and you're there."

That breaks it for Electra. She hasn't a hope of stopping the tears, anger and frustration driving them more than anything else. "You're not being helpful," she says, and Rex softens in the chastisement.

"I'm sorry," he says. "Don't cry."

"I need to go. *Today*. I need help."

"I'm sorry," he says again. "Just hoping you wouldn't. You shouldn't be out in this."

"I *have* to."

The mechanic relents. "OK," he says. "You have tire chains?"

"No."

"I can sell you a set. You know how to put them on?"

"No."

"I can show you."

She points next door. "Can you just do it for me? I'm over there. I'll pay you."

"Lady," he says, "I'm the only one here. Can't just leave. Bring the car over and I'll be happy to do it."

"I could barely bring me over, it's so slick."

"So," he says, "I'll show you how."

There is no holding Nathan off further, so when Electra gets back, she helps him into his coat and mittens and laces up his shoes and tells him, "OK, you can play in the snow next to me." They go out into the parking lot, hand in hand, the slips and slides a merriment to the boy, a response she thinks she might admire if not for the overbearing fear that she's carrying for them both. She goes into the phone booth—"You stay right here with me," she tells the boy—and she engages the operator and places the collect call and gets Charley on the line.

"On the road?" *He's watching the clock*, she thinks, *same as I am. I should be cutting the corner off New Mexico by now.*

"No," she says, and the tears come again. She squeezes her eyes closed and then opens them again, trying to stop the flow. The window of the phone booth explodes into a white star, and she jumps, then looks through the streaks of snow. Nathan has thrown a snowball at her, an act that makes him giddy.

"No?" Charley asks.

"Snowstorm," she says. "Goddammit."

"Oh, honey. Just stay another night."

"No. No way." She's full-on crying now, and she's ashamed of it, for no other reason than it's in her way. "I already spent thirty dollars on tire chains, that's the breakfast money and then some, and another night in a motel would be—"

"I'll wire you some money."

"*The money isn't the point.*" The words fly out of her with ferocity. "I'm not sitting around here in this . . . this—"

"Purgatory," he says.

"Yes. I'm not doing it. I'm leaving now. I'm coming. I said I would, and I am. I'm just going to be late, that's all."

"OK."

"I'm just calling to let you know."

Another snowball smashes against the booth, and Electra cups the mouthpiece and leans out and makes eye contact with her boy. "That's enough now, Nathan. You hear me?" His shoulders slump.

"OK." Charley sends soothing words her ear. "You come to me. I'll be waiting. I've got a bed made up for Nathan. Refrigerator's full. You're wanted here."

"So I'll be there."

"You know how I feel," Charley says.

"You know how I feel, too."

The motel proprietor has come by with a wide-mouthed shovel and cleared some working space for Electra behind the Firebird. She backs it out, maybe ten feet from the sidewalk fronting the row of rooms. Even at a gentle speed, with the brake applied tenderly, the car slides the final couple of feet. Electra emerges, jelly-legged, stepping with care. Nathan sits on the stoop, observing with full concentration, like a cat studying a bird in a tree outside.

"I'm cold," he says.

Electra drags the chains, one at a time, halting steps, and positions them alongside the four wheels. "I know, honey, me, too. You can go back inside."

"No."

"OK, then."

She zeroes in, bears down, remembering what Rex showed her and told her, and she sets to work. The chains laid out so, the V links set in a way that, once she gets them on the tires, will make contact with the road surface—or, more specific to the misadventure she has in mind, the ice atop it. Next, she lays them like blankets on the wheels, left back and right back first, the whole ballgame right there, if she can get those on good and tight, the front ones will be a cinch, and if she can't . . . she doesn't want to think about *can't* just now.

She's had some good luck, taking mechanical lessons from men, when they've set aside their own inflationary self-regard long enough to explain the things in a useful way. She remembers now her father, teaching her how to hang a door, a useful enough skill if also one that hasn't come up even once in the intervening years. How to drive a manual transmission, that was a better example of Sid Griffey's admonitions to his only child, his contention that any damn fool can drive these newfangled automatics, but what was she going to do if the only car she had access to was a shifter and she couldn't operate it? A good question. She'd insisted on an automatic when Ronnie, desperate to fend off her discontent, had bought her the Firebird. A hedging of her bets, you could call it.

She sits herself in the front seat and starts the car. *Mom and Dad, among the first calls once we're there*, she thinks now. They'll be disappointed, of course. Her dad loves Ronnie, because Ronnie understands raw certainty and the pleasures of whiskey, and her mom loves that Ronnie provides all the things she thinks are important and none of the ones Electra actually wants, the ones Suzanne Griffey can't see anyway and that her daughter has been unable to sufficiently explain. An unwelcome remembrance charges in, the only other night she'd run away, a couple of years before Nathan, when she'd shown up on the doorstep in Monterey and they'd taken her in and let her sleep and then told her the next morning that they loved her but that she had to go back. It's a commitment you've made, they said, and commitments are important.

"Not now," Electra says, and she sets the Firebird in drive. It's a light touch on the accelerator—Rex's voice in her head, *real slow, just turn the wheels one rotation*—and the back wheels fight her at first and then engage and the links find purchase, and . . .

A thump stops her, her foot stomping through to the floorboard on the brake. She sets the car shifter and she's out of there, to the front of the car, where Nathan lies on his back, planted in the shoveled snow.

"Nathan!" She's with him, on her knees, grabbing him, holding him, crying, frantic.

"You hit me," he says.

"My baby, my baby, my baby." She hugs him and she just as quickly holds him away from her, examining him. "What did you do?"

"You hit me."

"What did you do?" Her voice rises to its highest pitch, angry and frightened and flattened and hysterical. "What did you do?"

"You hit me."

She pulls him into a clench again, then lets him go. "I told you to sit there. I told you not to move."

She hadn't seen him. She hadn't even looked.

"I wanted to see what happened."

"And I hit you!" She hugs him again, and he strains in her embrace, and she lets him go. "Are you hurt?"

"I fell in the snow."

"Are you hurt, Nathan?"

"No, Momma."

She pulls him in again and hangs on this time, and he nestles his head under her chin, and she can feel that he's letting her have this, letting her get her heart rate down, letting the relief come screaming behind the terror, and she loves him for it. "We're almost there," she says, leavened words intended for herself as much as for him. "We're almost there, we're almost there."

When, at last, she lets him have free space again, she sends him inside. "You're not in trouble," she says, for the benefit of a boy who takes things to heart, for outcomes good and bad. "I've almost got this finished, and then we'll go, OK?"

"OK."

"I'll come and get you when we're ready."

"OK, Momma."

She sets back to work, with shaky fingers that have gone cold, her body riven by adrenaline, frozen air still being taken into her lungs in great gulps. The ends of the back sets of chains are connected, the cams tightened, the bungees crossing the front of the hubcap and pulling tension, just like Rex showed her. She goes inside, finds Nathan asleep in his coat, on the bed, legs askew, and she warms herself and heads back to the waiting work, and she lays into it, trying to remember every little step.

Electra takes down the twenty miles from Trinidad to Raton in an hour and a half, the Firebird cutting a path in the deep fallen snow, on a heading slow and deliberate and safe. She grips the wheel until her hands drain out, and Nathan sits in his seat, the hood of his coat cinched up around his face, blessedly quiet, as if he understands how fraught it all is.

When the Sangre de Christos fall away behind them, it's as if they've moved from one world to the next, seamlessly. She pulls into a sunny, wide spot off the road, and she tells the boy to sit quiet, then she gets out and works the chains off the tires, Rex's lessons played in reverse. She casts off her coat and sets it on the ground near the door, and she lugs the chains onto her shoulder, one at a time, and carries them to the trunk.

Here, the day is coming up warm, a radical departure from what they woke up to. She looks to the wide arc of the highway, the miles she can see in the clear light, the many more beyond that are yet invisible to her. A line from Robert Frost, a schoolgirl memorization, comes to her. How true it is.

She climbs back in with Nathan. "Piece of cake," she says.

"Piece of *pan*cake," he says.

"I know."

"With blueberries."

"I know, Nathan. I know."

In a couple of hours, they're in Clayton, in a booth at a truck stop, a plate stacked high with hotcakes and compote in front of him, coffee and two over-easy eggs and bacon for her. She looks out the window at the big rigs lined up. It's not like before, when the specter of Ronnie hung heavy. They're in open country now, not yet home free but just the driving, a whole damn lot of it, left to do. She sips her coffee, and the spring inside her unwinds.

"You like those?" she asks, and Nathan gives her a yummy-noise affirmative.

"Good," she says. "Real good."

The food will warm him, and he'll sleep. She'll be grateful.

Ten miles more, and they're across the line. She reaches right, blindly, her eyes fixated to the asphalt, and she rubs the sleepyhead. He wriggles away and puts his weight into the door.

"Texas," she says.

He stays down for hours, and she lets him, granted a chance to stay inside her own head and heart and all that abounds in each. Amarillo comes up, short buildings on a flat plain, and they're five hours in with seven still to go. She feels the grind, a gray headache that's sprung up. She pushes on.

When Nathan awakes, he looks at the vast horizons that spill across the hood of the car.

"Where are we?" he asks.

"Texas."

"This is Texas?"

"Yes."

"This is where we will live?"

"Well, not here. Another part of Texas. But yes."

"I need to pee," he says.

"Can you hold it? Just a few miles to the next town."

"Now," he says.

She eases onto the shoulder at a mile marker.

"Need me to help?" she asks.

"I can do it."

"Stand behind the door so people don't see you." She feels foolish for saying it. There are no people. Just a road and an overhanging sun and time.

"I know," he says.

"OK."

When he's done and back inside, he asks her how much longer, and she says "not long now." A convenient lie, that. She looks at her watch. Six hours if they make good time. She looks again. It's coming up on three o'clock, and then she realizes she hasn't made the change to Central time. Almost four o'clock. The shadows have lengthened, where there are shadows to cast. Ronnie will be home soon, will see what she's done, will read the letter she left for him. And so it will end, even as it begins.

She checks her mirrors and gets moving again.

11

October 1952 | Three Forks, Montana

Ronnie inches himself across the bench seat of Tom Foley's pickup, closer to Louann Harper, who sits with her hands entwined in her lap. She fixes him with a sideways look as he approaches.

"What are you doing?" she asks.

"I want to kiss you."

"Oh, you do?"

"I do."

"On the cheek, then." She's now a coquette, jutting her jawline toward him and tilting it upward. He puts his lips on her skin and lingers.

"One kiss," she says, pulling away. "Now, go back over there and be good."

Ronnie does as he's told. "I want to kiss you more," he says.

"I'm sure you do," Louann says. "I'm sure that's what you brought me up here for, for kissing." The lights from town blink below them, a small galaxy. Outside the truck, night holds them in a tight hug. She's a high school senior, a year beyond him, and the daughter of friends of the Foleys. He's balancing the incompatible interests of preserving familial harmony and seeing just how far he can get.

"Yeah, I did," Ronnie says. No point in lying about it, especially not to Louann, who has been as aggressive in her intentions at times as he has been. He remembers when Tom and Berta first took him to church—they're not really churchgoers, except for the big occasions, nor do they carry any particular expectations for his religious or educational rigor—and how she locked in on him as the new boy. Everything he had said, which wasn't much, was of interest to her. Everywhere he went, even if it was just a quick visit to the plate of cookies in the narthex, was the place to be. She's been plenty clear about some things and opaque about others. She has him on a string, and he suspects she knows it.

"Well," she says, "I want to talk about the movie."

"So talk." The flick didn't make much of an impression, for Ronnie's money. And it *was* Ronnie's money, four bits a ticket, more for the popcorn they shared and the two Cokes they didn't. What they got was something called *Horizons West*. That it was a western interested him. That Rock Hudson was on the bill interested her.

"I thought it was good," she says. "Did you?"

"I guess."

"I sure like that Rock Hudson."

"I know you do," he says. He cannot evade the implication, in the way she says it, that he most assuredly has no prospects of measuring up to someone like Rock Hudson. He's not tall enough, he's not good-looking enough, he doesn't have enough muscle on him by a damn sight. On the other hand, Ronnie thinks, he can sure enough hold a gun better than Rock Hudson can. That distinction, he knows, probably isn't going to mean much to Louann.

"You don't like him?" she asks.

"Not particularly, no." The truth is, Ronnie found Robert Ryan the more interesting of the stars, and by a goodly bit. The lines cut deep into his weatherworn face, that's a man right there. The wanting something beyond himself, beyond what the world says he ought to have, that's something Ronnie can feel in his own longing. A woman who wants him as much as he wants her, circumstance and what's proper be damned, that's how Ronnie *wants* to feel.

"I should be getting home," Louann says.

"I want to kiss you."

"One, but then I should be getting home."

She leans across to him, eyes closed, lips puckered, and he takes the offer. It's not quite the way Robert Ryan kissed Julie Adams up there on the screen, but it'll have to do.

"You smell like flowers," he says.

"I do?"

"Yeah. I like it."

Louann pulls away, though Ronnie picks up on some hesitancy to do so. She goes back to her spot on the bench. He retreats to his.

"It's called Arpege," she says, and he repeats it back to her, "Arp-idge," and she giggles. "It's French," she says. "My grandma got it for me at Hart-Albin in Billings."

"It makes me want to kiss you again," he says.

"So don't talk about it," she says. "Do it."

He leans toward her, and she toward him, and they touch lips, longer this time. He reaches for her, and she pulls away again.

"That was nice," she says.

"Let's do it again."

"I really have to go home."

"Nuts."

"Take me to the Harvest Dance next Saturday?" she asks, hopefulness brimming. "We can do more of it then, if you want."

"Yeah," he says. "OK."

It's early yet, earlier than Ronnie said he'd be back, anyway, and he resists the impulse to go downtown and see if he can finagle himself a beer. He probably can't, he thinks, but if it were his time and his pickup and only his neck, he might give it a whirl. He's not much known in town, barely a name or an age attached to him, but it's the physical that would give him away—the callowness, the gangly frame still toting a boy rather than a man, the upper lip that couldn't grow whiskers if he loaded it up with manure and gave it a month of rain.

What turns him toward the ranch, though, is more gratitude than superior judgment. The Foleys are awfully good to him, awfully generous. Tom has tossed him the pickup keys a few times for nights out with Louann, told him to have fun, slipped him some money, told him they'll see him in the morning. It wouldn't be right to push too far into the night or, worse, crack up the pickup while a beer sloshed around in his belly. Wouldn't be right at all.

And yet, Ronnie knows, it's also the lent pickup and the handed-over money and the rest of it that's pushing him away. Nothing is really his here, not even his time. He's been granted benevolence, and that's more than he ever thought he had coming, but more and more, he finds himself wanting something else, on terms he outlines, with the reasons all his own.

When he gets to the farmhouse, he parks the pickup, douses the lights, and shuts it down. He walks gently into the house, a courtesy rather than a precaution. If the Foleys have ever heard him, they've never said, and they've never come down to see him, to welcome him back, to volley questions at him or make him uncomfortable. They'll leave him be until morning and breakfast and tread lightly even then, and for that he's appreciative.

He shimmies out of his clothes, shirt and socks in the hamper, jeans still belted on the bedpost, ready for another round. He pulls a fresh T-shirt from the bureau and slips it on. The drawer still open, he takes apart a pair of tube socks and carries one to the bed. He turns back the covers and climbs in.

He reaches for himself and imagines what it might have all led to had Louann been willing to entertain his intentions a bit. Imagination is what he has, having never gotten past a deeper version of the kiss he negotiated out of her tonight. But, much like with the ideas of his own wheels and his own money, he has a brain that's gone addled with the prospect and the attendant mystery of sex. Put directly, he wants it. Put more directly, he sometimes thinks he'll up and pop if he doesn't get it, and therein lies the explanation for the light touch with himself and the soiled sock he'll hide in the laundry basket.

It's a shameful, if irresistible, thing to Ronnie, clouded each time with the remembrance of Dick's catching him in the barn when he first started doing it. The sweaty memory always comes, of Dick's holding him down, calling him a dirty monkey and kidney-punching him, hurting him where Ma would never see it. And later, at the dinner table, there's Dick, saying, "Mother, you will not believe what your son was doing this afternoon out in that barn."

"What's that?" An expectant look toward Ronnie, who had scooched down in his chair.

"Well, I just think it would be in bad taste to say," Dick had said. "Nasty. Just nasty."

"Well, OK, then." She always was an ignorance-is-the-better-part-of-valor woman.

"But boy," Dick had said to him, "if you need relief, why don't you just climb up behind one of those cows and take a turn? They won't mind." He'd had himself a good laugh at that and shoveled mashed taters into his mouth, and Ronnie had burned with shame as Ma had studiously avoided looking at him. Little Linda, thank god for small favors, seemed not to understand the fuss being made about the whole thing.

Ronnie finishes and cleans himself with the sock. He gets up again and carries it to the hamper and stuffs it deep into the pile, then retrieves its mate from the bureau and dumps that, too, so everything comes up even in the wash. He returns to bed, curls up into himself, swaddled in the covers, and tries to find sleep.

It's early afternoon the next day when Berta rides out to the field Ronnie helped Tom clear and level the year before. It's good to see her, respite as she'll be from the froze-up tractor engine they've been rebuilding, to little satisfaction yet. It's a hell of a smart setup Tom has here, a tractor running full-throttle day and night during the growing season, connected by a flat belt to a pump that pushes slough water up a pipe and out, down into the irrigation ditch. And now they stand upon the cleared-out results of that industry, another ten acres that get irrigated for alfalfa. The problem is that the wearing out comes sooner or later, and here they are, trying to overcome it. Ronnie finds himself relieved that it didn't happen in the summertime, when the stalled pumping would have cost real money and surely a greater expenditure of frustration and mild cursing from Tom.

Berta's appearance saves them from that, at least briefly. It's a chance to walk away from the job and see to her and let the ongoing frustration settle for just a little bit.

"That's quite a hoof," Tom says. "To what do we owe the pleasure?"

She pulls herself tight inside her coat. The morning frost has burned off, but the chill lingers, and the scant evidence of the sun hangs gauzily behind the clouds, a foretelling of a change in the weather that'll be nigh unstoppable.

"There's a letter," she says. That brings Ronnie from idly standing by to full-on attention.

"From?" he asks, hesitant hopefulness swelling inside the word.

"Yes," she says. "I didn't read it." She hands the envelope to him. "It's addressed to me, but it's for you, I imagine."

The particulars are written in a pretty cursive, with the letters taking on a northeastern lean and the loops tight and well-controlled and feminine.

Oscar Ray
Billings, MT

Mrs. Tom Foley
Three Forks, MT

Ronnie shows the envelope to Tom. "He didn't write this."

"No," Tom says, "I reckon he didn't. Well, open it, and let's see what whoever has to say."

Ronnie gives the envelope two quick shakes in his hand to push the letter to the edge. Then he rips the opposite side, careful not to take off too much off the top of it. He blows on the hole, widening it, and sends fingers inside to retrieve the single sheet of paper. Then he seizes up, unable to unfold it.

"Come on," Berta says. "Don't drag it out."

"I can't help it," Ronnie says. "I figured it was a lost cause."

When the inquiry Tom put in around Great Falls came up empty and the newspaper ads in Bozeman and Helena and Butte fetched nothing, same as the ones in Missoula and Kalispell, Ronnie had swallowed his disappointment and turned his thoughts toward May and his coming birthday. He'd talked about it just last night with Louann, fending off her mild suggestions that he stick around. *No, he'd said, when I'm seventeen, I can enlist with parental consent, and that's sure enough what I'm going to do.* He hadn't quite worked around the particular problem of that, the absence of parentals, but he had to figure Tom and Berta would stand in as the next best thing. They'd already found their way to acceptance that he was antsy to go. Surely they wouldn't stand in the way once he'd settled on a path.

So Ronnie had balked when Berta had suggested that they try the Billings paper before giving up. "Just more of your money gone," he'd said, and being how she is, Berta had replied, "Well, if we don't try, he certainly won't ever answer. A lot of people in Billings. It might work."

It had worked. Imagine that.

"You want me to read it?" Berta asks him.

He hands her the sheet. "Please."

She unfolds the paper and holds it close to her face.

"Dear Missus Foley. I am Oscar Ray. My son is named Ronald. He would be 16 or 17 years old, I think. I haven't seen him since he was little. He was born in Conrad, Montana. If you have information, please let me know, for I'd like to see him again. I'm working on Opal Knudsen's farm in Yellowstone County. Her number is 9-9127. Thank you."

Berta refolds the letter and wordlessly holds it out to Ronnie, who accepts it and examines it for himself. The same cursive as on the envelope spells it all out. Oscar Ray with dictation, Opal Knudsen, whoever that is, with transcription, seems like. He folds the letter again and puts it in the envelope.

"Well," Berta says, her hand going to her heart. "Isn't that a surprise?" Tom draws her in with an arm around her shoulders, and he kisses her forehead.

"It worked," Ronnie says. "How about that?"

"It worked," Tom agrees. He points to the tractor and its spilled guts on the ground. "Now, we need to get something else working." He turns again to his wife. "Dear, do you want me to drive you back?"

Berta pats his arm. "No. I think I'll walk. It'll do me some good. I'll see you in a bit."

"Good enough. We shouldn't be long."

"Ronnie?" she says.

"Yes, ma'am?"

"I'm happy for you, son."

She takes her leave, and Ronnie and Tom pour themselves back to the problem before them. It's the same now but different as they set into work again. Tom isn't so frustrated by the job anymore, a sort of sobriety having settled over them both, and when he needs a fresh tool, it's a request with a "please" attached and not a directive.

When, at last, the tractor engine fires and holds steady, Tom grips Ronnie's shoulder with a strong hand and says, "That was some fine work there, my boy," and it feels like misplaced praise. Ronnie hasn't done anything but follow directions. But he'll take it.

"You go back in the pickup," Tom says. "I'll drive the tractor to the barn."

"Yes, sir."

On the way back to the house, the pickup bouncing along two-track, Ronnie watches the sun's descent through the windshield glass, pinks and purples and oranges poking wide holes in the gray of the western sky and shining down on the hills. "Spotlights from heaven," he remembers Ma had called them one day when Dick had been gone. That had been a good day, but not the kind that can hold you. It wasn't a month later that Ronnie was gone for good.

He pats his shirt pocket and the envelope lying within. He's found himself a notch in the rhythms of these days and this place and these people, the sun coming up and lighting his way through the work, then darkness bringing on sleep before it all begins again, with plenty to eat and human kindnesses to sustain him during the intervening hours. *Why am I going?* he wonders, and he answers himself in the same thought. *Because I just can't picture many more tomorrows here.* Things with the Foleys have become a constant thrum, like that tractor engine helping to draw water into the ditch. Nothing wrong with it, but might be nice to hear something else, to see another horizon. *Maybe the Army will send me somewhere like Germany. Probably Korea first, the way that's going, but maybe Germany after. Wouldn't that be a hoot? Or maybe it'll be something else. Who knows?*

He wishes for the next sunrise, the next turn of the earth, and then the one after that and the one after that—however many of them he'll need until he's standing in front of his father and can at last say to him, *I'm here and I'm your boy.*

12

July 2002 | Billings, Montana

Another load is in the trailer and carried out—back to the dump, back to the scale, no sneering Jeff this time, thank god—and Cherie is at the house again before Anna pushes herself up from bed and rejoins the living. It's a well-worn pattern, Anna's complaint about the headache, as if it's chance that she'd have one, and her grumbling into the morning that's already making a hard turn toward noon, and the apologies and the subsequent promises that won't be kept.

"Sit down," Cherie says. "You want some breakfast?"

"No."

"How about some toast? Something?"

"OK."

She takes her mother gently by the elbow and guides her to one of the chairs at the kitchen table. *Might as well sit on them before they, too, are gone,* she thinks. *Probably tomorrow, definitely the next day, because that's the end of it, even if I have to do it alone.*

Next, she fetches coffee, puts it in front of Anna with a packet of sugar, and starts a fresh pot.

"You've made progress," Anna says, warming her hands on the cup and considering the room. The magazines and chipped end tables and fraying rugs, the cumulative treasures of an unremarkable life, have all been carried out and sent away. In their wake, order, almost.

"Some," Cherie says from the kitchen. She plugs in the toaster, roots through the fridge, finds the loaf of wheat bread they brought with them, retrieves a slice, drops it in, and sets the timer.

"We forgot butter," she says.

"I'll dip it in my coffee."

Cherie sits adjacent to her mother, at her left elbow. Anna looks like charbroiled hell, also predictable, also avoidable.

"How you feeling?"

Anna says nothing.

"You think you can get started in here, maybe?"

"Yeah, I'll try."

"I've been putting off the basement," Cherie says. "But it's time."

Anna's head swings low, her shoulders rounded into a slump. "I'm sorry," she says.

"I know."

"I keep doing it."

"You do."

"I'm sorry."

The toaster pings, a timely point of departure, for Cherie really doesn't want to go hurtling into this dead end again. In her own head, she's managed to cast the morning as one of accomplishment rather than abandonment, which pushes her toward motivation for the rest of what's to be done. She doesn't want to go riding off into the ditch that forever runs alongside them, filled to brimming with insufficient amends and unsustainable promises.

She gets up, finds a plate for the bread, cuts it diagonally, and totes it over to Anna.

"Thank you, dear."

"I'm going downstairs," Cherie says. "See you in a bit."

"OK."

It's unfinished down there, a dank mirror of the main house above. From the concrete floor, posts are framed up where there's drywall and plaster upstairs, forming the outlines of a small handful of what would be rooms here were there walls. A single bulb dangles parallel with the main fixture in the living room. Alvin Knudsen was a capable enough homebuilder—the structure's longevity attests to that—if not a particularly artful one.

Cherie first lights up the darkness and at once thinks of something Mr. Harrison was fond of saying, a memory straight out of eleventh-grade history, from the man who gave the hardest tests and had the best one-liners. *How do you eat an elephant? Carefully, and one bite at a time.* Cherie opts for the pile method—she'll go from area to area, sorting out the messes. Stuff that looks like trash in the garbage pile. Stuff that looks like keepers in the stay pile, the in-betweens to be examined and judged once the piles are set. And so on.

She's appalled—and a bit awed, truthfully—by the magnitude of the job before her. The principles of physics held that Opal had to at least retain space to live upstairs, to beat back the tide of possessions enough to walk or sit or set her head down at night. Here, though, she was bound only by the dimension of the space, and she damn near tapped it out. Old suitcases, zippers and latches loose and compartments misaligned, lie in a stack, slathered with dust and touched by a latticework of cobwebs. A formidable row of bankers' boxes, their corrugated bodies caving in from the weight of time. Knickknacks and abandoned furniture and other detritus. Cherie tries to shake her memory banks, because she doesn't recall it being such a critical mass when she'd visit as a little girl, but she can't hold the vision. Like so many things examined in the rearview, the pictures are fuzzy and unrefined, an impressionistic scattershot that she didn't retain in full because it wasn't an extant consideration.

From upstairs, she hears water running, the bathroom or the kitchen sink, no matter, because either option means her mother is at least moving. That's something.

Cherie heads to the back of the basement, below the two bedrooms, and plunges into the maw, because, if you're going to finish, you first must start.

At lunchtime, Cherie makes them bologna sandwiches, mayonnaise on wheat, a handful of potato chips on the side. As they've considered of the job at hand, she's managed to chase her mother off the idea of taking *all* the dishes—there's not room in the car, and besides, what happens on the other end? A cabinet fills with something no one ever uses, and soon you end up with the sort of pigsty from which they're trying to escape now. Anna seems to have taken it to heart, having boxed up the vast preponderance of tableware for the next dump run, with a small stack of pretty floral plates set near the door, bound for the car.

Anna looks much improved from morning despite the work she's put in. Another well-trod pattern. If Cherie can keep her away from the alcohol for a day or two, she'll shed the physical leavings of her chronic drunkenness. A day or two beyond that, and Anna will be chirping happily about the prospects of a sober life, with liberal citations of stock phrases such as "new day" and "new me," but she'll do so without dispensation of all the old that hangs heavily on them. A day or two beyond that and . . . well, Cherie thinks she would like to see that, or thirty days on, or a season, or half a year, those remote possibilities she dares not dwell upon. She's not hopeful.

"How's it going downstairs?" Anna asks.

Cherie considers how she must look, her blue MONTANA STATE UNIVERSITY T-shirt gone gray with marauding dust bunnies, the grime on her face, the sweat that's pooled under her arms and in her crotch.

"Getting there," she says. "About ready to bring some stuff up and take away another load."

"Do you want me to come with?"

"Better if you stay," Cherie says. "We'll get more done."

"OK."

Cherie munches a chip. "I found all the photo albums, I think."

"Oh, good."

"Was hard to resist taking a break and looking through them."

"We'll do it at home," Anna says.

Home. It's a word that pushes Cherie fully forward into what's coming, and fast. She needs to get back, get her fall classes lined up, settle on work-study, all of it. She can feel time sprinting away from her. It's all the more reason to finish up here, put the keys in the real estate agent's hands, let it go, so the next thing can be embraced or survived.

"Let's go out tonight," Anna says. "I'll be good."

"I was thinking pizza. In."

"You sure?"

"I'm sure," Cherie says. She stands, takes her mother's plate and her own to the sink, uses her hand to brush the crumbs away. She slips them into the box with the others headed for the scrap heap and seals it up with the tape roll lying beside it. She lifts the box, then clenches it tight when she feels the weight, and says, "Can you get the door for me?"

She waddles behind her mother, straining, and out the opened door, onto the porch. It's a race now, a contest between how deliberately she can move and at what speed and the load's seeming determination to work itself loose from her grasp.

She doesn't make it. She's on the grass when gravity finally wins, the box crashing to the earth, the shattering within obvious.

"Shit."

"You OK?"

"I'm fine."

"I can help."

"No need."

Cherie lowers herself into a squat, tips the box forward with her shoulder, gets her arms under it, and stands again. Once she's steadied, she makes a run at the trailer, a throaty growl that rises with each step, and she launches the box over the gate. It lands heavily, with more crashing porcelain. Cherie raises her arms, triumphant.

That evening, after two more dump runs and the pizza delivery and the six o'clock news, after Cherie has satisfied herself that they really are going to make it now, after she's praised her mother's industry and left Anna to relax with her paperback upstairs, she heads down again, to the last of the tasks in the basement. Every scrap of paper in the bankers' boxes must be gone through, for reasons practical and fanciful.

The real estate agent, whom they'll meet tomorrow, has requested anything that might clarify the history of the property. "These old houses, you never know," she'd said. "People sometimes balk at the unseen. If you can say, 'Well, the roof was redone here' or 'The electrical panel was upgraded in this year,' sometimes that will make a difference."

Cherie herself wishes for something grander, more dramatic, more heart-stopping in the files, even though she knows it's a silly hope. She imagines a cashier's check for some fantastical amount, say twenty grand or so, you know, something that was just misplaced, and something that can change trajectories, save her from the loans she's taken out to augment the meager scholarships she's won. Or a hand-drawn map to a treasure buried out back. Wouldn't that cast a new light on Opal, whom she loved well but who wasn't, in any sense, a woman who'd surprise you? Forrest Fenn, she wasn't.

It's tedious work, a slow system of retrieval and examination, one that leaves Cherie arm-weary from the repeated motion of pulling paper, holding it to the light, then finding the stack where it belongs. The one she thinks of as HOLY GOD, DID SHE KEEP EVERY RECEIPT? outpaces the piles of DESTROY THESE FOR THEY CONTAIN SOCIAL SECURITY NUMBERS and INTERESTING FAMILY ARTIFACTS by a long stretch.

"What's this?" Cherie asks no one. She's on her knees, hunched over the boxes. She spreads the single typewritten, yellowed sheet on the floor, under the light. She notes the names, the one she knows and the one she doesn't, and the date, and she recognizes the well-controlled signature.

She stands and brushes the dust from the knees of her jeans. She carries the paper up the stairs. Anna snoozes noisily in Opal's favorite chair.

"Mom?"

Anna surfaces. "Hmm?"

"Who's Oscar Ray?"

"Who?"

"Oscar Ray," Cherie says.

"I don't know."

"What's a quit claim?"

"I don't know."

"Well, look." She hands the paper over. Anna sits up, finds her readers, and puts them on. She scans the item. She frowns.

"I can't make sense of it." She looks at the date. "Nineteen fifty-two? I wasn't even born." She hands it back.

"Yeah, but you were on your way. It looks like she was transferring interest in the farm to this guy, this Oscar Ray, whoever he is," Cherie says.

"It was her parents' farm," Anna says. "She wouldn't have done that. No way."

"I'm just saying, that's what it looks like. Who is he?"

"I don't know. Never heard of him."

"Well, aren't you curious?"

"No," Anna says. "I mean, maybe, I guess, but . . . no. Her mom, your great-grandma, died in '51. Your grandma, she'd just lost her boyfriend. Can I look at that again?"

Cherie gives her the paper.

"October 28th, 1952," she reads.

"Larry Teasdale died—" Cherie starts.

"October 15th," Anna finishes. "So maybe that's it. Grandma had just lost him. She's in pain, she wants to start over, she's going to sell to this guy and then thinks better of it."

"That's a lot of supposing from a fifty-year-old sheet of paper. She didn't say anything about this?"

"She never talked about any of it, not much. You know that. Unmarried woman, pregnant with a soldier's child," Anna says. She stops, as if the shame Opal carried from her twenties to the grave suddenly makes a different kind of sense to her. "Me. Jesus. Me."

"But Oscar Ray," Cherie presses.

"I don't know. Never heard of him." Anna waves an arm across the room. "But clearly she never sold the place."

"I guess," Cherie says.

"Just throw it away." Anna gives her the paper again.

"I guess," Cherie says.

"Are you almost done with everything?"

"Getting there," Cherie says. "I'm going to go back down, really put a dent in it."

"OK, sweetie." Anna stands and stretches, then leans over and kisses Cherie's forehead. "I'm going to bed."

Electra Stidham

1939-1976

When you awake, a rarity anymore, for you mostly sleep, and you feel OK relative to what is happening inside you—what has started and advanced and has been bombed to the end of your tolerance and has kept eating away at everything you have to feed it—you ask him to bring the boy to you and sit him there where you can see him and to leave the two of you be for just a while so you can say the things that have gathered in your head.

You wrote Nathan a letter weeks ago, one he'll get when he's older and can grasp what you put in it, maybe when he has some perspective he can apply that makes the words land the way you intend them. You wrote it when you realized that the chemotherapy was clouding your thoughts, to get out in front of them as best you could in case you didn't have the ability later. You were still ambulatory—a doctor's word, that one—and still trying to work and still trying to hope, and all those things have left you now, one by one and then all at once. Hope, especially, has lit out for the territories. When you're angry, and you sometimes are, it's about the life you brought into the world and won't be able to follow anymore, not about the one being snuffed out. It's not a saintly thought; damn right, you'd prefer to live to be old, but it's not happening, and it's what you'll miss that tugs on you, not what's going to be lost. You won't know after it's done, and that right there, after the four months you've had, is pure relief.

He comes and he sits, and he holds your hand, though he balked at first, thinking he would bruise it up, as he's done before, clutching too tightly. *It's OK*, you tell him. *I'm tough. I might bruise easy, but I'm tough.*

You ask him about school, and it's fine, he says, he's struggling with the long division, that fourth grade is harder than third grade, but Charley, he's keen on words and grammar and is a big help there. He asks you when you're coming home, and here it is, the reason he's here now. You tell him you aren't, that you'd hoped so and the doctors had hoped so, and it's just not going to go that way. He cries when you say that, for he knows what it means. It's one of the cruel jokes of the universe, that he'd come to you not a year and a half ago and said, *Am I going to die someday?* He knew what death was in the abstract, having lost his grandfather to a heart attack the previous spring, and you'd had to sit him down for one of the Big Talks that's in all the child development books, and you'd had to explain that, yes, he will die someday, we all die after all, but not for a long, long time. *Are you and Charley going to die?* Yes, but not for a long, long time. *Daddy?* Yes. But again . . .

You wish for those answers back, so you can supply the caveats and the disclaimers, so you can tell him that no one can know all that might come. You gave those answers in a time when you thought you were just a little rundown, that you were a little over-busy, because you were. When you didn't know what you know now.

You tell him not to cry. He's strong, like you are, and he'll need to be stronger than he even knows. You tell him you love him. It's an impossibly big love, bigger than anything there has ever been. You tell him to remember that. You tell him to go and get Charley now, that Charley will take him home, that you will see him again.

He looks at you, his face red, his cheeks wet, and he asks you not to go. *For as long as I can*, you tell him, *I won't. Go on now with Charley. Let me sleep. OK?*

13

October 1972 | Euless, Texas

Electra, in the final throes of her coherence, thinks it'll be an absolute scream if she's made it this far, only to wither away on some lonely, barely lit avenue in Texas for want of a pay phone.

"Do you see anything?" she asks Nathan, whom she's enlisted in the search. He sits in the seat, face pressed to the window, scanning the right side of the road as she takes the left. Being assigned a duty has helped his disposition. These past few hours, he's been fussier than normal, which she supposes is his right. Two days in the car is a lot to ask of anyone, let alone a five-year-old whose natural state is wide-armed runs through the yard, like a dog with the rips.

"No," he says.

"They've sure rolled up the sidewalks," she says. "It's deader than Casper." She hadn't expected this, especially as they approached from the northwest and came upon a nighttime view of Fort Worth, the lit-up windows from the buildings rising like jagged teeth on the horizon, a suggestion of the multiplied tens of thousands who call this place home, more people than one can find in all of Wyoming. The effect had only been heightened by the highway they took due east, toward Dallas, a few dozen miles away. Electra had cackled at the sudden memory of one of her boy's favorite cartoons, the one with the preening, braggadocious rooster who says, "That girl reminds me of the highway between Dallas and Fort Worth. No curves." It really is true. Everything here is a hard angle, from what she can see.

"Just get off at Euless and find a phone and call me," Charley had said, a couple of hours earlier when she'd called from Wichita Falls. "I'll talk you in. Or I'll come get you."

"I will," she'd said.

But she hadn't. She'd had a brainstorm, a compulsion, one born from those calls with him when all of this seemed like some unreachable fantasy. She'd asked for his address and carried it down to the Casper Public Library and availed herself of the maps there and put her finger it, the place where he lives, and she'd traced the route from where she was to where she now knew she wanted to be. She'd imagined what his life must look like there, where he goes, what he does, and she wondered if she could make a place for herself, and for Nathan, inside it. She's had a *picture*, one in her head, anyway, and that's something you can cling to when there's nothing else. Many has been the day when she has imagined herself driving to him, finding him, walking up to his apartment door and knocking, and saying, "Hi there, Charley." The only thing she wants now more than seeing Charley at all is finding her way to him like that, to witness his surprise at seeing her. So many times, she has imagined it.

She hasn't imagined this, though, being this close and at the same time this far away, being punchy and sleep-deprived and child-stressed and ready to cry.

She swings the car right at the next light, thinking that will at least lead her back toward the highway—she hopes—and a chance at resetting and trying again. She'd seen a convenience store there on the access road, a phone booth out front, and she'd taken a pass on using it. Foolish. *Try again, Electra.*

"This is where we're going to live?" Nathan asks, and she says, "Yes, right here, in this car probably."

The boy recedes into silence, as if contemplating the gravity of that awful prospect. "I'm sorry," she says. "I'm only kidding."

She stands on the brake, pitching him forward, her arm shooting out to keep his head from crashing the dashboard. A car trailing her whips around, horn blaring.

"Mom!"

"I think that was it."

She checks the Firebird's mirrors, waits for an opening, and draws the car through a U-turn. The headlights cut the darkness and land on the street sign.

"That's it!"

"What?" Nathan asks.

"The place."

"The place?"

"The place, the place, the place."

She knows it from here as much as she knows anything. Turn right, first left, last set of apartments on the left, first door facing the parking lot, 3B. She fractures speed laws in getting there, her heart beating fast, oxygenated blood flooding her extremities and coursing back again through her chest for another round. The moment sparks and crackles and burns and renews and burns again.

They're in a parking space, and then they're on terra firma, and then Charley comes out the door as she admonishes Nathan to stand still and wait for her to get their things. She closes the trunk and sees Charley there.

"You were going to call," he says.

"I didn't need to."

He leaves the landing. She heads for the sidewalk, pulling Nathan along by hand, and she and Charley embrace upon reaching each other. He presses her shoulder with his forehead. "I've been waiting for this." She breathes him in. How she's wanted to. "Me, too." She presses his back with one hand and keeps her boy tethered with the other. Nathan tries to wrench himself free.

"And this," she says, detaching, "is Mr. Nathan." A memory tumbles into her head, the night she left Sally's and walked home from that chance meeting with Charley, everything the same and everything different, in ways she couldn't have imagined. How she paid Tracy, the teen girl from down the block, and asked how Nathan had been ("a little fussy before bed, but no real problems"), and had gone to him, asleep in his room, and whispered to him: "I think everything has changed now." And then Charley had called the next morning and said much the same, and she knew.

The boy now leans into her hip. Charley tilts himself downward and offers a handshake.

"Hi, Nathan. I've heard a lot about you. I'm Charley."

The boy shakes the hand and lets go in the same motion and says nothing.

"Welcome to Texas," Charley says.

"I don't like it."

"It'll grow on you."

"I don't like you."

"Nathan!" Electra says.

Charley smiles. "I will, too, if you'll give me a chance." He brings himself to fully standing, hands on his hips, rocked back on his feet. "I'll help with your things."

Charley gives them the five-cent tour of the place, the kitchen and living room on the first level, both bigger and newer than the ones she had back in Wyoming, and the patio enclosed by particle-board walls painted brown.

He tells them of the swimming pool just yards away from the door—"I don't think they've closed it up yet"—and the park with the swing set just a little beyond the door and the nine-hole golf course and the walking trail.

"Do you play golf, Nathan?"

"No."

"I could teach you."

"*No.*"

Electra notes the tell-tale vacuum cleaner lines in the carpet and the antiseptic scent of Pine-Sol in the bathroom upstairs, a cramped space with a toilet and a sink and a standup shower. He's worked at cleaning up for them. "We'll have to share," Charley says in apologia. "Maybe, once you're settled, we can look—"

"It's fine," she says, and it is. What he's described to her for weeks now, what she's imagined, and what she's seeing—all are in alignment. It works. It's *going to* work, she tells herself.

"I want to go home," Nathan says, and Charley winces, and Electra kneels to the boy and says, "This *is* home. Remember how we talked about this?"

"No, it's not."

"Somebody's tired, I think."

"No!"

The boy crumbles to the floor and begins crying. "I hate it."

"Nathan . . ."

"I hate it!"

Charley looks to her, stricken by the suddenness of the fit. She closes her eyes, shakes her head.

"Can you show me the kitchen again?" she asks.

"Um, sure."

On the stairs, Nathan's wails still rising behind them, she tells him the score. "It's a matter of wills sometimes. You ready for this?"

He slips a hand along her hip. "Of course. But you're just going to leave him up there?"

"He'll figure out soon that he doesn't have an audience and it will be done."

After they've gone downstairs, after Electra has made her assessment of the pantry, after she's pictured the days stretched out before them, after Nathan, red-faced and watery-eyed, has come down and asked for a glass of water, after Charley has fetched the rest of their things and stacked them by the door for sorting out later, after they've come back up the stairs, quieter, the three of them lie askew on the king bed. Charley is on his side, head propped up by an angular arm. Electra lies far opposite of him, attentive to her son, and Nathan sleeps in between, curled like a kitten's paw and under a loose blanket.

Electra reaches across the distance, and Charley takes her hand.

"Probably not what you expected."

"It's everything I expected," he whispers. "You?"

"It's what I want," she says.

"Me, too."

"He's really a good boy," she says.

"I know."

"It's a lot to deal with."

"It is." Charley sits himself up, careful not to jostle the boy. "Kids are resilient, though. I ever tell you about when we moved from Vernon to Wichita Falls?"

"No. I'd remember."

"You went through both towns," he says.

"I know."

"I wish I could have been there."

"I know," she says.

"Fifty-some miles, might as well have been moving from earth to the moon. I was nine. Everything I knew, every friend I had, they were all in Vernon, but my dad, he was a history teacher, and the high school in Wichita Falls, they offered him $15 more a week, so we moved. I didn't have any say."

"Had to be hard at that age." She's thinking now of Nathan's best friends, the Miles boy two doors down and the Fletcher kid, the one she doesn't much like but whom Nathan adores, and how she plucked him up and took him away without his getting to say goodbye. She hurts for him in a way that she hasn't allowed herself to think about until now.

"Hard at any age," Charley says. "But the thing is, in the end, I made new friends. Wichita Falls became home, every bit as much as Vernon had been. I adjusted. He'll adjust, too."

"Tomorrow," she says, more thoughts she's held at bay rushing toward her now. Enrolling Nathan in school. Finding a job. Learning where the supermarket is.

"It'll all get done," he says, as if inside her head. It's a talent he has.

She leans across and kisses him for the first time.

She leaves them in the night and goes downstairs and sits at the dining room table and makes the call, to tie off the last of her obligations before the next one queues up.

He answers with "where are you?"

"Where I am."

"Cute," he says.

"I'm going to tell you. But not tonight."

"Your folks?"

"You've already called them, so you have your answer." She knows this, surely as she knows anything. She knows they'll be sympathetic to Ronnie, that they'll think her impetuous. Of course Ronnie called, for validation if not for information, as they have none to offer him.

"Yeah. So where?"

"Not now."

"Just come back," he says.

"No."

"Where's Nathan?"

"He's with me. He's safe."

"I don't much care for child stealing."

"Ronnie," she says evenly, "he's my son. I didn't steal him."

"He's *our* son."

"Yes. I never said he wasn't."

"Come back."

"No."

"You know you will."

"I won't, not ever. Listen to me: You'll be receiving papers tomorrow." She looks at the clock on the wall. "Today. I haven't taken Nathan from you. I'm not asking for anything he doesn't have coming. You're hurt now, and I understand that, but I'm being fair. You need to think about this and be fair, too."

"*Where are you?*" he spats.

"Ronnie."

"I will fight you on this."

"And you will lose. And it will get ugly. Don't make it ugly."

"Fuck you."

She hangs up. Her hands quiver. She sets them in her lap and folds them tightly, smothering the tremors.

"Electra?" Charley is at the foot of the stairs. *How long? How much did he hear?*

"I should have waited until tomorrow," she says. "It felt undone. It felt unfair to let it linger. I should have waited."

He comes to her, and she leans in. He holds her head against him. "It had to be this way," he says, and she knows. She remembers how he told her, at the beginning when they adorned her perhaps foolish idea with words and schemes, that if she could get herself out and moved *of her own volition*—his phrase—that he would walk the path with her. That he couldn't be a direct party to the wrecking of another man's marriage, having seen his own cast upon the rocks by such disregard, but if she could come to him on her own, of her own determination, he would be her landing spot. It's why she structured things the way she did—the runaway and the plotting beforehand—and why, when her lawyer said, "Electra, it's a risk," she'd decided it was worth the stretch and had structured the offer of dissolution in a way where the material wealth, save for Nathan's support, accrued to him. And when Amy had said, "You could get so much more—you *deserve* so much more," and had gone on and on about "an equitable division"—not community property, for Wyoming doesn't see it that way, but basic fairness. Whatever the two of you have together, Amy had said, you both built. You should have your part. And Electra had parried that, saying, "I don't want more. I want out. That's everything."

And here she is. She stands, takes Charley's hand, and leads him back upstairs.

14

August 2012 | Billings, Montana

Nate comes out of sunken sleep, tossed and discombobulated, and into the dull, gray hum of a hangover. The red digits of the alarm clock morph and shift and at last clarify, and he blinks until he can read the display. Nine-seventeen. Daytime hours by the light flooding in. He sits up in bed, and the headache crush comes again.

A scrap of paper sits on the end table, carrying a splash of handwriting: *Call me when you're ready to get your truck. Rhonda. 406-794-1978.*

How he arrived here evades imminent recall, but there are enough dots in the line for him to imagine how they all connect. Back they'd gone to the house after cooler heads and coffee had prevailed, apologies made in the Ray men's usual way of making them—drink and more of it—and another tumble into the breach. He looks to the opposite bed, pristine, as the hotel staff left it. *So the old man didn't come back. Well, good.*

Nate gets up, a yawping ache in his hips. He grabs the flask from next to the TV, and he opens it and takes a long slug. Then he finds his phone and makes the call.

They ride high into a bright morning, the straight shot across the gut of central Montana before the turn northward, Bob at the wheel, Ronnie in the opposite seat. The silences are long, punctuated by words here and there, mostly from Bob, most of them lighter than the air they're breathed into. Seventy miles in, twice that still to go, and Ronnie chews on doubt while Bob keeps nervous hands on the wheel, hands clenching and disengaging and pulling away and grabbing hold, over and over, to the point of Ronnie's irritation. What seemed like a capital idea in the darkness is a burden in the sunshine.

"Been a long time since I've been up this way," Bob says now.

"However long for you, much longer for me."

"Weren't no reason after we cleared out," Bob says. "Good job, good town, Billings. Everything you need."

"Everything," Ronnie says. "No need to go back."

"And yet here we go," Bob says.

"Here we go."

"Where'd he go?" Nate stands in the gravel of Bob's driveway, his hands upturned, questioning her.

"You don't remember?"

"Clearly not."

Rhonda goes through it, the renewal of the festivities, the "fuck it, Bob and I are going up there, we've decided" declaration from his father, Bob's surprise that he'd been enlisted, the onward flow of drinks until father and son were at loggerheads again, each disagreement dumber and more pig-headed than the one preceding, culminating in a punch by Nate that wouldn't have connected in a hundred years from the bleary place it was thrown, another scrum, another retreat by both men. "That's when I took you back to the hotel," she tells him now.

"So he's in Great Falls?"

"Yeah. Or headed there, anyway."

"Well, goddammit. I'd have liked to go."

"Sorry," she says. "I don't think he had much interest in your company after all that last night."

Nate squeezes his eyes in the cup of his hand. "Yeah. Not the first morning I've felt foolish like that."

"I see."

"Well, what about you?" Nate asks.

"What about me?" she asks.

"What are you doing today?"

She flicks a thumb rearward at the pickup she ferried him in, a lawnmower graphic and RHONDA'S GROUND MAINTENANCE stenciled on the side, mowers and blowers and weed whackers in the back of it. *You didn't notice, you big dummy?*

"Yeah, OK," he says. "That'll work."

Bob worries that he won't be able to find it, a concern inverse to the one Ronnie lugs.

"A lot of years," Bob says, "a lot of people moved in. A lot has changed."

"Get me up on that hill," Ronnie says. "I'll find it."

"I never went up there much before Dick died anyway."

"I'll find it," Ronnie says.

Bob burbles happily about times long past, about his sweet Linda and how they met, him a city boy from Great Falls proper, her a farm girl, and thank god for the dance she came to that night—"Nineteen sixty-one," he says, "can you believe it?"—or else how would he have ever seen her, what with their different orbits? How could he have come to anything or anyone else?

He says he can't even contemplate it now that she's gone, and he weeps a bit, then gathers himself and apologizes and says, "I thought I'd gotten it all out."

Ronnie nods and clenches his lips. His own line of memory has hold of him. Bob puts the blinker on, a right turn toward the northern shot up by Judith Gap, and Ronnie, in his head, is seeing the Crosley station wagon, at the very intersection sixty-some-odd years ago, the wheels curved toward the west, Ronnie shivering in the backseat, the man in the fedora and his wife up front, saying they're bound for Livingston and Bozeman and Three Forks beyond them. "That'll be just fine," Ronnie says in his recall, and Bob makes his turn, and the man in the hat, in the ether of memory, makes his, and they go on and they go on and they go on, forever.

Nate stands on a concrete step high above the sport arena's main parking lot while Rhonda mows a strip of grass below. He fingers a number into his phone and holds it to his ear.

"Hey," Brandon says. "Where are you?"

"Montana."

"Still?"

"Yeah. Sorry."

"I thought—"

"I know. Your grandpa went up north for the day, so—"

"You've got a black-water leak on that trailer, you know," Brandon says. "Your shit, in my driveway."

"I'm sorry."

"Sure."

"I am." *Dammit.* Nate goes for brightness. "How's Kelly?"

"Tired. On bedrest till it's done." Brandon pauses. "It's been really hard on her."

"I'm sorry."

"OK."

"Brandon—"

"You need to get this thing out of here, like, yesterday."

"I will. I told you."

"Yeah, you told me. You tell me lots of things."

"Listen—" Nate says.

"Bye. Gotta go."

"It's the same damn place."

Ronnie sweeps an arm across the yard. They stand behind the tiny white farmhouse with the green trim and the insulated foundation being chipped away by the weather, same as it ever was. There, under the honey locust, the milk canister Ma would sit him on to cut his hair. Out by the road as they came in, a hay rake Dick had placed there and just left, its usefulness gone and the dead shell of it retired and put literally out to pasture. Between the house and the barn, the old single-wide, its roof caved in by time.

They'd knocked on the door upon arrival, but no answer had come. Curtains stretch tight across windows. The swirling scent of chickens and milk cows and manure and compost by the barn suffuses the air.

"Linda told me one time about how she dropped some eggs and Dick lit out after her, bawling her out," Bob says now. "She told him, 'Don't you yell at me or I'll cut out your other eye.' I can just picture that. She had a mean streak, that one. You didn't want to cross her."

"I remember," Ronnie says.

"You do?"

"Yeah." He recollects it in another shade, though, not as youthful bravado but as a marker for how different things could be, depending on whether you were Dick Littler's blood kin or just an acquisition he'd made along the way. He was Linda's father and Ronnie's stepfather, and into the gap between those degrees of separation spilled configurations of maltreatment. He remembers Dick laughing about it that night at dinner—"Don't anybody mess with my little girl if you know what's good for you." He also remembers punches to the back of the head when he was toting milk and the beatings that would surely follow if he allowed a drop to spill. Casual cruelties that linger past the point of pain.

"I know he was hard on you kids," Bob says, as if he has a hold on the same thoughts Ronnie does. "It was the time, I think. Hell, I've seen the business end of a belt."

"A belt?" Ronnie says, his quick-strike anger up. He reaches with his right hand, two fingers, and brushes the bandage covering the cut made by Nate's thrown whisky glass. He frowns, then goes back to it, quieter now. "A two-by-four. A brick. Dick would come at me with anything he—"

"Yeah, I know he would."

"Do you?"

"Don't be sore. I don't mean nothing by it."

"Come here," Ronnie says. "Come on." His oxygen tank is back at the car, and he's huffing through the meager effort, but he walks the line they came in on, down the dirt driveway, into the field beyond the house, stepping through the husks left after the silage was cut, headed for the yonder fence line. Bob calls after him—"Ronnie!"— and when he doesn't turn, he follows on his fat little legs.

Rhonda buys them lunch, a half-sandwich and some chips and veggies from a little place up around the college, where she's just finished another job while he strolled around the emptied-out grounds before the trampling of the fall semester begins. Nate is thankful to be fed, the wallet he's been leaning on having gone north for the day.

"So you make a living at this?" he asks. He crunches a chip.

"Pretty good one, most years."

"Impressive. I wouldn't have thought it would—"

"Be a job for a girl?" She says the last word with a troglodyte's inflection.

"Yeah, I guess." He goes flush.

"Well, you've heard of 'to the victor goes the spoils,' I guess."

"Huh?"

"I got it in the divorce," she says. She tosses a carrot at him, playful. "I was running it anyway. Used to say JIMMY'S GROUND MAINTENANCE on that truck, but he never did anything but come up with the idea. So I took it. He kept his job at the refinery, I gave him the house, I took the business. Yay me."

"Why do women do that?" Nate asks.

"What?"

"My mom, same thing. My ex-wife, too. Walked away from the house, just gave it up." He looks down at the table, ashamed, the part he doesn't want to give to the words coming up behind: *And a year and half later, it's in foreclosure.* "Mom could have kept it. It's a frappin' house. That's a big deal."

Rhonda sets down her soda. "Well," she says, "maybe your mom had a reason. Your ex, too. Maybe I did, as well. Pretty presumptuous to think I didn't know what I was doing, isn't it?"

"I guess—"

"I can do a lot more with this business than I can a damn leaky-roof, deferred-maintenance, shithole of a house," she says now. "Maybe just mind your own business, Nathan."

He raises his hands, surrender. "OK, OK."

She reaches into his basket and retrieves the carrot that bounced off his chest and landed there. She pops it in her mouth and chomps away and turns her eyes and lips into a wide smile.

"You're messing with me, aren't you?" he says.

"A little," she says. "Maybe."

"She called me that."

"Who?"

"Mom. Nathan. Ex called me other things."

"I imagine."

"Be nice," he says, and he throws a chip, which she catches and eats with a big chomp.

"So you do this alone?" he asks.

"For now, yeah," she says. "Had help from time to time. Never seems to last very long. Would be nice to find somebody reliable, I guess, but not necessary."

Nate says it, then can't believe he says it. The words fly away from him faster than he can put a net on them. "What about me?"

"What about you?"

The gumption already splashed out of him, he pushes on. "What if I went to work with you? Just supposing."

"Right."

"I'm serious," he says.

She bundles up the leavings in her basket. "No, you're not."

"What would you say if I was?"

She stands up. She asks for his basket, and he passes it over. She sets it inside hers, then puts her hands on the tabletop and leans in toward him.

"I'd have to pass."

"Pass?" he says, stung.

"You're a drunk, Nate. What would I want with that?"

Once Ronnie begins, there's no bailing on the story until it's out of him, no moment for reconsideration of what he's undertaken, no creative editing as the words surface so he can shape them into something easier to say and hear. And it's strange, because he doesn't feel like the narrator. It's like he's the audience, the same as it was the only other time he allowed himself to tell it. Electra. She'd heard and cried and held him. Bob just stares.

"We came right down this drive, right here, nineteen-thirty-nine," he says, scraping an arc in the dirt with his foot. "Me and my dad in his flivver, I remember that, old car already, and he's got on this cap that they gave him when he came out of jail. I remember it, clear as anything."

"You were, what, four?"

"I was three. I can't remember what happened yesterday like I remember that day, OK? And he's telling me things about Ma, how she wants to meet me, how I'll spend a week with her, it's her right, and then he'll come back and get me and—"

"I never knew—" Bob starts.

"Bob, just . . ." Ronnie stretches his arms behind his back, locks the fingers. He walks a tight circle. "I come here for a reason, OK?"

"OK."

"So just shut up."

"OK."

"Dick and Ma, they come out in their own car, meet us right up there." He points a bit up the drive, closer to the house. "Dad stops, Dick gets out, he's got a shotgun, and he puts it on us. I can see my dad, he's got his hands up, he's saying, 'What's this?' Ma, she come over, opens my door, grabs my hand, pulls me back to their car. Dick says, 'He's our boy now.'"

"Jesus. You remember that?"

Ronnie nods.

"Jesus."

"So now you know," Ronnie says. He grips his hands and holds them to his face, breathing the earth on them. "Now I've told somebody."

"Why'd you tell me?"

"I don't know," Ronnie says. "You're here."

"You should tell your son."

"No."

"He's got a powerful anger against you," Bob says. "Might help to let him into it. You see the way he was looking at us last night?"

"No."

"He doesn't know us. Thinks you're to blame for that."

Ronnie's hands clench. "Watch yourself, Bob."

"I don't mean no disrespect."

"He's weak," Ronnie says. "That's his problem. As weak as anybody I've ever seen, always crawling down into that bottle."

"He's your son. He has a right to know about this."

"Maybe."

"Not maybe. He does."

"Stop saying that." Ronnie kicks the ground. "Let's just go back, OK? I want to get out of here."

"OK."

"I was three," Ronnie says, stopping and turning around again, ferocity in the words. "You ever feel like you never had a chance, Bob? Tell me again about the business end of that belt. We're not the same, you and me. You hear me? So don't tell me what you think you know."

"Ronnie, I—"

"I can't sleep at night, Bob. All the time, waking up, my mind running away from me, and it's . . ." He closes his eyes. "It's not all here, OK? But it started here, and it went to shit everywhere else. Goddamn it. Don't tell me about Linda and some fucking cracked eggs, OK?"

"Jesus, Ronnie."

The words chase a man who's not there anymore. Ronnie walks with the wind at his back toward the farmhouse, hacking and spitting and cussing.

For the second time, Rhonda takes Nate to his truck. Hers sits idling next to it in the driveway. Nate sits slumped and silent, the way it's been the whole ride over.

"Day's done," she says. "You don't have to go home, but you—"

"I am," Nate says.

"You are what?"

"I'm a drunk."

"First step is admitting it."

"I wasn't always," he says.

"Most people aren't. You don't have to be."

He smiles at that. "Thanks, Mom."

"What was she like?" Rhonda asks now. "The Penneys—well, Bob and Linda, anyway—they talk about her like she hung the moon."

"Yeah," Nate says. He considers it a bit, how to arrange the words in a way that encompasses Electra Leigh Stidham. "She was strong."

"A good quality," Rhonda says.

"The best."

"And Uncle Ronnie?" she asks and then, as if she has only a second to get back on the right side of the line, she says, "It's none of my business. I mean, clearly, it's—it's just, you don't usually see a guy take a swing at his . . . Shit. I'm sorry."

"No, it's—" he says.

"I'm sorry."

"No, it's fine. He's my dad. Mom died, and he's the parent, you know? It's not what I wanted, but I was nine. I didn't get a vote, right? He moves down to Texas, because some lawyer told him he'd have an airtight case if he didn't take me away from my school and my friends, and he claimed his right. Whatever. I'm sure he thought he was just stealing me back from someone who stole me in the first place."

She nods, then she opens herself to him, turning in her seat, attentive, as if inviting him to drop more between them if he wants to.

"I used to get so excited when summer would come around, because that's when I'd see him, maybe a week or two after school let out," Nate says. "He'd show up in his truck, and I'd go out with him for a couple of weeks, just me and him on the road, staying in the sleeper compartment, sometimes a hotel, and fast food and pinball machines and riding around. I loved it. I just loved it. And then I'd go back home—by then, you know, my mom and Charley, they had a proper house, so I'd go back and it was just . . . boring. But I was a kid, you know? Of course it was boring, because that's everyday life. It didn't mean I wanted to be with my dad all the time."

"Sure."

"I think he thought I wanted that. So Mom dies and he moves down, and Charley's out of the picture and—"

"Why? Why was Charley out of the picture?"

"Dad told him to get out. Said 'he's my boy,' and booted him. That's the story."

"But . . ."

"But it was fucked up. That's all." He looks at her. "That's all. That's everything."

"And you'd have rather stayed with your stepdad?"

Nate nods and looks away, out his own window. He never has far to travel when he thinks of this, which is why he tries not to. Charley Stidham sitting him down, kneeling in front of him, putting a hand on Nate's knee and telling him what was what, when there wasn't anything to do but that, the decision already made and no fight to be had over it. *In my heart, you'll always be my son.* He thinks of what followed, the prefab house Ronnie moved them into, jammed into that same sprawling suburb where he'd been growing up, but a corner of it he didn't know. The long hours alone, his father on the road, the sundry girlfriends to whom Ronnie could never commit and thus who could never commit to looking after the boy he was in the way his father expected they would in his absences. Instead, Nate was left to trying to raise himself up without the tools for the doing. He thinks of how it all eroded, slowly and then swiftly, how at some point he let himself loose from aspirations and just limped through it, at best. He thinks of how, later, as an adult and free to do as he wanted, he chose to stay away from Charley for shame of what he'd made of himself. One time, no longer bound to another man's control, he thought maybe it could go another way, but it didn't. Charley asked him to call, but he couldn't. He just couldn't.

"Absolutely," Nate says now. "Yes. That's what I wanted."

"I'm sorry."

"It was a long time ago," he says, opening the pickup door and sliding out. "I'll get out of your hair."

He goes around the front, between the truck and the garage door, and she opens her window and leans out. "Nathan?"

He comes over and sets his hands inside the window frame.

"I had no right to say what I said," she says.

He leans through and kisses her flush. She pulls back, looking horrified. "You shouldn't have done that," she says.

"Well, now we're even," he says.

She sets her truck in gear, backs out, and whiplashes into the street. He walks down the driveway, hands held up, palms up, questioning, and he follows on the sidewalk until she's at the corner, where she turns right and is as gone as she can be.

15

September 2002 | Bozeman, Montana

Cherie holds the bottom of the tacked-up flyer and pulls it in for a closer look, trying to put herself in the words on the photocopy and trying to stay out of the direct fire of those aimed at her ears.

"Saturday. After the game. You should come."

"Mmm hmm," she says. She lent a pencil and ended up with a puppy. First day, Introduction to English, and the skinny guy with the longish hair and the goatee—cute, she'll certainly acknowledge, but not enough so as to punch a ticket on the time he's been taking, two lunches to which he's invited himself, and now whatever weekend scam he has in mind.

"What is this?" he asks. He pulls the paper away from her, ripping it from its bulletin-board tack. "'Volunteer for the Bozeman PD.' Yeah, right."

"Maybe," she says, taking the paper back from him.

"Cherie the Narc."

"Shut up." He—*Adam? Aidan?* She can't remember—smells of patchouli and insufficient ambition. She needs an exit strategy.

"So," he says, "about the thing Saturday—"

"What is it again?" she asks.

"Party. Off-campus. It'll be off the hook."

"Ah."

"You'll come?"

"No," she says.

"Really? Why not?"

She sets her backpack down, then folds the flyer into a square and finds a pocket for it.

"Here's the thing, Aidan—"

"Evan."

"Evan?"

"Evan."

She tries again. "OK, EV-an, here's the deal: I'm going to be busy Saturday."

"Too bad," he says.

"Not just Saturday, either, but every other day that ends in D-A-Y. Forever."

He looks at her as if he hasn't yet processed what she means by that, exactly. When it finally registers, he says, "Harsh."

"Sorry," she says, and she picks up her backpack, claps him on the shoulder, and leaves him to the swirl of the student union, a mingling of souls that, if he's willing to put forth the effort, surely would yield at least one woman willing to do keg stands come Saturday. Heaven help her.

Between classes, she summons her aging Honda, the one extravagance she undertook with her meager share of Opal's only slightly more than meager estate, and she pilots it from campus to a tucked-in street behind the Hotel Baxter on a prominent corner of downtown.

She comes up the sidewalk along Willson Avenue, backpack on one shoulder, cuts across Main Street with the light, bears left, past her favorite bookstore, and falls into the midday autumn bustle. She dodges mothers pushing carriages and dogs on leashes and buskers with hats on the ground, sprouting cabbage. It's everything she loves and everything she loathes, in one squirming mass. The boutiques and the coffee shops and the lunch spots she adores. The dive bars she's pulled her mother out of, right here on Main, a more rugged time coexisting warily with progress. The restaurants where dates have too often believed they bought themselves more than a dinner and some conversation. She has had, as yet, only first dates and has come closer than she might have imagined, at just eighteen years old, to waving the white flag on those.

Two blocks down, she ducks into a nondescript office building, skips the elevator, and takes the stairs, two at a time, to the third floor, where she's spat into a carpeted hallway neutralized into nothingness. It's been a while since she was here, and so she picks her way down the hall, scrutinizing stenciled doors and windows until she gets to 317, WILLIAM J. BOWDEN, ATTORNEY AT LAW.

She lets herself in and tosses a "hi!" to the receptionist. "I'm Mr. Bowden's three o'clock," she says. She looks at the clock perched off the woman's right shoulder. It looks to be art deco. She's impressed.

"Your name?"

"Cherie Bowden."

"Oh," the receptionist says, then a beat of recognition. "Oh! Well, please, sit down. I'm sure he'll be ready for you soon."

Cherie finds a chair and considers the periodicals, the *Kiplinger's* and the *Bloomberg Businessweek* and the *Fortune*. MAKE A MILLION | WE KNOW YOU CAN DO IT! one headline cheerleads, and she considers how many uncountable worlds inhabit a single planet. She's never pined so thoroughly for a copy of *Sports Illustrated*.

"So you're his daughter?" the receptionist asks.

"Hmm?"

"His daughter?"

"Oh, yes," Cherie says. "As far as we know."

That throws the woman a wicked curveball. "What a curious thing to say."

Bill Bowden's emergence from his office spares them the further degradation of the matter. He's neat and trim—thinner than Cherie saw him last, a compulsory drop-in last Thanksgiving or Christmas, she can't remember which, but surely not both. A little grayer, too. One can't hope to keep all the rigors of aging at bay. He's holding his own nonetheless.

"Come on in," he says, and she rises, carrying her backpack, and follows him. On the other side of the closed door, after he pulls a chair away from the desk for her and deposits himself on the other side, she says, "She's nice."

"I think so."

"Younger than the last one," she says. "And the one before that."

"Cher."

"Way younger than Mom."

"Come on."

She sits. He scatters papers on his desk, then aligns them into a neat stack. "You said I could help with something."

Cherie unzips her backpack, roots through it a bit, then finds what she seeks. She pulls the paper out, sets it on the edge of the desk, and smooths the creases as best she can. She pushes it across, and he takes it.

"It's a quit claim," he says. "An old one."

"I know."

"Unfiled. No stamp."

"I know." The title search when the house in Billings was sold settled that matter for good. Owned free and clear by Opal Knudsen before she up and croaked. Reverted on death to Anna Lynn Bowden. No encumbrances. Clear to close.

He peers closer. "Who's Oscar Ray?"

"I don't know. Here's where I need help."

"From me?"

"No," she says. "From Miss Perky out there."

"Cher, come on."

"Don't call me that."

He rolls back his chair, laces his hands behind his head, and leans back. "I'm an estate planner. Not a gumshoe."

"You went to *law school*, didn't you? You know how to dig into records, don't you?"

"Yes."

"Well, then."

"Are you ever going to stop being angry at me?" he asks.

"I hope not."

He pitches forward again. "What have you found out so far?"

She returns to the backpack. "Not much. He's dead. I'm pretty sure he's dead." She comes up with a handheld notebook into which she's scratched her notations. "I'm pretty sure I found him. He had a Social Security number. Found that on the Social Security Death Index. Pretty cool. Public record. I got Kurt Cobain's, too. You want it?"

"Nah, it's fine."

She reads her handwriting. "Oscar Julius Ray, born 1905, Great Falls. Died 1970, Madras, Oregon. He's buried out there, too. Found that out. But I'm more interested—"

"Montana," he says.

"Yeah. And what his involvement with grandma was."

"I can look around. Might be a few weeks. Wouldn't get my hopes up about the Opal connection, though."

"What do you mean?"

He folds the document and pushes it back to her. "It's two signatures on a piece of paper that was never filed. So who knows what was going on there. Somebody had second thoughts."

"Still," she says.

"I'll look," he says. "I'll see what I can find."

"Thank you."

He leans forward, elbows on the desk, wrists out, hands forming a bridge. He smiles and nods, and she doesn't care for it.

"What?"

"You sent back the check," he says.

"I didn't need it."

"It was a graduation gift."

"I didn't need it."

"It was a gift."

"I didn't want it. I want this, though."

"OK," he says.

"We done?" she asks.

He blows a blast of air through his lips. "Sure."

She gathers her things, stands, and leaves. Her hand is on the doorknob when he says, "Cherie?"

She turns, tilts her head, waits.

"Is your mom doing OK?"

"Don't waste my time," she says. "You know how she's doing."

Cherie comes home after seven and finds Anna in a flurry of preparation, the air fragrant with perfume, her mother in a summer dress—"I think I can get one more wearing out of it before the coats come out," she says—and her mood bouncy and light and luminescent. "Got a date," Anna says, and she points at Cherie and winks and makes a clicking sound with her tongue.

"On a Wednesday?"

"Last minute," Anna says. "Nice guy. You'd like him."

"I doubt it."

"Oh, pooh." Anna frowns, but it's exaggerated and pouty, then it's gone. She's on her own ride. "How do I look?" She lifts the corners of the dress, gives a little spin.

"You look pretty, Mom. Where are you going?"

"Ale Works."

"Nice."

"I think so." Anna flits off to the bathroom for a last bit of primping, and Cherie follows.

"Maybe lay off the ale, though," Cherie says, and she knows it's heavy-handed. She also knows what the end of an evening sometimes looks like when she doesn't say it explicitly. She's hedging her bets by being upfront.

"Of course," Anna says. "You know I'm off that."

No. What Cherie knows is that her mother hasn't had booze in a while, and that's great as far as it goes. She also knows that the problem isn't stopping in the abstract. It's stopping once she's gotten started. She also knows that the black dog stalks Anna in other ways. She knows, and well remembers, the crying jags—sudden and extreme and unrelenting—after Opal died, after the house sold, after anniversaries significant and picayune came up and brought memories with them, something into which the depression could gain a foothold. Alcohol, added to that, is an accelerant, and these bursts of outsized joy, as now, sometimes cause Cherie to wonder if she's gone mad or somehow harbors latent resentment. *Who wouldn't want her own mother to be happy?* Someone who's seen what Anna does when she reaches those heights, the recklessness that ensues, and how steep the fall that surely comes. That's who.

"What's this guy's name?" Cherie asks.

"Norm."

"Heh."

"I know. But he's a nice man."

"What's he do?"

"Analyst in the finance department." City government and all its oniony layers. Finance, that's a new one. Cherie remembers her mother dating a firefighter, a guy from public works, the parks department guy—a peach, that one, a dude named Kyle who propositioned Cherie when she was but sixteen. She didn't say anything, just made herself scarce, and when he'd broken it off a week or so later—they all break it off, some early, some late, but there's always uniformity in the outcomes—Anna had cried for days.

"Will you say hi to him?" Anna asks now.

"Sure, of course. I'll be here." *Bring it, Norm.*

"I'm sorry I didn't have time to make anything."

"It's fine," Cherie says. "There's leftover Chinese."

"OK, good."

Anna presents herself again. "Good?"

"You look terrific."

"Aw, thanks." She leans in, right cheek leading, and Cherie kisses it. "I really like this guy."

"Mom, it's Norm from finance."

"I know."

"Maybe keep the expectations in check."

"Oh, shush."

"I mean, if it was Tyrone from legal . . ."

"Shush!"

"Just have a good time, OK?"

Norm from finance turns out to be something other than what Cherie expected. Short—shorter than Anna, certainly, and thus much shorter than Cherie, who carries her father's stilt-like frame, while her mother holds the northern European peasant look passed down from Opal and her forebears. Bald, hilariously so, like TV's Murray Slaughter. Pudgy and unathletic. Certainly not Anna's type, as it were, but it's not like her type has been any great shakes. She thinks of George Costanza, in the endless sitcom reruns, and how he finally did the right thing by going against every instinct he had. Come to think of it, Norm looks a little like Costanza. Maybe it tracks.

He's polite and deferential, and he tells Cherie he's heard a lot about her, which she rather doubts but appreciates just the same. Cherie sees them out with a "you crazy kids be good," and she closes herself up, alone inside the house, and she feels the amped-up tension swept away with her mother's departure, and she's thankful for that.

If not for the vagaries of whom she might end up with as a roomie, Cherie would be inclined to get a dorm or an off-campus rental, just as step one in a two-step release from current circumstance. She thinks about it sometimes, then she just as quickly thinks of what falls out from there, in all likelihood: increasingly fewer visits home, Anna's restlessness and loneliness and inability to cope with the crisis of the moment, disaster. It's what made Annapolis finally seem so unreachable, and it's holding her here, the gravity of it like a tether.

She goes to the kitchen, digs in the fridge, finds two-day-old General Tso's chicken and white rice, and some crispy green beans. She arranges the leftovers on a cranberry-red plate, pushes it into the microwave, and sets the time. She watches the food spin under the light. The peppers activate, pungent in her sinuses. The plate comes out hot, the food sending up swirls of steam. She carries it to the table, her hands exchanging the weight of it, back and forth, never allowing the heat to penetrate her fingers too deeply. She pulls a knife and a fork from the drawer, pours herself a glass of water, sits down and eats, blowing on the food, cooling it, then taking it in, a forkful at a time. She fixes her eyes on the wall and blesses the silence.

Later, after Cherie has made a considerable dent in the English paper she has to turn in next week, she goes into her backpack and finds the flyer she took—that *EV-an* took and she reclaimed—and she pays it a deeper mind. Volunteers needed, for a range of duties. Crowd control at Bobcats games. Bike registrations. Paperwork. For those interested in police work, ride-alongs. Now they're talking.

She remembers an article in the *Daily Chronicle*, not so long ago, the police chief making a plea for community involvement. "If I had six or eight reliable volunteers," he said, "we could do some great things." She saves her classwork on her laptop, then pulls up her email program and begins composing.

To whom it may concern:
My name is Cherie Bowden, and I am a freshman at
Montana State. I'm definitely interested in being a
department volunteer.
I'm in general studies right now—I haven't
chosen a major yet—but think I would be interested
in a career in public safety. I was admitted to the
U.S. Naval Academy in Annapolis, Maryland,
earlier this year but had to decline the appointment
because of a family situation. I'm responsible,
despite my young age, and motivated. I think I
would be a very good volunteer, and I would be
happy to discuss it with you at your convenience.
Thank you,
Cherie Bowden

She reads it over and makes a few alterations, then appends her contact information at the bottom. She decides she'll let it sit overnight, that she'll hew to what her English professor says about the gulf between first drafts and second ones, how in the initial composition you say what's on the surface and in revision, after you've had time for consideration, you find the heart of the matter.

Cherie hears steps on the porch, and the motion-sensor light floods the yard. A key shakes in the lock. She stands up. Anna comes in, quietly at first, and then, when she sees Cherie, with a bright smile and a flourish. She closes the door and presses her backside against it and closes her eyes. She's disheveled, the dress on not quite right, the lipstick gone and the hair fallen.

"Good time?" Cherie asks, sitting again.

Anna exhales. She opens her eyes.

"I think I'm in love."

Cherie glances away, puts her finger on the track pad, guides the cursor to "send," and clicks.

16

October 1952 | Three Forks, Montana

Berta Foley comes into Ronnie's bedroom as he's finishing up with the packing. She carries three shirts, a spectrum of plaids, pressed and neat and folded into sharpness. "I got you these in Bozeman," she says. "Do you have room?"

He turns to her, sees her downcast eyes and nervous hands, and feels his own insides churn over what the day holds. It's been pressing on his gut all morning, through his chores and a quiet breakfast, and now, alone in his room, he fears the sadness might break the skin.

"You didn't have to do that," he says.

"Chambers-Fisher had a sale. I wanted to."

She holds the shirts out, and he takes them from her, then lays them atop the clothes he's stacked in his suitcase. He flips the lid closed and latches it.

"Thank you for these," he says. "You've been awfully good to me."

"You've been good to us, Ronnie. *For* us."

He finds the edge of the bed and sits himself upon it, not certain he can keep standing under the circumstances. She comes over and sits next to him. He smiles tightly, then looks at the wall opposite. She does, too.

"We haven't talked much of personal things," she says. "It's not our way."

"I know. I've appreciated that."

"You've never asked questions."

"I've tried not to," he says.

"A farm like this." She sweeps an arm in a wide arc, as if to take in the immensity, then brings her hands back to folded in her lap. "There ought to have been children. A lineage. Someone to receive it when we can't do what needs doing anymore." She pauses, considers. He can feel the tremble next to him, or maybe it's his own tremor, radiating. "Two more months of fall, but I can feel winter in my bones. That time for us, it's coming. You've delayed it some, and we're so grateful."

Ronnie squeezes his eyes closed.

"Anyway," she says, "children just weren't in the cards for Tom and me. When the time comes, we've got a cousin up the valley— shirttail relative, we don't know him much, but kin—who'll probably be happy to buy us out, let us find a little house in town where we can live out our days."

Ronnie, softly, says, "I can't picture that."

That brings a chuckle out of her. "We can't, either. We even talked once, just thinking out loud, wondering if we could adopt you."

Ronnie snaps his attention to her. "You did?"

She nods. "That supposing runs out of room after you follow the thinking for a bit, though. You're somebody else's boy, and that would have had to be untangled, and . . . well, you can see where that goes."

"Yeah," he said.

"They didn't do right by you. That's their loss. We've tried to."

"You *have*," he says.

"There's no chance you'd—" She stops herself. "No. I'm sorry. It's unfair."

"I would," Ronnie says. "If it's what I wanted, I would. But I can't."

"I know. Forgive me."

They sit a spell longer. Silence settles on them, comfortable and crushing at the same time.

"There's something else," she says. She digs into the pocket of her apron and pulls out a handful of folding money. She gives it to him. "Tom wants you to have this. Wages for your time here. Not enough, but what we can do. He didn't think he could say the right thing, so he asked me to give it to you, said that I'd have the words. He overestimates me."

Ronnie looks at the bills in his hands, tries to add them up. He gets to six hundred dollars before he's overcome.

"I can't," he says.

"You have to. It's yours. This world you're heading into, things cost. Beds and meals and gasoline. You take it. You might need it."

"I'll pay you back."

"Son," she says, "you already have."

He stands. She stands with him. He presses the money into his front pocket. "I'm grateful," he says.

"Ronnie?"

"Yes?"

"Can I hug you?"

He steps into her, reaches around her ample back until his hands meet where the apron is tied off, and he sets his head into her bosom, and she's so warm, like home as he's always imagined it to be, and she begins to weep, and he holds on and fights himself not to and loses.

When it's done, she lets him go. "Tom'll be ready for you now."

The eastward route sits frosty and gray outside the pickup windows.

Ronnie sets his head against the glass and watches it go by, the broad valley they leave behind, and Bozeman, eleven thousand souls strong, yawning at the foot of the Bridger Mountains. Tom takes it slow through the pass, mindful of the lurking ice invisible against the blacktop. On the other side, near Livingston, the clouds hang low on the Absarokas, silver and threatening, and the hurled wind whipsaws the pickup. Tom grips tight the wheel. "Goddamn," he says.

Ronnie is there and not, alternately in the moment and in his head. He stares out across Tom Foley's rigid arms and through the opposite window, at the railroad town sliding by. He thinks of what and who awaits on the other end, the short telephone call they've already had, accommodation requested and granted, plans shared, hopes given some illumination.

I want to enlist in the Army next spring.

Enlisted man. Good for you.

In the meantime, I can help.

Plenty of work here with Opal.

It's been a long time.

Yes, indeedy, boy. A long time. It'll be good to see you.

"Gonna rain," Tom says. "Or worse."

"I hope it holds off till you're back home."

"I'm not picky about rain."

"No. Me, either."

Up ahead, the road comes to a crossing. The Crazy Mountains, half-blanketed white from high-elevation snow, sit distant on the port side. Ronnie recognizes where he is, that if Tom were to bear left, he'd circumnavigate the Crazies, hit White Sulphur Springs and go north, north, north, eventually reaching Great Falls. Ronnie has ridden that route, only in reverse, with no idea where it would take him. He realizes now, in a thunderclap, that it brought him right here, to this pickup, on this day, riding shotgun to this man.

"This the way you came when you went up to the Fairfield Bench?" Ronnie asks.

"No," Tom says. "I went up through Helena. More direct."

"I guess I don't know my way around."

"You're young yet," he says. "It'll come."

"I guess."

The highway intersection falls away, the Crazies rise up, and Ronnie feels the newness of the earth running below their penned-in feet. Every inch in this direction is something he hasn't ever seen. He settles in again and lets it come to him.

In Laurel, maybe an hour from where they're headed, Tom leaves the highway and angles the pickup into a space in front of a diner. "Feed you one last time," he says. To Ronnie, it feels abrupt and preempted, as if the steady progress to some mysterious goal has been short-circuited, but he doesn't wish to be ungrateful. He goes inside, plops into a booth with Tom, and smiles when the waitress comes around.

"Ham sandwich," Tom tells her. She jots the order, then looks at Ronnie expectantly.

"Coca-Cola."

"That all?"

"Yes, ma'am."

She leaves them. "You should eat," Tom says.

"Thank you, sir. I'm not hungry."

Tom nods. "I understand. You don't mind? I'm a little peaked."

"No, sir."

They sit, polite but also outside the boundaries of conversation, not that it's ever come easily between them, not the way it has with Berta. Ronnie has been around Tom enough now to have seen his interactions with any number of people, to know that his silence isn't intended personally. Some men spew their words freely, and some keep them in reserve until there's a compelling reason to rub them together and speak them into being. Having had some exposure to both types, Ronnie can say he prefers the latter.

Not that Tom hasn't sprung the occasional surprise. It wasn't long into their arrangement—just enough time for Tom to realize he had a real worker on his hands, not a layabout—that Ronnie wound up his nerve and asked why Tom lingered so over the sports page on spring evenings.

"Baseball!" Tom had said, with a propulsion to the word that someone else might pin to, say, "fire!" or "Santa Claus!"

"You play baseball, boy?"

"No, sir."

"And you call yourself a real boy."

Ronnie might well have been wounded by that had Berta not clucked at her husband and said, "Oh, hush. He's a real boy. He certainly eats like one," and pushed the mashed potatoes to Ronnie and bid him to take another helping.

The admonition didn't slow Tom down. He was off, burbling happily about Stan the Man and the mighty St. Louis Cardinals, his favorite team on account of you could get them on the radio way out here, with Stretch Miller and Gus Mancuso calling the action. Babe Ruth, he had to concede, had been a fine, fine player—"a shame he had to go so quick, such a young fella"—and times sure were changing, what with the Dodgers signing that Negro kid and the Indians, too, and now a bunch of teams following suit. Players come and go, he said, but no matter what, the game was the beautiful thing. Later that week, Tom brought home a couple of mitts and a ball, and the two of them would sometimes play catch into the dusk.

Ronnie watches Tom eat and thinks of ways he can stash away that memory and keep it safe and even bring it out and look it over when the mood strikes him so. Under the table, his right knee fires like a piston, his heel laying down a frantic rhythm on the floor.

Tom looks up as he finishes a bite. "You want to go, don't you?"

Ronnie's first thought is to deny it, but then he figures now is no time to start lying to this fine man. "Yes, sir."

"OK, then."

Tom calls for the check and asks if Ronnie can take the bottle of Coke with him. "Pay the two-cent deposit, sure," the waitress says.

"I'm feeling rich," Tom says, and he digs in his pocket to cover the freight.

The stomach churn accelerates for Ronnie as they drive through Billings. The haze of the in-between season—still fall by the calendar, winter sucking in a mouthful and preparing to blow—hangs low over the city, gray and gloomy. The byproducts of industry penetrate the cab—roasted sugar beets, oil refining, animal slaughter. Ronnie takes it into his senses and feels a slight case of sickness coming on.

"Some town you've chosen," Tom says, dismissive. "Nothing but banks and car lots."

"I think it chose me," Ronnie says, and he's not altogether certain what he means by it, but Tom smiles, a rarity, and says, "Maybe it did, at that."

The fairgrounds, empty and destitute, pass by as the pickup climbs the hill out of the downtown bowl. The farther they go, the more the sickly smells dissipate, and soon, it's just them and the strain of the engine and the countryside, dotted by the odd house here and there but otherwise like so much of the country they've passed through along the way.

Off to the east, Ronnie catches glimpses of the Yellowstone River, running parallel to them. The anticipation inside him, like the cola he hasn't sipped, has been shaken up for hours, even days, and he'd imagined that it would find release once they arrived in Billings. But the road goes on, well out of town, and he feels ready to burst.

"They're out here a good little bit," Tom says.

"Yeah."

Ronnie fortifies himself against the possible difference between what he's imagined the coming moment to be and what he'll experience when it arrives. When he closes his eyes and thinks of his father, of the singular memory he has of the man, it's less the angles of his face or the quality of his eyes or whether he had a beard, because Ronnie honestly cannot remember. He remembers the hat he wore, just a cheap cloth one with a cardboard bill, and the terror in his face and the chaos and the tires spitting dirt and the crying and, back at the house, the first blow from Dick, the backhand that dropped his little body just inside the door, and Dick's telling Ma, "Delia, you keep that boy quiet now, you hear me?" The truth of it: Ronnie isn't sure, if he were now to walk past his dad on the street, that he'd see himself, his past and his future, in the man's face. He'd like to think so, but he just doesn't know. He's alternately fascinated and fearful to find out.

Tom turns left off the highway, onto a dirt road. He points toward the windshield, an angular finger pushing southwest. "There it is, I guess." They're a hundred yards out, if that.

"Listen," Tom says. "I'm going to stop a little bit short and let you out, OK?"

"OK."

"You walk up there, and when he comes out for you and I know you're OK, I'm gone. Understand?"

"Yes, sir."

"OK, then."

He eases to the side of the road, maybe twenty yards shy of the chain-link fence out front of the house, a little white clapboard place. Ronnie grips the door handle. The full Coke bottle between his legs is an obstacle.

"What do I do with this?"

"Take it," Tom says.

"I won't drink it."

Tom holds out a hand, accepting it.

"Don't forget your suitcase," he says.

"I won't." Ronnie clambers out, goes to the rear of the pickup, and gets his things. He comes back to close the door.

"Sir," he says, with nothing come up behind.

"I know. I know, son," Tom says. "Me, too."

Ronnie trudges toward the house, his steps plodding, the suitcase heavy in his hand, creasing the soft skin on the underside of his fingers. As he nears, the door opens and a tall drink of water with a potbelly and white wispy hair steps onto the landing. The man's jeans sag, and the tail of his shirt, the only part untucked, flaps behind him. Ronnie picks up the pace.

Behind the man, a woman peeks out from the door frame.

"Well, there he is," the man who must be Oscar Ray booms, leaving the porch to bound across the patch of browned grass and open the front gate. He offers a handshake that Ronnie accepts by transferring the suitcase to his left hand and gripping hard his father's hand with his right.

Behind Ronnie, Tom's pickup crunches the gravel in a U-turn, and when Ronnie spins around to look, after the claps on the back and the smile at Opal Knudsen, he sees only the dust that's been kicked high and is raining back down.

Oscar Ray

1905-1970

You've seen some hell on earth in your time, sure enough, but for sheer boredom and no prospects, you're not certain anything exceeds eastern Oregon. Maybe eastern Washington, the same endless high desert and igneous rock and windblown empty spaces. The same slow-moving idiots. They should have divvied those two states vertically rather than horizontally, you think. Coastal paradise on the left, the bullshit you gotta drive through to get there on the right.

Anyway, you set your current lack of being impressed aside. What eastern Oregon has going for it, you know, is that it's not Idaho. You've played that one out, a good thing you had going for a while in Wallace, damn near the payoff, and then it turned. An old man and his wife—older than you, if you can believe that— almost relieved of their house, until their kid comes in from Boise and starts sniffing around and catches the scent of you. Another shotgun under your nose—third one—and the best deal you were going to get, under the circumstances: *Leave now, don't ever come back, and I won't call the law and I won't blow your head clean off your shoulders and onto the lawn.*

That's the thing about rooking people out of what's dear to them. It doesn't always work—and when it goes wrong, it's sometimes spectacularly so—but the cops almost never get called. The shame of it all is too great. How could they be so stupid, so naïve? It's what you count on—that they are, in fact, so stupid, and that when the deed goes down, one way or another, their primary concern is making sure nobody else finds out.

Your pickup bounces on a dirt road, jostling the hamburger you just had in Madras, not the worst thing you've eaten of late. You're thinking of swinging back toward town, finding a flophouse, considering your damn meager options, when you see her in the yard, scattering feed for a group of scrawny chickens. You pull up behind the car parked there—Jesus, a '51 Nash Statesman, looks like, and you wonder how the wheels ain't come off it—and you step out of your pickup and you make a proper introduction of yourself. Then you tell her that the trim on her house there—*nice place, ma'am, really nice*—looks awfully weather-worn. You're handy with a saw and a bucket of paint, you say. Happy to help. Better to get it now before the rodents move in and you've got a real problem.

"What's it to you?" she asks.

Nothing, nothing at all, you say. You're a handyman and she looks like she could use one, that's all. Unless, of course, she has a husband, and maybe he's just been busy with other things. You know how it is with men.

"Nah, ain't got one of those."

Well, then, you say, maybe you can help. With the trim, you say, not the husbandin', and you laugh, and she doesn't.

"I don't know you," she says.

Well, you say, we can fix that. Oscar Ray, Coeur d'Alene, Idaho, originally, but moving out here, always liked it. You move to the chain-link fence and offer a handshake. She steps toward you, eyeballing you, but doesn't accept your offered hand.

"I still don't know you."

Well, you say, OK, how about this? I'll climb up there, pull down those rotted boards, paint you up some new ones, put those up, and then, if you like my work, you can decide what it's worth. How about that?

"Maybe."

And after that, if you want, I could do some other stuff. That fence could use some patching.

"Maybe."

Well, all right, you say. That's a start, Miss . . . you didn't catch the name.

"I didn't fling it."

Well, all right, then, you say, you'll get started. Ladder and tools're in the truck.

"You're pretty old to be climbing up ladders, aren't you?"

Only as old as you feel, ma'am, you say. Only as old as you feel.

17

November 1972 | Euless, Texas

Electra walks home with Nathan, her hand enveloping his. The pathway bends to the left ahead, hugging the shape and the flow of what they call a river around here, utterly without irony. Electra thinks they give themselves and their waterways too much credit by half; it's an irrigation ditch without water, a muddied-up, weed-strangled, browned-out crack in the ground. She thinks of the North Platte back home in Casper, the steady flow northward, and then she thinks, *dammit, I have to stop saying that word, home.*

The ditch aside, it's a pleasant interlude, her daily stroll with Nathan after she's walked alone to his school and stood outside at the fence and waited and collected him when he tumbles out and asked about his day. Normal, one could say.

They walk back between subdivisions and hulking apartment homes with names evocative and incongruent, with hints of Old Spain and Greece and flora that doesn't grow here. El Dorado. City of gold. Not yet, she thinks. Not so far. But maybe. Keep plugging, and maybe.

She grips his hand tighter and makes another round of inquiries, about that nice Miss Lowrance and the games and the puzzles, and she braces for what the answers will be. Nathan's responses, when he's had them, have had a particularly negative lean so far. *It's too big* (fair), *I don't know any of these kids* (just takes time, son, just takes time), *I miss my old school at home* (stop saying that word, the both of us).

There'd been more banging of the heads between him and Charley that morning before school, more sullenness about an unwanted breakfast, a mood that went from grumpy to nasty without a stop in between—"you're the worst mom!"—and Charley had scooped Nathan's bowl of cereal from in front of him and dumped it in the sink and told him to go to his room while they finished eating. When Nathan had refused, Charley had taken him by the shoulders and lifted him, feet kicking, and carried him there. He'd come back and told her, "It has to be done," and of course, she knew he was right, but that didn't make the screaming any easier to take, didn't make her heart calm down any.

"Any new friends?" she asks.

Nathan shakes his head.

"It'll come," she says.

He drops her hand and moves slightly away from her, though still parallel. Her chest walls cave in.

Since the unpacking and the settling in and the confronting of changes subtle and abrupt, she's had a reckoning with herself in as many ways as she's had to guard his feelings. It was unfair what she did, pulling him from his first school, only kindergarten, just a month and half into it. Throwing these changes at him like errant fastballs and saying, in essence, new school, new friends, new town, new *man*, just deal with it, Nathan, because it isn't going to go any way but this way here. Hadn't she and Charley foreseen some of these things, when her idea was but a hatchling, and hadn't they said, hey, maybe we should point our nose to next summer and ease into this thing?

And hadn't she said, no, no, it's now or I don't come at all? Not because I don't want to, and not because you don't want me to, but because I'll suffocate under months more of knowing what I want to do and not doing it, and I will give up. Don't you see? I'm already giving up. This is the fight I have left, enough to get there to you, and I have to spend it now or lose it.

She reclaims her son's hand, and she points ahead to the footbridge spanning the ditch and the playground beyond and, a short stretch farther, the apartment. Home the way they both need to start thinking of it.

She wishes Charley were with them, not in his car, headed south to Waco to talk to a football coach, only to turn around and go back come Saturday. There's been a fair amount of that these two weeks—more absenteeism from him than she'd hoped, though he'd certainly warned her it would come irregularly—now that things were in this shoulder season where football is in the thick of it and basketball is just stirring up and baseball is murmuring in its sleep. He's on some practice field or in some gymnasium or stadium somewhere three or four nights a week, and she's lonely when he's gone, which is mostly how she knows the thing they have is good, in its fundamentals if not always in the moment. In those final years with Ronnie, he would head out on a delivery and the stifling pressure would leave the house with him, drafting in his wake. Here, the air isn't right when Charley isn't in it.

He had said his goodbyes to Nathan that morning, after the boy had calmed down, a peace offering of sorts. "You'll be asleep when I come back, but I'll bring you a treat."

"What?"

"I can't tell you. It's a surprise." A wink at Electra.

"Tell me."

"Kolaches," Charley had said.

"What are those?"

"They're from Czechoslovakia. Well, no, they're from Waco, but they're made by people from Czechoslovakia. Do you know where that is?"

"What are they?"

"Do you like Twinkies?"

"Everybody likes Twinkies."

"They're better than Twinkies. You'll see."

It had been encouraging, then it had crashed. Nathan, pouting, given a banana after his cereal had been tossed, the walk to school still in front of them, had said, "I don't think I'll like them."

"Yeah?" Charley had said. "You didn't know what they were five seconds ago."

"I don't like them."

"Fine. Fine. Your mother and I will eat them, then."

Nathan, dug in: "Fine."

Later, upstairs, after the boy was safely deposited at school, she and Charley made their way back to each other.

"That was stupid," he said.

"It wasn't."

"I can't argue with him all the time. It won't get anywhere."

"I—"

"But he's *so headstrong*."

"He is. I told you."

"You did," he said.

Now, Electra tugs her boy along, covering the last stretch they must cross, for now.

"It'll get better," she says. "I promise."

The call comes as she's putting away the last of the dinner dishes. Nathan lies stretched out on the floor, on his stomach, building something modern and well-angled with his erector set, a gift that keeps on giving her peace and quiet. She reaches for the handset, then stops and twirls her fingers, wondering who it will be. Charley, she hopes. Ronnie, possibly. He's called a few times since she gave him the number—"His boy is here and we can't duck him forever" had been her rationale, which was, well, rational, but perhaps not very smart.

She answers, a too-timid "hello."

"Electra, it's Amy."

Relief and dread flood in, incompatible, grappling for space in a single gut. Electra takes a breath.

"Hi, Amy."

"He's retained counsel."

"Oh, no."

"Stay with me."

"OK," Electra says.

"We talked about this."

"I know."

"I still think it's posturing," Amy says. "The best deal he's going to get is the one you presented him. A good lawyer would tell him so. But if he wants to spend money, there are certainly lawyers who'll be happy to take it from him."

"OK," Electra says. Her pent-up breath leaves her in a long release.

"There's more," Amy says. "He wants a visit. He's going to be in Texas in a couple of weeks and wants to see Nathan."

"Oh, no."

"He's entitled. Peril ahead if we fight this."

"OK."

"I can put some boundaries on it. A few hours, no leaving your apartment, but—"

"Yeah."

"I'll set it up," Amy says. "I'll call again soon."

Electra thanks her, says goodbye, hangs up. She goes to Nathan, matches his posture on the floor, and examines his work. With a delicate finger, she touches a hinge point on his contraption, and the metal structure bows from the intrusion. He reaches over and sets it right.

"What is this?" she asks.

"I call it The Whirler."

"What's it for?"

"Whirling," Nathan says, and she lets go a sputtering laugh, and the giggles get him, too, and they're rolling, both of them, off their stomachs and onto their backs and there's no stopping it now, the laughter coming in heaving convulsions, and Electra's tummy hurts with the most wonderful pain she has felt in days.

It's past one a.m. when Charley is at the bed, getting ready to move in beside her. The belt buckle and keys flopped onto the bureau stir her, and she rolls toward the nightstand and the light.

"Leave it," he whispers.

"I didn't hear you come in."

"I was quiet."

Aided by a slice of moonlight flooding in, she sees that he's down to a T-shirt and boxers, and she imagines those chicken legs of his down there in the deeper darkness, the only thing that truly surprised her the first time they got naked together. His movement on them is so graceful that it seems a shame they are so scrawny in the raw. But there are always surprises in that first moment of such vulnerability, aren't there? It's a hell of a thing, to fall in love before matters of flesh get involved, to have unshakeable trust before the clothes come off. A first for her, and for him, he'd said. Things with Ronnie had gone the other way, blind gropes in a Chevy on a first date, intimacy before knowledge, unencumbered lust barely beyond acquaintance. You go to bed, or the vehicular approximation you have of it, and later you figure out the rest. With Charley, it's been precisely the opposite.

He slips into the bed and takes her in, kisses her deeply with coffee on his breath.

"You drink the whole pot, mister?" she asks, giggling.

"Long drive. Had to."

"I'm glad you're here."

"Me, too."

She sets her head on his chest, her ear to his rabbit cage, listening to his heartbeat and feeling the rise and fall as he tells her about his long day ninety-some miles south, sitting down with the new Baylor football coach for a chat about what seems the impossible job of making a church school in central Texas into anything worth watching. "I doubt he can," he tells her. "I doubt anyone can." After that, some time spent with the basketball team at practice, dinner with the athletic director, gathering string for a coming winter of coverage. Write his column, send it off by Western Union, come home, where he wants to be.

She nuzzles in.

"How was your day?" he asks her.

"Fine," she says, and she kisses him again.

At breakfast, Charley folds the sports section in half and puts it in front of Nathan. He taps a small black-and-white picture with a finger.

"Do you know that guy?"

Nathan peers in. "No."

"Look closer."

Nathan squints and presses his nose forward, almost into the newsprint. "No."

"That's Charley!" Electra says as she sweeps around for a look. "Don't you recognize him?"

Nathan looks to the page to Charley to the page and back again to Charley. "You're not wearing glasses here," he says, pointing at the newspaper.

"No," Charley says.

"Vanity?" Electra asks.

"Yes," Charley says, and that makes her laugh.

"Why are you in the newspaper?" Nathan asks.

Charley pulls out the chair next to him and sits so they can look at the page together. "That's my job," he says. "I write about sports, and the newspaper prints my words with my picture. I'm called a *columnist*."

"That's a weird word."

"I guess it is," Charley says.

"Just sports?"

Charley shrugs. "So far."

"You wrote all this?" Nathan smears the page with cherry filling from his pastry as he manhandles it.

"Just the words under my picture."

"That's a lot."

"Yeah."

"That's neat."

Charley picks up the section, unfolds it, then flips the page and shows the boy more, where the words go when they leave the front page, the small type with the scores and statistics ("That's called agate," he says, a weirder word for Nathan to absorb), how the editors in an office downtown work all night putting pictures and words and agate together, positioning it all around the advertisements, then how the whole thing gets printed on a big tumbling machine and put on trucks and taken to vending boxes and stores and thrown onto front porches, like theirs, every morning. "It goes out in a two-hundred-mile radius," Charley says, and Nathan asks what a radius is, and Charley tries to describe it as best he can, and the boy's eyes grow wide at the scale of what he hears. Electra picks up their dishes, carries them to the sink, and scrubs them down, and she takes a moment, lingering in a squat below the sink as she gets the detergent, welling up for what just might be a breakthrough. And if it's not, it'll do until the real thing comes around. She then stands and gets busy again.

She tells Charley of the phone call and the coming visit from Ronnie when they're alone on the walk home from the school, Nathan safely dropped off with Miss Lowrance, who has reported that he's coming along, if a bit slowly. "I've had to send him to the gray line a couple of times," she says, invoking the wide ribbon of duct tape on the floor, bisecting her room. Little boys and girls who misbehave must sit there silently for a time commensurate with their infraction, in full view of the others in the group. "Nothing that can't be fixed—talking out of turn, mostly," she says. "He's a bright boy, maybe the brightest in the class."

They go on, and Electra relays the development and watches as a storm gathers in Charley's response to Ronnie's pending visit. "I suppose it was inevitable," he says, and she thinks that's true enough, given Amy's view on it. He apologizes to her—again—for any preemptive hostility toward her ex, and again she demurs. "I haven't exactly been charitable in my assessments."

"So what's the story?" he asks. "He's coming here? Right here?"

"Amy says maybe the best thing is that they sit in our living room for a few hours, alone." She silently thrills at the possessive pronoun, one she hasn't yet flung into a casual conversation.

"Yeah," he says, smiling. "That'd work."

"Or we could all go have lunch or something," she says, surprising herself. "Though that seems like it would be uncomfortable."

"Détente, Mr. Brezhnev?" He nudges her, but she doesn't laugh, and he covers up with "yeah, that's no good."

At the playground, he jogs through the sand to the swing sets, settles into the wide rubber seat, and starts kicking himself into motion. "Come on," he says.

"Really?"

"Come on."

He's traveling in a swift arc now, rising forward and falling back, the action giving him lift on both ends of the pendulum. She takes the seat next to him and starts playing catch-up. Their rhythm is off—when he's on the downslope, she's reaching her apex—and they talk past each other, full beats punctuating each completed phrase.

"Where are we going to go?" he asks. "When this visit happens?"

"I'm going to be right here, where I can see our front door." She feels her stomach drop away, the swing or the *our*, it matters not which one.

"No, let's go see a movie or something."

"No chance. I'm going to be right where I can see them."

"Really?"

"Really."

"OK," he says, "watch this." At the top of his swoop, he disengages himself from the seat and the chains tethering it and takes flight, his feet and knees a little too forward, his ass end making the acquaintance of gravity, and he overcorrects, hitting the sand on his tippy-toes and pitching forward, his mouth grinding the grain when he lands.

"Charley!" She arrests her movement and lights out to him, dropping to her knees as he flops onto his back.

"That was easier when I was eight," he says.

"What were you thinking?" she asks.

"I was thinking I'd show off for you a little bit."

"Yeah? Flowers are cheaper than back surgery." She touches his forehead and he smiles big, and she tries not to laugh so she doesn't give him further license for such recklessness.

He sobers up. "You're really worried about this, aren't you?"

"Yes." Her mouth tugs tight.

"It's that bad?"

"Here," she says, "get up." She stands and offers him both hands, arms crossing in front of her, and he crosses his in a mirror, grasps her hands, and rises. He dusts off his shirt and his butt and his thighs, then sees the hole in the trouser knee and the widening red stain in the khaki.

"You're bleeding," she says.

"I'm fine."

"Let's go," she says.

They walk off, holding hands. He limps for a bit, then finds his stride. Just outside the door, he stops.

"Lec, listen. Is it that bad?"

"No," she says, then she reconsiders. "Well, I mean, yes. The loneliness about crushed me, and it got worse, not better, the longer it went on. But he's not a bad person. He's ..."

"Immature?"

"Incomplete. He thinks because he never struck me, never struck Nathan ..."

"Jesus."

She puts a hand on his chest. "There are some things. Ronnie is—" It stops there for her. She's told some of it already and some she hasn't, caught between the promise to herself to deal honestly in all things with Charley and other promises to hold tight to stories that aren't hers to tell.

"What?"

"He isn't bad."

"He's not?"

"Good husband? No, not really. Attentive? Not particularly, but sometimes."

"I'm sorry," Charley says. "When does the not-bad part come in?"

"Stop it. Listen."

"I'm trying," he says.

"OK. Look, the thing is, he's got some particular views of things, some things that happened to him. Dammit." She stamps her foot. "This is hard."

"OK. I'm sorry."

"I don't hate him."

"Of course you don't," Charley says.

"But I don't trust him, either."

"I understand."

"Do you?"

"I do," he says. "I'm an understanding guy." He moves into her. He trails kisses on her forehead, on her cheeks, on her mouth, where he lingers awhile.

"Mercy," she says when she draws breath. "I believe the answer to your inquiry is beyond that door, Mr. Stidham."

She thinks it a good line. He's impervious. He stares through her, and she looks away, then presses her head into his chest.

"Electra," he says.

"Yes?"

"I love you."

She moves into him again and closes her eyes and holds on.

18

August 2012 | Billings, Montana

Nate props himself up in a sitting position, his back braced by pillows against the headboard. On the TV, the well-coiffed sports yakkers carry on in a low-volume hum. His attentions sway from the screen to the phone in his hand, from which he beams out his messages.

I'm sorry.

I shouldn't have.

Come on.

Call me, OK?

Nothing comes back. He considers—then rejects consideration of—calling Brandon. It's an hour later there, for one thing, and his timing lately has been for shit when he calls anyway. For another, he doesn't think he has it in him to go around and around again. The way Nate figures it, they'll be on the road tomorrow morning—not much reason to be sticking around, assuming the old man gets back at a reasonable hour—and he can call then and actually have something to report: *I'll be home tomorrow and will move that rig then, and excuse me for living.*

Her words blink in.

I don't think that's a good idea.

Nate sends air through his lips, thrumming them like an outboard motor. He pecks out a reply: *I just want to leave on good terms.*

The phone rings, startling him. He answers.

"Thank you," he says.

"So you're leaving tomorrow?" she asks.

"I guess so, yeah," he says.

"Well, have a safe trip back."

"Thanks."

The connection hangs silent between them.

"Anything else?" she asks.

"I just wanted to apologize."

"OK," she says. "Accepted."

"I just—"

"What?" she asks.

"I don't know why I did it."

She laughs.

"What?" he asks.

"*I* know why you did it."

He sits up straight. "Why?"

"Let's see," she says. "No impulse control. No boundaries. You think you're more charming than you actually are. You—"

"Jeez, lady."

"What?" she asks. "Am I wrong? Go ahead. Tell me how I'm wrong about this."

He begins to speak, but no arrangements come. He scrambles to the safe ground of a repeat. "I just wanted to apologize, that's all."

"So you did," she says. "And I accepted your apology. I thought you wanted to talk."

"I do."

"So let's talk."

"OK," he says. "You first."

"Fine. Let's talk about how shook up I am that this guy I barely know, met just last night, in fact, proposed coming to work for me twenty minutes before he kissed me. OK? Do you have any thoughts on those things? Do you want to talk to me about why you did that?"

"No," he says.

"That's too bad. Because that's what I want to talk about. That's what I want to understand."

"I don't know," he says. "I don't know why."

"We've already been at *I don't know why*," she says. "And I already told you why. How about you give me something honest now that I've told you the reasons."

"Like what?"

"Like *why* you have no impulse control or boundaries," she says.

"And I'm a drunk," he says. "You forgot that."

"I haven't forgotten anything."

He laughs, an almost involuntary response to the way she's cut down the space on him. He cradles the phone to his ear with a lifted shoulder and turns his palms upward, questioning no one.

"But listen," she says. "Why are you a drunk? I mean, as long as we're being honest."

"You won't like the answer," he says.

"Try me."

"I don't know."

"I said *try*," she says.

"No, really, I don't know. You think I haven't thought about it? It wasn't a decision. I wasn't all 'hey, getting hammered all the time sounds good.' It's a pretty damn short step from drinking wine coolers at lunch in the school parking lot when you're sixteen to not being able to face work at twenty-five unless you're blitzed out of your head."

"Well, that's just fine," she says. "You can pretty much give yourself a license to do anything with that attitude."

"I think you're being unfair," he says.

"Yeah? I think you're being cagey and evasive."

He sits heavy on the bed. The words land in the places where they've always landed, the callused and impregnable places where he can keep them from sinking deeper into him.

"You don't think much of me," he says.

"You're wrong about that," she says.

"Right. OK. Whatever."

"Try to get this," she says. "We're sitting at lunch, and you say to me, 'Hey, looks like you could use some help,' and I'm all, 'Yeah, yeah, well, he's not blind,' but I'm thinking, 'Well, he's not wrong, either,' and then you say, 'What about me?' Well, what *about* you, Nate? You're just going to move to Montana to mow grass with me? What did you think, that I was just going to say, 'Yeah, sure, come on and join me, Nate'?"

"No."

"Then why did you say it?"

"It was a joke."

"A joke," she says. "I must have missed the punch line."

He says nothing. There is nothing to say.

"See," she goes on, "I think you said it because it's no cost to you to say something like that. And if it stirs me up, well, that doesn't cost you anything, either. The payoff for you is if I say something like, 'Oh, gee, Nate, that would be *so* wonderful, wouldn't it?' You can feel all warm inside. Too bad it didn't go that way for you."

"I'm sorry," he says.

"And then, when I'm trying to apologize to you about my own overstep, you kiss me," she says, "which I did not ask you to do, didn't imply I wanted it, nothing. You just did it. Again, no cost to you, but maybe there's a big payoff, right? Maybe I kiss you back. Or maybe even I go to bed with you. Let you fuck me. It's worth a shot, right? Never mind how I feel or what I want. Never mind how it affects me, right? As long as it works out for you."

"I'm sorry," he says again.

"I know you are, but I don't think you know what you're sorry about," she says. She sighs heavily, garble on the connection, and she puts the straight razor of her words away. "Nate, listen, when I was a younger woman, I might have given you every payoff you wanted today. I might have. But I just don't have the time or the inclination anymore to play at things. I can't. And I don't want to. You understand?"

"Yes."

"You said I don't think much of you," she says. "You're wrong. I think a great deal of you, actually. You're sensitive and funny. You're interesting."

"Thank you."

"And you're going to be dead soon, I'm afraid."

She goes quiet. He doesn't fill the gaps. The room feels like it has pulled away from him.

"Anyway, have a safe trip back," she says.

The phone goes lifeless in his hands.

Nate pushes off the bed, zeroed in. He sweeps the flask from the bureau and gives it a shake, and there's nothing. Dry. He sets it down again.

From the back wall, over the bed, the rippled, leathery, black-and-white face of a rodeo cowboy considers him in profile. Third night here, it's the first he's really looked at the picture. The man has a weathered weariness about him, coexisting uneasily with attentiveness to whatever is going on in the arena beyond the camera eye.

Nate side-skips twice toward the cowboy's face and launches a haymaker of a right hand that lands square on the chin, shattering the glass in the frame, and the pain is like a blooming kaleidoscope, all kinetic shapes and colors, and he falls sideways onto the bed, rolls onto his back, and holds the hand aloft. Blood runs in zagging rivulets from his hand to his elbow and falls in dots onto his shirt. Glass grows from his knuckles. He winces and rolls again and finds his feet, and he stumbles toward the sink.

He thinks it's the damned stupidest thing he's done yet.

Nate is nearly down for good when the knuckled rap on the door comes. His right hand lies limp at his side, wrapped in a hotel-grade towel, the bleeding stanched, the little pieces of glass—most of them, anyway—picked out of the wound and swept down the sink.

The knocking comes again, and he rolls onto his feet. "Dad?" he calls out.

"No." It's a man's voice. He can't place it.

"Who is it?"

"Jimmy. Come on, Nate, open up."

"OK, just a sec."

Nate steps to the door with an outsized measure of caution. *She wouldn't have called him up and spilled, would she?* He doesn't think so. He also doesn't know. She's surprising in ways he hasn't cataloged yet.

Nate throws open the door, and Jimmy stands there, lopsided goofy smile, oil-smudged work clothes, heavy boots. The smile diffuses when he gets an eyeful of Nate.

"You look like shit," he says.

"Yeah, thanks. Come on in."

Jimmy steps forward, his girth overtaking the small room. Nate hadn't appreciated—or considered, truthfully—just how substantial the guy is, clearly someone who can handle himself. That's good to know, as Nate is the other kind of guy, one who loses a fistfight with a photograph. He sits back on the bed. A headache's coming on, the kind for which he lacks the most reliable cure.

"Dad called," Jimmy said. "They're staying up in Great Falls tonight, having dinner with the cousins."

"Great."

"They'll drive down early in the morning. I thought we could go have a beer. Been a long time, cousin."

"Last night doesn't count, I guess," Nate says.

"Yeah, that was weird. What happened there?"

"I don't know."

"Well, anyway," Jimmy says. "Beer?"

"Yeah," Nate says. "Sounds good."

The cowboy bar downtown isn't much of a salve for a headache, what with its too-loud thumping music and jammed-in revelers who carry fifteen to twenty years fewer than Nate and Jimmy do. What it has in abundance, though, are free-flowing taps and plenty of bottles ready to be poured out. Nate takes his best crack at it, quickly going three shots in, with beer chasers.

Jimmy clinks a shot glass against Nate's fourth and shouts above the onslaught. "To family."

Nate lifts his glass with his damaged hand. That had been quite the story on the drive over. A guy can't unwrap a bloody hand and say he fell down the stairs or something equally impotent, not when the evidence of what he's done is plain enough to anyone standing in the room. So he'd just copped to it, minus the leading details. "Got pissed off. Punched a picture," he'd said, pointing at the wreckage on the floor. "Not the smartest thing I've done. Not the dumbest, either." Jimmy, by all appearances the sort of fella who understands the negotiating power of blunt-force trauma, just laughed and said, "Well, all right, man. Shoulda seen the other guy, right?"

Now, Nate says, "To family, such as it is," and he throws back the liquor. The warmth of it coats his throat and swims down his gullet, nice and easy. He feels his bonds to the world loosening.

"What do you do, Nate?" Jimmy asks. "For a living."

Nate smiles and squints and leans in so he can be heard. "I'm between opportunities."

"Ah."

"What about you?"

"Pipefitter."

Nate, feeling fine, stands himself up, rigid and straight, and says in a choppy, exaggerated voice, "Big strong man work."

"Something like that."

His compromised faculties aside, Nate looks at this inexplicable blood relation and tries to find whatever it is in there that Rhonda once responded to, whatever might have caused her, in her winsome youth, to say, "Yeah, OK, this one will do," and whether she found out later she was wrong about that thing or she simply reconsidered her wants and escaped accordingly. He thinks of Annette and how she came to find her ticket somewhere else and a clear-cut reason for punching it. When you're young and in the full roar of lust, you can hide from or look past a lot of blemishes, even the most disfiguring ones. Charades isn't a game for older folks. *Nate, you're a drunk and I can't anymore, I just can't.* She went, twenty years ago, Brandon, too. Inside of two years, she's married again, to a nice guy, Brandon says, and Nate figures the proof lies in how Brandon got raised in his absence.

"What's the deal with you and Uncle Ronnie?" Jimmy asks.

"Deal?"

"You know." Jimmy feigns a punch, and Nate groans.

"Oh, yeah. How long you got?"

Jimmy flags down the bartender. Nate sits heavy on the stool. "Two more," Jimmy tells the guy.

A gesture toward Nate, who's listing left. "He ain't driving, is he?"

"No, I am," Jimmy says. "Last one for me."

"OK, then." The bartender makes the pours and sends the glasses across to them.

Jimmy again touches his glass to Nate's. They throw the drinks down in synchronicity.

"Oh, that's good," Nate says.

"Now," Jimmy says, "you were saying . . ."

"Right." Nate makes a quarter-turn on his stool, facing him. "The first thing you have to know: Ronnie is an asshole."

"Don't say that."

"You asked. Listen, men in general are assholes, aren't they? You and me, we're assholes, right? Well, he got a double helping."

"Not all men."

"All men!" Nate fires up an arm in an abrupt arc, punctuating his belligerence.

"You're drunk."

"No shit."

"Let's go."

Nate touches his arm. "No, wait. For real. Wait." He swallows hard and sits up. He pushes his shot glass back across the bar. He finds his bearings and starts again.

"My dad's biggest problem is that he outlived my mom. Be a lot easier to take what he is if I still had her." Nate, gone glum, suddenly brightens. "Hey, we have that in common, right? Dead moms."

"Yeah." The punch connects on Jimmy. He's glad of that.

"That's not all," Nate says. "We've both been divorced by women who are better off without us. A couple of winners, you and me."

Jimmy, with no in-between from befuddlement to sadness to anger, says, "Mind your business now."

"Seriously," Nate doubles down. "We got to be the stupidest motherfuckers alive. I'll bet you're stupider, though."

"We're leaving now."

Jimmy pays the tab, then yanks Nate from the barstool like he's nothing. Jimmy has him by an elbow and the opposite shoulder, and that's sufficient to immobilize him. They push through the dance floor, parting the sea, and out the back door of the place, into an empty alleyway. Jimmy spins Nate a half-turn and digs a right uppercut dead center of him, just below the breastplate. The air leaves him in a shrill *whoosh*, and it's the next blow, as he falls away, a right hand to his naked jaw, that brings down the lights.

19

October 1952 | Billings, Montana

"You two get in there closer." With one dangling hand, Opal holds the camera, the box of it and the attached bulb straining her. With the other, she directs. "Oscar, put your arm around him."

"OK, OK," Oscar says. "Come on, boy."

Ronnie has scarcely had time to set down his suitcase and say his hellos before the camera has come out, and he feels ill-prepared and self-conscious in this place unknown to him, one with its own odor and a general untidiness that the likes of Berta would have never countenanced. He'd have changed his shirt, had he known it was going to be a production.

"I'm documenting the moment," Opal says now, as she brings the camera up and holds it with both hands, lining up the shot.

"She's a pip with the camera," Oscar says.

Ronnie's father tightens down on his shoulders and pulls him in and the flash goes off.

"Now the two of you," Oscar says, releasing Ronnie and walking toward her, his hand out.

"No," she says.

"Come on, Opal."

"I don't even know him."

"I don't mind," Ronnie says.

"Well, OK." She hands the camera off to Oscar and comes to him. "Sorry to put you through this," she says.

"It's fine."

"OK," Oscar says, "get in there."

She nestles into him. The flash goes off as she asks, "You hungry?"

"Dang it, Opal, you turned your head."

"Sorry."

"Let's do it again now," Oscar says. "Look at me."

She and Ronnie stare straight ahead, grinning.

"You hungry?" she asks again, side-mouthing the words.

The flash goes again, and Ronnie's eyes chase the purple spots around the room.

"Dammit, Opal!"

"Oh, just leave it," she says.

Ronnie blinks, squeezing his eyes with a thumb and forefinger, and says, "Sure, I could eat something."

They munch on bologna sandwiches and carrots and make short work of their shared memories, each Ray man filling in the details for the other, and betwixt them comes some semblance of full recall.

"When my wife and me busted up, she didn't have no interest in looking after him," Oscar says, a carrot dangling from his fingers like a lit Lucky Strike. "Vile woman, that one."

Ronnie frowns, and Opal rallies to him. "Don't say that about the boy's ma."

"Just dealing in facts."

"No, he's right, mostly," Ronnie says. *Vile* isn't exactly the word he'd settle on to describe her. Fact was, separated from Dick Littler, she could be downright pleasant in her way. He carries a particular memory of her splashing around in the Missouri River one fine summer day when it was just the two of them, before Linda had come along, Dick uninterested in joining them, and that little scrap leavens the darker recall, of those times when Dick had him in the cross-hairs and he knew he'd be on his own, that Ma would either stay out of it entirely or egg it on in some way, like scolding him harder for some perceived infraction so as to curry Dick's favor. Ronnie had come to despise and fear the weakness in her, and the danger it held for him.

"Anyway," Oscar rambles on, "it was just us men, except when I was otherwise engaged—"

"In prison," Ronnie says.

"In *jail*," Oscar corrects him. "You remember that?"

"Sort of."

"Jail?" Opal asks.

"Horse rustling," Oscar says. "So they said. They were *my* horses."

"Who are you, Pancho Villa?" Opal asks. That makes Ronnie squirt out a laugh.

"*Anyway*," Oscar says, exasperated, "my mom looked after him, and then Delia, she wanted to spend some time with him after I come out, so . . ." He trails off.

"I don't remember that," Ronnie says. "My grandma, I mean."

"You were just a little tyke. Anyway, she's gone. So I took him out to see her . . ." Oscar ends it again.

"And that was thirteen years ago," Ronnie says. "Last time we saw each other."

"Well," Oscar says, "it's good to see you now."

"You, too."

Opal stands and collects the plates, then carries them into the kitchen. Oscar stands, too, and beats out a rhythm on his tummy with his hands.

"Thinking we could go find us a dinner out tonight," he says. "Just you and me."

"Sure. Opal could—"

"No," she says, "you two go and spend some time together."

"Ready to see your accommodations?" Oscar asks.

"Sure."

"Well, grab your suitcase and come out back. We're in the barn."

"I thought . . ." Ronnie stops short, lacking the finishing words, and just points at them, Oscar first, then Opal, as if he had a notion.

"You thought we're a couple?" Oscar asks. Opal sputters a laugh.

"Well, yeah."

"No, boy," he says. "You and me, we're the help. We come here for three squares and portraiture."

"You come in whenever you want, Ronnie," Opal says.

"Well," Oscar says, "ain't you just got the key to the city?"

The setup out back isn't as austere as Ronnie had imagined it might be. His father has rigged up a proper bunkhouse in the far corner of the barn, with walls and a door, two windows to the outside and a stove for warmth. A cot is made up for Ronnie, with his father's unkempt one adjacent. *It'll do*, he thinks.

"I come here in answer to an advertisement," Oscar tells him, "was just knocking around in the railyard, doing odd jobs, and I see it in the newspaper, and I come out here and I tell her, 'Well, lady, I ain't sleeping in the yard.' To her credit, she sprung for the lumber and whatnot, and I framed it up good."

"It's nice," Ronnie says.

"It'll do for forty winks, for sure."

Oscar leads him outside and shows him the terrain of the place. A few dozen sugar beet acres. Alfalfa. Chickens. That's about the size of it, he says. "Ain't really enough work for one man, let alone two, but there's always something coming up. She wants to paint the house come spring, she says. I could use your help then, for sure."

"I can definitely help," Ronnie says. "Whatever you need."

"I got some other jobs cooking, too." He claps Ronnie on the shoulder and gives it a deep rub. "We'll spend some time, make a little cabbage, get reacquainted, before you go off and enlist. How's that?"

"Sounds good."

"Glad you're here, son."

"Me, too," Ronnie says. "Dad."

It's over dinner—broiled chicken, in a diner downtown—that Oscar tries to get down into the nitty-gritty of it and Ronnie decides that he's just going to deflect it all as best he can. They've trod carefully around the day Dick and Ma came out to the road and met them and made their claim, neither making a direct reference to it, both knowing what had happened and trying to bridge the in-between time for the other with informed imagination.

"What in the hell were you doing in Three Forks?" Oscar asks. "A long damn way from the bench."

Ronnie shrugs and shovels in another mouthful. "Lit out when I got the chance. That's where I ended up. I figured, why not?"

"You mad at me?"

"No," Ronnie says. "Why?"

"Never came back for you."

Ronnie has occasionally considered the question of why Oscar didn't, but supplying an answer has never taken much time once he gets to pondering. A situation like that, you can head in the other direction or lie there more than halfway to dead out on Dick's road. An easy choice, considering the lack of alternatives.

"It worked out," Ronnie says.

"Boy howdy. I about shit my drawers when—" The rough-edged speech riles a dining couple at the next table, who turn and cluck at them, disapproving. Oscar lowers his voice. "It was a surprise, seeing that advertisement. I told Opal I'd easier find gold while digging a post hole."

"She's nice, Opal," Ronnie says.

"Opal? She's all right, I guess. Dumber than a bowling ball, but a nice lady."

"She didn't seem dumb."

"Well, she is," Oscar says. "Tough life out there. Folks owned the place. Dad died some years ago, I take it, and she and her mom kept it together, but then the old lady up and died, too."

"Never married?"

"You saw her. Nobody was beating down her door with flowers and a ring, no."

"Well, I liked her."

"Well, you're a nice kid."

They finish and pay up, and Oscar makes a big show at the register, telling the proprietor that this is his boy and it's a big day for them, and Ronnie stands there and takes it in, having imagined the day many times over but never quite picturing it like this, with a father this effusive, this loud, this boisterous. The whiparound of day to night is drawing tight on him, and Oscar is walking him out, saying just one more stop, one thing yet to do, did you have enough to eat, you're a growing boy, and we're going to have us some fun, yes, we are. Ronnie wishes mostly to put his head down, to slip from now into tomorrow, when he can take this thing he's dropped into at face value and start finding common cause with it, when his heart isn't clouded by what he's left behind. But he's here now, he says, so let's go.

It's full-on dark when they leave the diner, and Oscar wends through the downtown streets, zipping left and right, waiting out traffic lights and the odd pedestrian and navigating the vagaries of other motorists, and Ronnie wishes for vision beyond the hood of the pickup so that he might orient himself. Tom had given him the lay of the land coming in, how if he could find the rimrocks—the long sandstone wall holding the city like a mother cradles a child—

and turn himself toward them and stare, he'd know he was pointing himself due north. The pangs dig into him when Tom crosses his mind. Ronnie hopes he made it home safely, that he and Berta are far off into sleep—where Ronnie himself ought to be and would be were he still with them—and that they aren't missing him too awful.

He sees a hulking building hanging back from the road, shrouded in a soft light, three stories tall, it looks like, foreboding and cold. He points out the window. "That's—"

"High school," Oscar says upon a glance.

"How'd you come here?" Ronnie asks. "Billings, I mean."

"By this pickup here." Oscar shoots out an arm, shaking Ronnie by the shoulder. "I'm just joshing you. I don't know. Sort of came to it because I needed somewhere to go."

"OK."

"Great Falls played out," Oscar says now. "Figured I could go west or east. Decided to come east."

Just up a hill from the high school, Oscar swings a hard right turn and then another, and he brings the pickup gentle against the curb and shuts it down. Ronnie sits up, leans forward, and peers through the windshield. A couple of well-spaced houses are in his view, porchlights on, windows buttoned up and dark. As his eyes adjust, he sees concrete slabs in the gaps, several of them.

"What're we doing?"

"Waiting, for now," Oscar says. "Make yourself comfortable. Don't talk too much."

Ronnie scooches down in the bench seat, his back bowing inward, and he sets his head against the window glass. Only a few beats pass before he's gone.

Ronnie goes cold in the late hours, his body heat dropping in slumber right along with the temperature outside the pickup, and when Oscar starts shaking him, the movement first folds itself into his dream. He's walking through a winter field he doesn't know, ill-fitted for the conditions, the snow melting under his steps and saturating his thin socks, the sun a fuzzy orb throwing light but not heat, and the coming night chasing it toward the horizon. Hunger gnaws at his gut, and fear scarfs up the leftovers.

"Come on, son, wake up." The insistency penetrates the veneer of sleep, and Ronnie comes out of it, startled and attenuated, the set-in chill flushing to the surface of his skin.

"What time is it?" His breathing is shallow, rapid.

"Midnight. Maybe later. It's time."

Ronnie chases down his breath. "For what?"

"You know what a copper spool is, boy?"

"Yeah. I think."

Oscar points into the darkness outside. "Well, you can't miss it. There's one right alongside that second foundation up there. You get out, go find it, and you roll it up to the street here. I'll drive down and help you lift it into the back."

"We're stealing it?"

Oscar's hard scoff has the feel, at first, of ignited anger, and Ronnie braces himself for what, he doesn't know, and then his father laughs gently, a rolling chuckle.

"We ain't stealing nothing," he says. "Only one who's been stole from is me, when this crew took three days of my work and fired me without paying for my time. We're evening it up."

"OK," Ronnie says.

"Hell, you drive, and I'll go get it," Oscar says. "Don't make no difference to me."

"No, I'll get it."

"All right." Oscar reaches across him and opens the door for him. "Be quick about it, but not noisy. Don't waste no time, but don't rush around and make a mistake, either. Understand?"

"Yes, sir."

"All right, get. Don't slam that door."

Soon, Ronnie is on the street and cutting across at an angle away from the pickup, and every footfall is a calamity in his ears. The wind kicks up and blows hard against his back, cutting through his shirt and knifing below the skin, and he wishes for a coat to deflect it.

He makes his way to the second concrete slab, and there it is, a wooden spool standing on its two wheels, half his height. He puts a hand on what's wrapped tight around it, feeling the cold metal. He brings a palm to his nose and breathes in, and the smell of pennies sweeps through his senses.

He lays his weight into the spool, getting the wheels perpendicular to the road. It's a chore, just that quarter-spin, but now that he has it aligned, he sees how he can make quicker work of it. He grips one wheel with his left hand, the other with his right, and he digs in for traction, then gives a push. The spool cooperates, and Ronnie senses how he can keep the things steered right by applying even pressure, left and right, as it rolls along.

When he closes in on the street, he hears the pickup engine come to life and the crunch of gravel as it draws near, lights still off. Oscar pulls up parallel, hops out, digs behind the seat, and withdraws a small back tarpaulin, folded into a neat square.

"I'll get the gate," he says. "Wheel it to the back."

Ronnie has good intent but poor motor skills in the clutch. When he yells "shit!" he clamps a hand over his mouth too late, but it's no matter. The spool, rolling downhill away from them, with the curb as a guardrail keeping it in play, makes enough noise as it rambles into the night, occasionally illuminated as it passes below a streetlight.

He and Oscar beat it into the cab and take off in pursuit. An unwound line of copper tubing leads them like a line on a map to the termination point, where the spool has splintered against a concrete retaining wall on the far side of a bisecting street. Oscar whips the truck to a stop and they scramble out, pulling the loose tubing hand over hand and into the bed of pickup. It can't be more than a few dozen seconds, but it seems interminable, and Oscar's head whips around, on the lookout.

When the last of it is in the bed, Oscar covers the works with the tarp and orders Ronnie to lie down atop it all.

"It's freezing, Dad."

"Do what I tell you."

Ronnie scrambles into place.

"Hunker down there. Don't let anybody see you." Oscar shuts the gate, gets into the pickup, and tears off into the darkness.

Later, still shivering in his warm new bed, Ronnie blinks into the night that's fallen around him. Oscar's rapid, syncopated breathing cuts a sad song in the bed opposite.

"You still awake?" the older man asks.

"Yeah," Ronnie says.

"That was fun, wasn't it?"

"That was something."

Ronnie hears rustling as his father sits himself up. "I can get a buck a pound for that. It don't have to be fun, I guess, long as it's lucrative. Half's yours."

"I don't want it."

Oscar snorts. Ronnie properly interprets it as derision. "I wouldn't go thumbing my nose at a payday. We won't see a lot of them."

"I understand."

"You got money?"

Ronnie considers the question and shaves his answer appropriately. "A little."

"That's good. Real good. You keep it close for when you need it."

"I will, sir."

Oscar punches his pillow into softness. "OK, kid. Good night."

"Good night."

Ronnie waits until he's sure, until the breaths of his father recede into deep-throated snores, and then he comes out of the cot, inch by torturous inch, stopping with each creak and holding his breath and listening for the droning of the older man before he dares to move again. In time, he finds his pants on the floor, feels them in silence for the outline of his wallet, then extracts that with the nimblest of hands. He carries it to the cot and sets it in the middle of the blankets, then he pours himself atop it, the wallet notching against his breastbone, and he lets himself go with a promise, that from now on, not a sliver of air will come between him and it. Never, ever.

20

October 2002 | Bozeman, Montana

Cherie figures there's nowhere she'd rather be than where she is right now, on an unseasonably warm night, sultry even, with her head hanging out the open passenger-side window of a cruiser, its strobe engaged, doubling the speed limit on a downtown street, the Friday traffic peeling to the edges of the road to let them by. Carl Gunnarsson—"Gunny," the other officers call him, and Cherie does, too, which thrills her inexplicably—is locked in on where he's headed. The call goes out—firearm discharge—and a cop gets serious quick. Gunny lost interest in his hamburger in a split second. He's in the moment now.

"Bowden, roll that up," he says. "It's go time."

She loves that he calls her "Bowden." She loves that all of them do, all of them she's met so far at stadium parking lot duty and bike fairs. She loves that she can cruise by the department after class and hang out. She loves that the chief knows her by name.

And she loves go time, even when, for her, it's don't-go-anywhere time. Fine. Whatever. This is her second ride-along but her first gunplay. That's the juice. Traffic stops are fine, drunk-and-disorderly calls their own kind of interesting, but nothing stands the fine hairs on end like this.

Gunny parks at an angle in the street, just two blocks off Main, his cruiser and the two others already there juxtaposed like a hockey defenseman's teeth. He turns up the radio before he gets out, for her benefit, and tells her "you stay right here," for his. The crackle and pop of the radio transmissions spell it out for her even as the cops outside the windows play it in pantomime. Gunny and Jonesy and Zukes—officers Melvin Jones and Rex Zukar, for the uninitiated— duck low behind Jonesy's car, service pistols drawn, and talk it out while Sergeant Hall, having just arrived, joins them. The size of the situation seems to be a domestic squabble, an unintended shot, a neighbor's call upon hearing it, then the shooter's subsequent call, upon the gathering of the fraternal order of police convention in front of his house, to say it's all a big misunderstanding.

That clearly isn't going to cut it now.

"Subject advises he's coming out."

The officers lurch rigidly into firing position. Cherie feels it as her breath catches.

The front door of the house, a square, low-slung bungalow, comes open just a bit, and when it does, Gunny's voice cuts the evening air. "Come out slow. Hands up."

A twig of a man—older, Cherie thinks, maybe fifty—steps out, quivering. Gunny keeps barking. "On your knees. Hands up."

The man goes down. He's trembling, the movements shaky.

"Now your stomach. Hands out."

He faceplants. For the first time, Cherie allows herself a look around at the scene. They've attracted an audience—people on their own front stoops, a TV news van, folks on the sidewalks farther down on either end of the street, out of the action but witness to it. It's quite the gathering for something that ends so quickly and ignominiously. Gunny and Jonesy are atop the man in short order, his offshoot arms pulled back and cuffed, a reading of his rights after Gunny stands him up for the walk to the cruiser. Gunny folds him in half and deposits him. While the officer is getting into the car, Cherie regards the man in the rearview mirror. The tininess of him all but sinks into the upholstery.

"Am I in trouble?" the man asks when Gunny is strapped in and the strobe is off. It's a deep, resonant voice, incongruous with the tiny, birdlike man from whom it emerges.

"A fair amount, yeah," Gunny says.

"How much?"

"I don't know. More than you should want, in any case."

"Who's she?" Cherie's eyes flash to the mirror again at her invocation.

"My biographer," Gunny says.

"Funny. Funny cop."

"Shut up."

Things go quiet. A bite at a time, Cherie swallows an urge to bust out with a laugh.

"I didn't mean to fire," the man says now.

"So you said. We'll write it down that way, not that it matters, since you did."

"I didn't even know it was loaded."

"Old story, pal," Gunny says. "Ignorance isn't the defense you think it is."

"I just wanted her to shut the fuck up," the man says, hitting the final four syllables like a pom pounding a bass drum.

"Dude, seriously," Gunny says, "the whole right-to-remain-silent thing is for you. You hear me?"

At this, the man goes weepy, having been on the edge of it all along. His head hangs low, shoulders go down, nose tucks into the collar of his shirt, back heaves. Cherie watches him in reverse, caught between pity and disdain. She imagines some far-off day—but nearer than it's ever been, now that she's found a way to give shape to her aspirations—when she's in the driver's seat and it's her perp to book and she has some in-between time with him, after the event and before the teeth of the justice system start chewing on him, and she wonders what she might impart in their interlude. Maybe a good deal of what Gunny has said—she rather liked the Miranda reminder—and maybe something else. Maybe she'd tell him that nothing is irretrievable, not even a better day in the aftermath of the worst day you've ever had. Her mind blossoms into vast configurations of what would be proper and what would be comforting, if the bird man were in her cruiser cage.

Gunny takes things in a different direction.

"You believe this guy?" he says to her. "We wasted a perfectly good dinner on this candy-ass."

Later, after it's done and the bird man is booked and after Cherie has had a Coke and a chat with Sergeant Hall and Gunny has done his paperwork, the patrol officer tells her she can go home if she wants, that it's been a full night already. That's when she tells him that she's not going anywhere, that things are just getting good now, and Gunny says, "You're one of us, for sure." Cherie thinks she can live for days on that utterance.

"What's going to happen to him?" she asks Gunny when they're out again, riding Main Street to its far western edge, keeping an eye on things as they wait for the next dispatch call, the next assignment.

"Who knows? Prosecutor's call."

"Yeah," she says, "but your best guess."

"Probation. I mean, he didn't hurt anything but his drywall. Just another dumbass with a gun. Too many of those, and they're multiplying."

Gunny turns around in a strip mall parking lot and heads back the way they came. Bozeman lays out before them, twinkling. She's never had a particular love for it—like most any kid, she has viewed where she's from as a place to be escaped, with tentacles that seem to only grip tighter as she tries to pull away—but these weeks with the PD have brought a clarity of purpose. Could she imagine staying forever? She's maybe not quite there yet, but give her this responsibility on the nightly, let her drive herself into the evening, self-possessed and in service, and maybe the scales finally weigh out in Bozeman's favor.

"I'm trying to figure out what brings a man to that point," she says now. "How does an otherwise reasonable person get to, 'You know what, I'll just scare her with a gun'? I mean, what's the thought process there?"

"Oh, we're assuming he's reasonable?"

"He seemed reasonable."

"Reasonable? Crying and carrying on like that?"

"He was scared. That doesn't mean he's unreasonable most of the time, does it?"

"Yeah," Gunny says. "I don't truck with what might be. He had a gun and he used it, maybe not in the way he intended, but there isn't a lot of reasonable there that I can see."

"Fair," she says.

"The thing is, Bowds," he says, and she thrills again at the nickname they've given her, a limitless well of dopamine, "I figure you can be a cop or a social worker. If you're a cop, there are rules, and it's your job to make sure they're followed. I don't go power-tripping on it, like Jonesy, but I figure that's my role: I'm a dispassionate dispenser of the consequences for rule-breaking. I don't concern myself with why people act the way they do. It clouds the issue. They do. And some of them are on the wrong side of the rules *when* they do. My job is dealing with the infraction, not the factors that brought them to a moment of choosing to do the wrong thing."

"But aren't the reasons interesting?" she presses. "Doesn't it help to know them, if they're knowable? I feel like maybe you could see things start to change if you had that knowledge."

"Liberal."

"I'm not," she protests.

"You sure sound like one."

"I'm just talking it out here."

He sits quiet with it awhile before he tries to paint out his position again. "I couldn't fit a piece of paper into the gap between what's a reason and what's an excuse," he says.

The radio crackles, a call for help, alleyway between Willson and Tracy avenues. Gunny says they'll roll on it.

"Good talk," he tells her. "Back to work."

They pull up alongside a thirtyish guy at the mouth of the alley when he flags them down. Gunny retracts his window.

"I called it in," the man says, leaning in. "Guy down there, he just pitched over."

"You talk to him?"

"Hell, no."

Cherie looks ahead, sees the lump in the middle of the asphalt next to a rogue shopping cart, looking like a bag of discarded trash.

"OK, thanks," Gunny says. He rolls up the window again and noses the cruiser into the alley, off the street.

"Stay here," he tells her.

"Let me come."

"No."

"Come on, Gunny. It's a homeless guy. Probably drunk. Let me come with you."

"Yeah, yeah, OK. But if shit starts to fly, you get down, you understand me?"

"OK."

They get out of the cruiser and start stepping, at half-speed, toward the figure. Gunny talks at him. "Hey, you. You OK?" There's no response. He gets on the radio, calls in, makes the request for an ambulance.

They're upon him now, the stink of too much alcohol and not enough showers radiating off the lump of him. Gunny shakes the man, to no effect. Together, they roll him over, and he's yet unresponsive. Gunny puts an ear to the man's chest. "Nothing."

"CPR," she says.

"EMTs are coming."

Cherie drops to her knees beside the man and lifts up from the back of his neck, tilting his head.

"Bowden."

She pinches his nose and puts her mouth on his and tastes the liquor. She shoots two quick breaths into him.

"Don't do that, Bowden."

She uses the butt of her right hand and positions it into the notch of his chest. He's an old guy, this much she knows from the weathering of the face and the whiskers gone ghost-white, and she says, "I'm sorry, sir," and lays into him, deep compressions, and she feels the ribs cracking below her hands. She compresses in rhythm with the song playing in her head, "Staying Alive," the title an amusing juxtaposition to well-on-its-way death and also the perfect beat for chest compressions. She remembers her CPR instructor telling her class that, making them sing along while they worked over the dummy torsos. After thirty, she pinches the nose and blows again, then goes back to the compressions.

"EMTs are here," Gunny says.

Cherie moves out of position and lets the professionals in, and it's just a few seconds more and the man on the ground is sputtering, his eyes rolling around crazily, and the technicians move seamlessly into the next phase of lifesaving.

"Holy shit," Gunny says.

It's hours yet before Cherie goes home. Gunny wanted to buy her a beer—they all wanted to buy her a beer, but she's eighteen and there are rules, she reminded them—and so a handful of them settled on a late-night breakfast at IHOP. When she finally breaches the door at home, she's exhausted and exhilarated and discontent, the latter because she is altogether unsure how she can bear down and write a personal essay—due Monday—when all she wants is to be in that cruiser, again and again.

She sets her things down, then goes to the fridge and roots around, wanting nothing and everything, simultaneously.

"You're late."

The voice startles Cherie.

"Time got away from me," she says.

"A good night?"

"The *best* night."

"I'm glad," Anna says. "Can I talk to you about something?"

"Sure." Cherie sits down at the kitchen table, waves a hand at the chair opposite. Anna comes on bare feet, in her fraying robe, and sits with her.

"You stink," Anna says. "What did you do tonight?"

"Long story. What's up?"

"OK. That might be a long story, too."

"Go," Cherie says.

"It's Norm," she says, and Cherie feels the old defenses lock in, ready to be deployed in whatever way the situation demands. There's no sign of crying, so that's good, but it's also not definitive. She can't draw a read from Anna's sober manner. "He wants me to move in with him."

"Really?"

"You sound surprised."

"Do I?" Cherie gathers herself. She doesn't want to be prejudicial. She also wants to be clear. "Just seems early, that's all."

"It's been three weeks," Anna says, and the unspoken parts filter into that, giving it context Cherie knows all too well. It's a longer gestation than she's given to other such arrangements. The rejoinder, of course, is that all of them came to a consistent end, not least of all because of the many things you can't know about someone after only a couple of weeks. Does Norm know what he needs to know? Doubtful. Does she know Norm and his idiosyncrasies? Equally doubtful.

"Still," Cherie says, "it's quick."

"It is. It definitely is. I love him."

"I know. Does he love you?"

"Don't be mean."

"I'm not," Cherie says. "Really, I'm not. I'm just asking."

"He does. I think he does."

Cherie says nothing.

"I'm lonely," Anna says.

"I know."

"You're gone all the time."

"Mom, it's not—"

"I know."

Cherie stands. "It's not up to me. This is you, Mom. It's your decision. It's your thing. I don't have any say. I don't *want* any say."

"Will you be OK?"

"Mom, I'm fine. I'm so fine. You don't even have to worry about any of that."

"OK. I'm going to think about it some more."

"I think that's a good idea," Cherie says.

"Good night, then."

"Good night."

Cherie waits for her to leave, then collects her things and carries them to her room. From her dresser, she pulls out a T-shirt and boy shorts and a pair of socks, and these she carries into the bathroom. She turns on the spray and waits for the room to steam up. She strips out of the day clothes, down to what the good lord gave her, and she considers herself in the mirror. She's been running daily and lifting weights since the first ride-along, when Zukes gave her a cursory look and said, "You're way too scrawny for a cop," and went through his maintenance routine. She eyeballs herself now, looking for any suggestion that she's changing her shape, but she sees none yet. What's happening, she knows, is more of an inside job. She's found her people and her thing, and the running and the lifting and the protein-loading are part and parcel of *becoming*. She can't imagine a setup where this isn't both what she does and who she is. She wouldn't want the half measure of it when she can have the whole. Gunny can talk all he wants to about the line between what he does and where others' responsibilities lie, but she doesn't want the line. She wants it all, what's on both sides of it, and what rolls out to the horizons she can't even see yet. And now, tonight, she's convinced that all of it, every little bit, is riding her way.

She climbs into the shower and turns her backside to the water and drops her head back, back, back and lets it flow over her.

Cherie Bowden

1984-

You sit, and Captain Hall plops himself down opposite you, behind his desk, and for the first time—honest to god, the first time—you're nervous and tentative around him. Not about the reason you've come to see him, you're resolute about that, but just the being in his presence, wondering how he's going to take the words you're about to spill out to him, what he'll think of you after you say them. And that's it right there, the crux of it. You don't want him to lose that feeling he has for you. It's nothing inappropriate—indeed, it's the purest thing in the world, the way he's taken you to him all these years, shown you the way, been the cooler head, been the wise counsel. You want to walk out of here, probably just a few minutes from now, and you want to know those things are still in your pocket.

Either way, you're walking. You have to. When the realization came, and with it the certitude of what to do, there could be no half-measure or partial cure. Someone overstays every party, and you came to the hard realization that person was you—that, Jesus, at *twenty-eight* you'd had both enough and too much—and that you couldn't take on any more, not here, that if you stayed you'd be forever discontent in the living and the working. So you'd asked for some time on Captain Hall's calendar, his being the only higher-up you trust to be wise in that rabbinical way you need, and here you are, all set to dump out the problem and your concept of what might settle it.

"So, what's up?" he says, and you do as you planned, you just vomit it out there as plainly as you can, that you think it's time to move on. New town, new force, new run at living. What you don't say is that you don't have the first idea about what you'll do with all the old. The clothes and the furniture and the assorted belongings you'll pack up. The attitude—still pretty good, considering the challenges, but a torment when you're alone with it too long. The memories you can't outrun.

"I see," he says.

You weren't going to say anything else, but in the moment there's so much more context to give it all. You're not discontent, you say. You like the job, the fellow officers, the beat. You like the people in the neighborhoods who've let you in, who know your name, who trust you. What you are is discouraged, and you've come to believe that it's a feeling sunk into the bones of this place, one that sits on every corner you'll ever drive to. You don't have anybody left here— your dad, he lit out for retirement in Florida—so what's holding you still? Nothing. So that's your conclusion, your one certainty amid a load of things you don't know and can't guess: Change the place, then by extension change the rest.

He works it over a bit in his head, then says, "I know how you feel. I ever tell you about my brother?"

You don't think so, you say.

"He's an officer, too. Was. Retired now. Worked in Billings for twenty-odd years. Raised him up some kids, established in the community, had him a church he liked. And come '92—I think it was '92—he had a powerful need to leave. Called it a moral imperative. Finished his career down in Colorado, small-town police chief, happy as a clam."

You nod.

"The point being, here's a guy who was a candidate to stay if there ever was one. You'd think he'd grown his legs down into the earth there. But no. So you want to go, then?"

Yes, sir, you say.

"Well, Bowds, where do you want to go?"

It's a good question, that one. Somewhere you don't have to love anybody or miss anybody so terribly hard, that would be nice. That would be a start. I don't know, you say. Where you got?

"I'm going to put some thought into it," he says. "You hang in here with me for a bit. I know it's hard to stay when you want to go, but hang in, do your job, and I'll find you something, OK? I promise. It might just take a little time. You think you can do that?"

Good enough, you think. And yes, hell yes, you can do that. You've done so much more than that already. Hang in there? No problem. No problem at all.

21

November 1952 | Billings, Montana

The rifle shot dumps Ronnie to the floor, startled, and brings Oscar groaning out of his own sleep. By the time Ronnie comes around to time and place, there's another volley, the second barrel.

"That confounded woman," Oscar says.

"What's going on?"

"Just stay here."

Oscar is up and padding to the door, wearing red long johns, working an itchy spot on his ass with right hand as he tries to shake the hitch out of his get-along. He slips into the darkness of the barn proper while Ronnie scrambles over to tend to the stove that's been reduced to smoldering in the night. Their tidy room has gone cold.

"Woman," he hears his father yell out, the words stretched thin by the distance. "Don't do that."

A reply, aggressive and shrill and garbled, comes back, and in manner it's quite unlike the version of Opal whom Ronnie has come to know in small snippets these past couple of weeks, someone who sidles up unexpectedly sometimes while he's on some chore and asks how it's going and whether he needs anything.

"They're crows, Opal. They ain't going south. They're stayin' right here where they are."

More protestations.

"They have *bird brains*, Opal. In five minutes, they ain't gonna remember you fired that thing. Put it away."

They both have more to say, but the words come Ronnie's way muffled, not enough pitch on them to cover the distance. There's Oscar's yammering and hers, and then there's quiet, until Oscar comes back in, carrying the shotgun and a pack of shells, laughing.

"Fool woman," he says.

"Crows?" Ronnie asks.

"Heh, yeah." Oscar looks around, considers the room, then slips the munitions behind the bureau drawers in the corner. "She can have it back in the spring," he says, and he lowers himself down to his cot and scurries under the covers. "Crazy lady said she was sending them home. What she don't know is them birds are gonna be here to pick at her carcass, more likely. Soon, if she keeps pulling that shit."

"Don't say that."

"It was a joke, son."

"I know."

Oscar props himself on an elbow, staring at him. "You got a soft spot for her?"

Ronnie shakes his head. He wouldn't call it soft. He pities her, out here on her lonesome, too young by far to be left traveling alone in the world. She's twenty-six, just a decade older than he is, a fact that caught him between the eyes when she told him, for she certainly looks another ten years or so beyond that. But he figures maybe that's just the way of farm life, that the daily struggle puts years on you prematurely, but then the never-ending duties keep you strong and well-preserved. He holds Berta Foley in his mind's eye. She'd never offered an age and he'd never been crass enough to ask, but the loose details that had come his way suggested a proximity to sixty, with Tom a few years beyond that. She didn't look much older than Opal looks now.

"She's been nice to me, is all," Ronnie says.

"She is nice. Dumber than every rock in the yard, but nice."

"Yeah."

After eggs and bacon and a couple of cups of strong coffee, Oscar says he's gone for the day, off to Miles City to see a man about what needs seeing. Ronnie gets caught between the twin impulses of asking if he can come—Miles City, a couple of hours east, will be new territory for him—and staying far away. The old man is talking in code about what he's got going on out there, and Ronnie wants no part of another scheme.

The closest they've come to a breach happened when Ronnie told Oscar to count him out of further shenanigans, after the attempted theft of a pallet of lumber left Ronnie hauling ass through an alleyway, the cops hot on him, and cowering in the shed in somebody's backyard on Yellowstone Avenue. He'd subsequently picked his way along city streets, sticking to the dark alleys and the secondary lanes, fully prepared to walk the many miles back to Opal's farm if he had to. Down near the fairgrounds, Oscar had rolled up in the pickup and let him in.

"We'll get her next time," he'd said.

"No next time for me."

"Come on, boy. Show some guts."

"I'd rather show some brains."

On and on it had gone, the back-and-forth all the way to Opal's place, Ronnie resolute in declining any and all future schemes, Oscar holding forth on the big things they could do together, Ronnie saying, hell, I can just go back with the Foleys and we can forget about it, and Oscar saying, no, no, I understand, no more, I get it. You'll be missing out, but it's your life, kid.

Out in the yard, after breakfast, Oscar lays out the work he wants done that day. It doesn't amount to much of a pile. Pull some rotted boards from the chicken coop and replace them. Make sure every living thing gets fed, same as every day. Don't stand around outside playing pocket pool too awfully much or the neighbors will talk. There are no neighbors, which Ronnie supposes is what makes the whole thing funny if you happen to be standing in Oscar's boots.

He sets to work before the pickup is barreling eastward, kicking dust into the gray sky.

She comes to him around noontime, another quiet approach that catches him by surprise, occupied as he is.

"You want some lunch?"

"Sure," he says. "Thank you."

He follows her to the house, watching her bearing as she travels on heavy steps. There's not an ounce of smoothness in her movements, but she makes up for the lack of delicacies with a determined manner, boring through in a straight line, gobbling ground with her strides. Raw determination is a virtue, too, and probably more useful than delicate graces, he figures.

It's a good meal, fried chicken left over from Sunday dinner, russets cut thick and battered and deep-fried, creamed corn, a bottle of pop. She's a lesser cook than Ma or Berta, Ronnie has decided after a large enough sample of meals, but she's also appreciative of his appreciation for being fed, something he's never allowed himself to count on. He's pleased to have his belly warmed, and she's pleased to provide it, and they have that, which isn't nothing.

He eats heartily and is well pleased when she offers him another helping of corn. He asks if she's going to eat, too, and she says, "No, I'll just sit with you." He catches her looking at him, a gaze more penetrating than pleasant, and he asks, "What?"

"Nothing."

"OK."

"Do you like it here?" she asks.

He laughs, then he feels guilty for it when she turns her eyes toward her lap, as if he's made fun. It's just not an original question, that's all. She's asked it a dozen times, at least, and he's fielded it the same way a commensurate number: "Yeah, sure."

"It's different from what I'm used to," he says, slicing his answer a little too fine amid the circumstances. "But yeah, I like it."

"Different how?"

"Well, you know—"

"Oscar," she says.

"Yeah. I don't really know him. Trying to. Like I said, different."

"I understand."

Ronnie goes back to shoveling food.

"He belittles you," she says. "I don't like that."

He drops the fork, flabbergasted. He was on the precipice of saying damn near the same words to her, but he didn't know the way in or if he wanted to go there, considering the blind offshoots.

"I don't think he means to."

"No?" she says.

"It's just how he is." *God*, he thinks, *let's leave it at that*. Ronnie has no stomach for getting into the ways of the men he's known, how belittlement is tolerable and downright preferable when stacked against physical cruelty and abject indifference.

Ronnie digs back in and finishes his corn. "That was good," he says. "Thank you."

"You're welcome."

"You got a nice house here." *Nice*, he thinks, might be an overstatement by half—it's really just a boxy, plain-Jane place, but it's hers, and he wishes to be kind.

"My daddy built it," she says. "Can I show you around?"

"Yes," Ronnie says, wiping his mouth with his napkin, then

setting it on his plate and rising to bus his dishes to the sink. "I'd like that."

Opal seems proudest of the pictures on the wall, the black-and-whites that she says she took with the Brownie Hawkeye her mother gave her the previous Christmas, their last together. He sidesteps down the hallway, giving consideration to each. He senses retreat in them—the shots are pulled back, a little out of focus in a way that conveys artistry rather than carelessness. Fog hanging in the valley. A glint off the river on a stark afternoon. No people, just some birds in distant flight and some cows stricken by indifference.

"I about run myself into the poorhouse getting things developed, at first," she says. "I've had to lay off that."

"They're pretty," he says, and he can see that receiving the kind word pleases her.

"This your mom?" He points to a grim-faced woman, a studio portrait.

"That's her. Nineteen forty-seven. Year after daddy died. She said, 'Well, I better get one last picture made.' There it is."

"You didn't take her picture with your camera?"

"No," she says. "She wouldn't let me. 'Go aim that thing outside.'"

"What's her name?" he asks.

"Hannah. What's your mom's name?"

"Ma." She looks at him quizzically, and he laughs. "Delia."

"Nice name."

"I guess," he says.

Back in the living room, he continues his closer look, wondering about the stories behind knickknacks or why this was kept and some other thing was discarded. It's funny, he's been in the house plenty, three times a day to eat, a once-through when he first arrived, but now it's as if he's seeing it all with newly peeled eyes. It makes a difference, for sure. There's color and light here. You just have to get in it and look.

He lifts a short silver canister from the mantel. "This OK?" he asks her.

"Go ahead."

"What is it?"

"Lift the top," she says.

He pulls the lid off the thing, and the plinking notes come, tinny and delicate at the same time.

"It's a Thorens music box," she says.

He holds it to his ear. "I like it. Nice tune."

"My folks got it for me in New York. I was just a little girl." She reaches out, and he hands her both pieces. "It's my favorite thing." She puts it back together and returns it to its spot.

"It's really nice."

"Do you have to keep working?" She's moved up into his space. He hasn't ceded it.

"Not for a while."

"You want something else to eat?"

"OK."

"I have some apples."

"Apple pie?"

"I don't know how to make pie," she says.

"I do," he says.

Ronnie teaches her the method as it was shown to him. A block of butter into the ice box to get it cold. Flour—she has flour, for sure, because she can make a biscuit even if she can't whip up a crust—and salt and cold water. Opal peels and divvies the apples into thin slices, and when he's stumped as to how to make the filling, she has the idea of boiling them and adding sugar and cinnamon and a little corn starch for thickening, and that's the ticket right there.

He then shows her how to get her hands into the dough, to really massage it with her fingers. He echoes Berta Foley's words with his own, "the hands are what make it taste good," and he reaches around her and puts his fingers in the bowl with hers, and they work it together. "That's it," he tells her. "Now you've got it."

They roll it out and cut the crust just so, fill it, then build the top layer and cut out the vents. He shows her how to pinch the junctures and seal it up, then into the hot oven it goes.

Ronnie feels lightheaded and disproportionately happy, which vexes him, and he tells Opal he'll go outside and tend to the last of the chores while the pie bakes. "If I lose track of time," he says, "yell for me in about a half-hour."

The duties out in the yard aren't substantial, just some feed spread around for the chickens and putting the tools back where they came from, because if he doesn't, his father will surely pounce on that oversight. He's more preoccupied with a notion he has, one that seems smooth enough in the imagination but lacks some how-does-one-get-there-from-here details in the visualization. If matters had played out in a linear way, he'd have already been there with Louann Harper—she'd all but promised it that night in Tom's pickup—but Oscar's appearance had interceded and the harvest dance and its associated pleasures had gone on without his presence.

He walks the yard, considering. Go in there and just kiss her? He's filled to the brimming with gumption, but even that seems outrageous in its boldness. "I really like you, Opal"? Too boyish. Ronnie flushes with inadequacies of a kid who's seen too much and done not nearly enough. *Go in and eat your pie and get back in the bunkhouse where you belong.*

He lets himself in the back door, the aroma of the baking apples folding him into the swirl. She sits at the table, waiting.

"Just a few minutes," she says.

"Yeah."

He sits down with her. His heart is beating out double time in his ears. He hopes she can't hear it. He smiles, and she smiles back, and they both ponder their hands.

After a time, he says, "Let's take a look," and they go to the oven door together and bring it down. The pie is a perfect bronze. The filling congeals at the mouth of the venting holes he cut in the top crust. The air gets a sprinkling of cinnamon and sugar. He slips on the oven mitts and extracts the pie and sets it on a rack to cool. "Wish we had some ice cream," she says. He nods. "Sure enough," he says. "That'd be perfect."

She presses into him, as if in a hurry and before he can react, and her mouth is on his. He's glad to have it, glad to reach around and feel the fullness of her, and to kiss her back when he catches up to the moment. He takes her hand and leads her out of the kitchen, into the living room, into the hallway beyond, to the room at the end of it, past the door, onto the bed, where he lays her down. Without words, they undress each other, removing the last of what's between them, and he says, "I've been wanting this," and she says, "I have, too," and they take what they've been waiting for separately, together.

22

August 2012 | Billings, Montana

She takes her assignment, says hello to the guys coming on shift and going off—they're all guys, she's noticed, and that's one thing she thought maybe would have changed by now but hasn't, to their detriment all around. She's tucking their names away, one by one, as she fills her head with the relentless new, just a little bit at a time, until one day she'll have it all memorized, she's sure. Tonight, she'll be downtown again, not surprising given the recency of her arrival. It's smaller in the main part of the city, easier to learn, not as daunting as the ever-wider civic spread, but two weeks in, she's gotten antsy for the nighttime action on the outskirts, where the people of Billings go when their day is done and where, sometimes, they reveal their darkness to each other. That's where she comes in, sometimes.

To her daily surprise, she likes the job and the city. She'd looked askance at it when Captain Hall had first suggested it, but she'd bowed to his insistence that it was the right thing—new, as she wanted, but familiar. "Bigger city, won't look like a lateral move," he'd told her, as if that last part had been somehow important to her. But she appreciated it all the same, and she does so especially now that she's here. And here, not being there, is a place she's finding her way into, bit by little incomprehensible bit.

She settles herself into the car, backs it out, and rolls on. It's full-on night now, and the streetlamps stand like beacons up the curve of 27th Street, toward the rimrocks and the airport. She'll stop short of there, though, and turn left in front of the college and work her way back down into the bowl, past the pretty houses in the North Elevation neighborhood, over by the community crisis center, a frequent trouble spot, she's coming to learn. Billings doesn't have the market on transience and homelessness and unchecked mental-health problems—she's heard about what goes down in Portland and Seattle and Los Angeles and wants none of it—but it sure enough is a dumping ground for what the rest of Montana doesn't want. Parolees on buses, the wandering homeless, all of them shunted into pockets downtown and on the north and south sides, the NIMBY attitudes keeping those folks out of the tonier places. She thinks of a long-ago, cherished colleague and his protestations that he didn't want to be a social worker, and it makes her laugh sometimes, as unfunny as it is, because she feels now that she never had a choice in the matter. You can't do the job and skip that part of it, the one with the stopgap measures and the actions you cannot take looming larger than the ones you can. More directly, you can't do the job. No resources, no strategy, no hope, no understanding of the correlation between services and the costs necessary to bear them.

The thought of Gunny brings a ripping off of a scab that never heals, a letting loose of the blood that sits under the skin, pressured up, looking for escape. She loved him, not only in the chuck-on-the-shoulder-and-a-bust-to-the-balls way that played out with such familiarity, but also real and blossoming love that she kept entirely from him. There were times when she thought she might confess it, even times when maybe he was angling for his own words to say to her, moments when she thought she wouldn't have to, but she seized up and he did, too. You think there will be more chances than the one immediately in front of you. More time than the clock will end up imparting. You think you have opportunities still to be optioned, and then you don't, because there's a wreck up on Main Street one snowy night a few years back and somebody has to tend to traffic control and is just there, a standing, arm-waving duck, when a Ford half-ton loses its grip on the road and comes sliding into a mess that's already big enough, and the final moments are squeezed out of Gunny before anyone has a chance to help him. After that, tell whatever it is you have to say to his marker in Sunset Hills. He's free to listen now, if he cares to, if he's there to. Make your other stop, too, and have that eternal conversation that never gets resolved.

She's back downtown now, in the lit-up night, straightaway Fourth Avenue, streaming past the Y and the First Interstate tower, to the juncture with North Broadway, where two banks, a church, and the newspaper offices post up on the corners. She swings a right turn on Broadway, holds her line, goes right again at the next light. She moves slowly across the silent storefronts, eyes taking in and processing details, and what she sees down an alleyway prompts an immediate left turn, down to the light at Second Avenue, another left there, and a nose into the alley.

She gets out, hand on the butt of her revolver, soft words into the radio transmitter at her breastbone, letting dispatch know she's good, where she is, and what she's doing.

"You OK?" she calls out.

She steps closer. "Sir?"

The lumpen figure rolls from his stomach to his back, and she closes the distance, wary but not afraid.

She stands over him, staring down. His eyes are closed, but he's with her, a hand massaging his left jaw, painful whimpers.

The pitching forward onto his face did the damage he hasn't yet assessed, she reckons.

"Here, let me help you," she says, and she gets herself under his arms and crouches low for leverage and pulls him to sitting against the back wall of the building. He lists rightward but holds up. Another drunk, she can gather by the whiff of him. She's seen what comes of this, many times.

"You OK?" she asks.

He rubs the jaw again. "Not particularly."

"Got some ID?"

"Am I under arrest?"

"Not yet. ID, please."

He digs in a back pocket for his wallet, extracts the driver's license, and hands it over. She gives it a cursory look, then a deeper one when a detail catches her eye.

"You're a long way from home, Mister Ray," she says. "You sit here. I'll be right back. Need some water or anything?"

"Yeah."

"Water?"

"Yeah. In the absence of anything stronger, water'll be fine." It's a good line, she thinks. Whatever happened to him sobered him up. It's to his benefit.

"I'll be right back," she says. She turns from him and walks back to the cruiser, not altogether steady, silently cursing the legs that want only to run.

She calls it in and waits, watching him. He has no ambition for further movement, it seems, with his head tilted back against the wall. No danger here, she tells them, no need to send anyone else. Soon, the information she seeks comes back to her, a history that's checkered, yes, but also unremarkable. She'll hear worse tonight, she's sure. More important, nothing he's wanted for, so no reason to bring him in. It's entirely her discretion, and she's already decided.

She carries the license back to him and squats. He opens his eyes.

"What happened here?" she asks.

"Nothing I didn't deserve."

"That's philosophical. Fight?"

"Not much of one."

"Who did it?"

"I don't know him," he says.

She reaches toward his face, and he leans away. "May I?" she asks. He nods.

She touches him lightly beneath the abrasions, looking for broken skin, finding none. She offers him a hand to grip and helps him to his feet.

"Just stand there for a sec," she says.

"Sobriety test?"

"Similar. I already know you're drunk."

"So I'm going in, then?"

"Maybe," she says. "I'm going to ask you some questions. Just answer, OK?"

"OK," he says.

"Your full name?" she asks

"Nathan Brandon Ray. NBR. Never Break Rank."

"Very good."

"Thanks."

"Your birthdate?"

"February 9, 1967."

"Your address?"

"Now, or—"

"On your license," she says.

"Seventy-twenty-five Crabtree Lane, North Richland Hills, Texas, 76182," he says.

"Do you have a headache?" she asks.

"Nothing special."

"OK," she says. "I think you're going to live."

"Sorry to hear it."

"Funny, Mister Ray, very funny. Can I drop you somewhere?"

She has him nearly to the Heights before she starts working the questions sitting on her head. It's a delicate thing, being mostly sure of something but not near enough to entirely, and the moment in front of her doesn't much match the one she's occasionally imagined, so the formulations don't come in the way she might have expected. The man in her backseat, unshackled, not headed to any unpleasantness she'll be involved with, has been quiet, withdrawn inside himself as the city has slipped the windows.

"What brings you to Billings?"

"Funeral."

"I'm sorry," she says. "Whose?"

"My aunt."

"I'm sorry again. That's hard."

"I guess. Didn't know her."

"Just you?"

"Me and my dad," he says.

"What's his name?"

The answer doesn't come in rhythm. She finds him in the rearview, makes eye contact, sends up an eyebrow.

"You're too friendly to be a cop," he says, and the apology is right on the heels of it, chasing down the words. "Sorry."

"Just making conversation. We don't have to."

"Name's Ronnie."

She nods. "I knew some Montana Rays once. Small world. Oscar Ray, you ever hear of him?"

"Nope."

"Unrelated, maybe. Big place. Common name."

She pulls into the hotel parking lot, and he points out the red truck with the Texas plates and says to drop him there. As he's getting out, she asks, "When are you heading back home?"

"Tomorrow, I hope."

"Hold on a sec." She pulls a card and a pen from her console and jots a number on the back of it, then hands it through a slot in the plexiglass. "That's my number. Text before you go. Let's have some coffee, you, me, and your dad."

He takes the card. "Why?"

"How about so your last memory here isn't getting the shit kicked out of you?"

He stares at her.

"I'd like to meet your old man," she says.

"You know," he says, "I'm old enough to—" and she cuts him off with "relax, stud, I'm talking about coffee."

He opens the door and slides himself out, then ducks his head back in. "You do this with everyone you bust?"

"I didn't bust you."

"Still," he says.

"You question every kindness? It's just coffee. Text me. Or don't."

"I might," he says.

"Up to you," she says. She sets the cruiser in drive, he closes the door, and she's out of there, well out of her zone, hustling to get back where she belongs. During the drive back downtown, she's calculating the odds, like she's sitting on hole cards that just might play, if the river runs favorably and the guy across the table holds what she thinks he has there under his hand. The cruiser interior has grown swampy in the thickening night, and she rolls down a window to give the air a stir.

Her mind bounces, inexplicably, to a statistics course she took sophomore year, when she was still trying to get her legs under her scholastically and had taken on a class well beyond her ability. It's the only thing, really, that piqued her interest at the time, the only thing that stuck as she limped out of there with a hard-earned C. "There are no coincidences," the instructor had declared, an attention-getter for sure but more prosaic in the fuller explanation.

Her point had been that the statistically inclined believe that coincidence, as it's understood, can be explained by the Law of Truly Large Numbers, the postulate being that if you get enough people together, any strange event is inevitable. The further point: Coincidences are utterly random, and it's only that they're memorable that these expectable events stick with us.

And Cherie thinks now that she should be damned because she let go of expectation and hope on this count a long time ago. You relearn something new every day, don't you?

23

November 1972 | Euless, Texas

Electra pulls a big sheet of plastic wrap across the razor teeth, cutting off big enough chunks to cover the four large trays of cinnamon rolls she's rolled out and filled and cut and frosted. One by one, the trays are covered and the plastic is cinched to the edges, then she carries them back and puts them on the tower rack, and finally she wheels that into the walk-in fridge, where they'll be ready for the oven first thing in the morning. She checks the clock; it's 3:42, later than she wants it to be. She stops moving around just long enough to catch the sound of Nathan and the Carson kid giving chase to each other between the lunchroom tables beyond the door. They're understandably restless. She gets it. She is, too, for reasons not rooted in being a little boy.

"All set, Wanda," she calls out to the back of the industrial-sized kitchen. "I'll see you."

"Sounds good."

She doffs her apron and hangs it, first taking her purse and her coat from the same peg. Had she time for vanity, she might slip into the restroom just beyond the door for a quick freshen up, but there's little she could abate now. She knows she's a sight, and she smells the lunchtime gravy on herself, feels the powdery leavings from the dough on her fingertips. Her stomach grumbles, denied lunch again, not that she could have kept it down, and she's just not as good as the other ladies yet at sneaking a few bites between the lines of hungry kids.

She comes into the lunchroom at large, and Christopher is running toward her, crazy-eyed, arms swinging frenetically like an out-of-balance windmill, Nathan hot on his heels. She holds up a stop-sign hand and says, "Whoa, whoa. Let's settle down now." The boys skid into obedience.

"Let's go," she says, and she offers a hand to Nathan that she knows he won't take, and he doesn't.

They're through the back door of the lunchroom and down to the street, crossing over, left turn. It's the last throes of autumn, and she's been surprised at how Texas lately has vacillated between warm days that punch ever deeper into the year and cold mornings that rival, in their bone-penetrating chill, anything that Wyoming ever tossed at her. The three of them walked to school hours earlier with gloves and jackets on. Now, the boys are slinging those jackets around their waists and tying off the arms in front.

Electra finds herself ever thankful that Nathan's first friend comes from the same apartment complex, just another building, and that these walks that started barely a week ago are now what they all do, to and from, five days a week. Christopher is a high-spirited boy. It's become a running joke between her and Charley, that first day he came over after school to play with Nathan, the subsequent questions that came at Charley like pepper being shaken out, for Christopher Carson loves the Dallas Cowboys generally and Craig Morton particularly, which by association makes Charley, the newspaperman, this fascinating adjunct to greatness. "Don't go all Christopher" is their private code, meaning, in general, "simmer down and take it slow."

She very nearly went all Christopher that morning, the anticipation of a necessary and unwanted event getting to her, and she knows she might well yet go all Christopher, depending on how closely Ronnie has hewn to her instructions about what time to show up. She hasn't told Nathan he's coming, a decision that prompted some respectful debate with Charley, who wondered why she wouldn't. For that, she had one answer, the only one she needed: I'm not building up his hopes and then, for whatever reason, having them dashed when Ronnie doesn't show up. *Let him be surprised.*

Well, here surprise comes, one way or another. His or hers. Ronnie had called the night before, late, and said he was in Oklahoma City and on track, a delivery in Dallas and then headed their way. She has no reason to believe otherwise, what she wants—that he would just head back to Wyoming and give them some time to figure this whole thing out—be damned.

Just before reaching the playground, they veer off the path and send tow-headed Christopher shuttling down the walkway to his mother's apartment. Jeannette comes out to greet him, offering a little wave that Electra returns. Christopher spins on the sidewalk and waves frantically goodbye, and then he and his mother are inside and it's done, and Electra's hand now is good enough for her son.

They walk the footbridge and cut across the playground between the swing set and the merry-go-round, finding the pathway again. She can see now the bright yellow back end of Ronnie's trailer. Nathan's little-boy eyes are less focused, more prone to distraction, or it simply isn't registering with him. She grips his hand tighter.

Ronnie climbs down out of the cab, and she goes tense. "Look," she says, nodding, and Nathan sees it now, his father striding toward him, arms wide, and Nathan shakes his hand free from his mother and throws himself into a gallop, and Electra stands there, frozen, watching the man she cut loose from and the boy she won't let go come together in a hug, and her heart drops straight out of her and heads for the depths.

Later, she and Charley sit on the swings again, oriented now toward their front door and Ronnie's truck, idling on the curb.

"I went out, asked him if he wanted to come in and wait," Charley says. "'Nope.' 'Want anything to drink?' 'Nope.' Well, OK. I went back inside and waited."

"Mmm hmm."

"When are you and he going to talk?"

"I don't know," she says. It had been two phone calls ago when Ronnie had suggested that they might. She had said, "I don't know why we're going to let lawyers have everything when we can get it done with a couple of signatures," sensibly as she could put it, and that had been the first evidence that maybe he'd put his head into the thing and could see the situation with clarity rather than rage.

Amy's first bill had come the day before, a few hundred dollars Electra didn't have and refused to take from Charley, and the two of them had gone around again about why she'd pulled that ad from the school bulletin board—*lunch lady needed*—and had been glad to have it. Charley's point, reasonable enough in his limited view, had been that she doesn't get enough sleep now, that their time together gets pinched on both ends. Hers trumped all of that. She's not ever going to be maneuvered into a place where she can't take care of herself and her son, period, end of discussion. That she spends her workday in proximity to where Nathan is just makes it easier, even if things for her and Charley are harder in the bargain.

Lec, we can't get where we're going if it's me, and you and me, and him and you.

The words hit her again, and she knows he's right, and she knows that doesn't prove up for eight cents right now against everything else that's swirling.

"You look tired," he says.

"I *am* tired."

He shuts up. She hasn't given him a glance. Every particle of her concentration rests twenty yards in front of them.

"I'm sorry," he says.

Ronnie goes down to the floor with his boy for a close-up view of the gas station in miniature. He watches as two round-headed figurines in a car, into which they fit like pegs, ride the elevator up to the top floor and the door opens and the car rolls out and careers down the ramp to the carpet beneath them.

"Ain't that something?" he says, and the boy squirms happily.

"I got it for Christmas last year," Nathan says.

"I remember," Ronnie says, a harmless lie, he thinks. "Hey, I saw that kid Richard, your friend, the other day. He says hello."

"He's nice," Nathan says.

"Yeah, he's a good kid."

Nathan bounces up and grabs his father's hand. Ronnie clambers to his feet.

"Come here," Nathan says, tugging him.

"OK."

Nathan pulls him to the window that looks out upon the suburban expanse. "See that?"

"Yeah," Ronnie says. "Buildings."

"No, *that*." Nathan points, insistent.

"What?"

"The blue thing."

Ronnie stares down. "What blue thing?"

"No, *there*." The boy redirects his indicator, trying to get his father to follow the line.

"The water tower?"

"Yes."

"Yeah, I see it," Ronnie says.

"That's where you live."

"It is?"

"Yes. I live here. You live over there."

"No, son."

"Yes."

"No." Ronnie makes a quarter-turn, facing the wall. He points at the blankness of it. "It looks the same as our water tower, but I live a thousand miles that way. North. Where you used to live." He turns back to the window and points again. "That over there, that's east. Understand?"

"No."

"Well, come downstairs, Sport, and I'll try to explain it, OK?"

"OK."

After some trying, Charley coaxes Electra into leaving the swings and taking a stroll on the sidewalk winding through the complex. "We'll stay close," he says. "Nobody's leaving."

Her strides are compact and hesitant, not the big, purposeful ones she usually takes, and they mostly walk in misshapen circles around the parking lot. Each time it looks like they might slip out of view of Ronnie's truck, she course-corrects and brings it back into their line of vision.

"I need to talk to you about next month," Charley says.

"OK."

"It's not for certain, but there's a good chance I'm going to be traveling."

"OK."

"The Cowboys, they're good," he says, "but I don't think they're better than the Redskins, so—"

"Do we have to talk about this right now?"

"No."

"Can we not, then?"

"Fine," he says.

They make another loop, then another one. On each pass, she looks to the front door of the apartment. They're closed up in there. She checks her watch. It's been forty-seven minutes, not that she's counting. Ronnie's truck still sits, idling, tossing exhaust into the air, a signal she interprets as he won't be taking his full allotted time. Nausea sweeps into her empty stomach.

"It's just—" he starts, and she goes to cut him off, and he says, "No, Lec, listen. I can't talk to you about what's going on in there, and I'm not going to just stand here and watch this thing eat you up, OK, so we're going to talk. About something, we're going to talk. We have to, Electra."

She faces him and cups his cheeks with her hands. "OK."

"I'm scared," he says. "I'm scared that you're going to need me and I'm going to be, shit, I don't know, in San Francisco or something."

She lets him go. "It's OK. We'll deal with it."

"Will we?"

"Yes."

"You're not here," he says, his voice pitched. "I'm sorry. It's just that, ever since this came up, in your head, you're somewhere else half the time."

"Can you blame me?"

"No, of course not. I'm just trying to be with you through it."

"You are," she says. "And one hundred percent, I am here. I promise." She takes his hand, laces her fingers with his. They walk another loop.

Afternoon cartoons flicker on the TV. Ronnie and Nathan settle into the couch, staring at the screen. A half-finished cup of milk and Ronnie's untouched glass of water sit on the coffee table.

"How's school?"

"It's fine." The answer is clipped and distant. Idle conversation has nothing on Huckleberry Hound.

"You like it here?"

"It's OK," the boy says.

"Good."

Ronnie pushes off the couch and goes to the TV, turning it off.

"I'm watching that," Nathan protests.

Ronnie returns to him and sits again. "I know. I need to talk to you about something." The boy fidgets and digs in the couch and scares up a green plastic Army man. Ronnie takes it from him.

"Nathan, listen to me. For just a minute, then I'll turn the TV back on."

The boy frowns.

"Your mom and me, we're getting divorced."

"I know. She told me."

"She did?"

"Yeah. I heard her talking to Charley about it. She told me. Christopher's mom is divorced."

"Christopher?"

"My friend."

"You have a friend here?"

"Yeah."

"What about Richard?"

Nathan shrugs.

"Well, here's the thing," Ronnie says. "Your mom and me, we've decided that from time to time, I'm going to come down here and see you, but you're going to live here all the time. Do you understand?"

"I think so."

"Maybe when you're older, you can come in the truck with me sometimes, if it doesn't interfere with school or anything. That would be fun, wouldn't it?"

"Yeah."

"Your mom wants to live here. She wants you to live with her."

"And Charley."

"Yes," Ronnie says. "And Charley."

"OK," Nathan says.

Ronnie goes back to the TV and turns it on again, and Nathan is subsequently entranced. He returns, leans down, kisses his son's head, and leaves through the front door.

Electra and Ronnie sit at a picnic table near the playground. She and Charley had been on the far end of the parking lot when he came out, and when they'd caught up to him, he'd said, "Can I talk to you? Alone?" and here they are. She'd touched Charley's arm, told him it was OK, to go and tend to Nathan and she'd be right back. Now, she sits with hands clenched in front of her, bled white. Ronnie straddles the bench, looking away.

"I didn't deserve this," he says. "To lose the both of you like this."

"Oh." Her fuse shortens. "Oh! We're going to fight? That's what you want to talk about?"

"No," he says. "I'm just saying, I didn't deserve this, to lose you and my son. I didn't."

"I was *alone*," she says. "We were alone. All the time. We were last on your list."

"You weren't last."

"We weren't first, Ronnie. We weren't." She has her back up now, anger soaked through her words, as she butts up against something she can feel more than she can articulate.

"You weren't last."

"Fine," she says. "Fine."

"I think he misses Wyoming," he says, and she looks stricken. "That's what I think."

"Did he say that?"

"No, not exactly."

"Oh," she says. "So you're just—"

"It's where he's from," Ronnie says.

"He lives here now. This is where he needs to be. With me."

"And Charley," Ronnie says.

"Yes."

"What if you're wrong? About what he needs. About this guy."

"I'm not wrong."

"What if you are?"

"I'm right."

Ronnie runs a hand across his face, top to bottom, brim of his cap to his chin. "He belongs with you."

"Damn right."

"But I'm his father."

Electra, softer now, says, "Yes."

"I did what I felt like I was supposed to do," he says, his own edge creeping in. "Did you ever want for anything? Did he?"

"No," she says, softer now. "Nothing material. A lot you can't put your hands on, though."

"Like what?"

"Like, everything."

"That's no answer," he says.

"It is. For me, it is."

"I didn't deserve this," he says again.

"Don't you talk to me about who deserves what. It's not the point. You want to fight, Ronnie? Over this? Over *him*? Fine. If that's what it has to be, let's fight. Let's settle it."

"No," he says. "I don't want to fight."

"Then don't start at deserve, and we won't."

He spins himself around to face her. "I'm signing the papers, Electra. Fact is, I already did. They're up in the cab." He nods toward the truck.

"Oh."

"I'm his *father*. I'm your husband, at least for now."

"No one has ever said you're not."

"But you went and found him another dad."

"Ronnie, no," she says.

"Yeah. That's what you did."

"I—" She stops short, realizes there's nothing she can clarify that hasn't been laid out in legal documents and in late-night, plaintive phone conversations. *You want this boy to have his best chance, what any parent should want for any child, and it's here, where I am, where I have chosen to be.* And if there's some of what she wants for herself in the spillover, she thinks, well, maybe it could have played out another way, but it didn't. This is how it went. She sees no way to say it that hasn't been spoken before, and she's tired. She says nothing.

"I need to get going," he says.

"OK."

They walk back, far apart, and when they get to the parking lot, Nathan bangs out of the front door, Charley behind him, and down the steps.

"Say goodbye to your dad," Electra says. "He'll be back soon." She looks to Ronnie. "Right?"

"A few months," he says, and he scoops the boy up and hugs him, then sets him down. "Go back inside, would you, Sport? We need to talk just a little bit more."

Once Nathan is compliantly behind the door, Ronnie says, "Just a sec."

He goes around to the truck door and climbs up, digs through manifests and maps, finds the paperwork he's looking for and brings it to her. "Signed. I'll send the first check when I get back."

"Thank you," she says.

Charley offers a handshake. Ronnie considers it, then makes another choice. The right hand, fast and rash and thrown before he can choose another way, lands flush on the point of Charley's chin and drops him in a heap on the sidewalk.

"You wanted 'em, you got 'em," Ronnie says, standing over him. "But don't you ever take anything else that's mine." He leaves them there and climbs up into the cab of his rig. Electra is on her knees, screaming at him, and Charley shakes his head and tries to come around as the big truck grumbles and pulls away.

24

November 2002 | Bozeman, Montana

The doorbell rings. Cherie remembers too late. Now there'll be some explaining to do.

"I wonder who that is," Anna says, crossing the living room and headed toward the door.

Cherie, at the kitchen table, deep into the math at which she was never very good, starts to answer, then lets it go. Anna's hand is on the knob. *Surprise!*

"Bill," Anna says upon opening the door, with equanimity that's admirable considering the long line of people—Michael Jordan, Bill Clinton, Meryl Streep, the pope, just for starters—she'd expect to see on her doorstep before finding her ex-husband there.

"Hi, Anna."

Norm, on the couch, speaks through half a handful of popcorn. "Who's there, hon?"

"My . . . Bill."

"Hi," Cherie says, standing up.

"Hi," Bill says.

"Come in," Anna says, standing aside.

"Who's Bill?" Norm asks.

Cherie and her father bunker in at the table, and Anna and Norm post up in front of the TV. Cherie has made her apologies, first to her father, a "maybe we should have met downtown," then to her mother for not saying anything between making the appointment two days earlier and promptly forgetting it in the swirl of everything else. "We're all adults here, right?" Cherie says, an attempt at smoothing over that only makes things weirder. There are handshakes and introductions, *Norm, Bill, Bill, Norm.* It's awkward and bewildering, the odd alignment of past and present in a single room.

Now that her father is here, though, Cherie is in it with him, eager to hear what he's learned on the errand she gave him.

"It's not much," he says. "Just some vapor trails in time."

"Show me."

He extracts a manila folder from his briefcase and opens it. She sees a stack of photostat copies. He picks up the first, looks at it, and passes it on. It's a Great Falls newspaper clipping, dated August 24, 1939.

Assault charges denied

Oscar Ray and Delia Ray both entered pleas of not guilty when they were arraigned separately before Justice Harry M. MacDonald on charges of third-degree assault. Trials in both cases are pending. One complaint alleges that Oscar Ray "struck, beat, and hit" Delia Ray with "intent to inflict bodily injury." In a counter-complaint, Oscar Ray contends that Delia Ray was the instigator and that he was defending himself. The Rays are divorcing.

"Who's Delia Ray?" Cherie asks.

Her father hands over the next page, also a clipping from Great Falls, dated May 15, 1940.

Littler-Ray nuptials here

*Richard Littler and Delia Ray wed on May 6 at the
Cascade County Courthouse in Great Falls. They
live near Fort Shaw.*

"Who's Richard Littler?"

The document production goes on. Next, August 12, 1965.

Richard Littler rites Tuesday

*Richard Littler, age 53, a farmer near Fort Shaw,
will be laid to rest at 2 p.m. Tuesday, August 17, at
Mount Olivet Cemetery.*

*Littler died last week when he was smothered by
a load of sawdust that fell atop him.*

*He is survived by his wife, Delia Littler of Fort
Shaw, their daughter Linda Penney, of Great Falls,
and Delia Littler's son, Ronald Ray, of Mills, Wyo.*

Cherie reads the last sentence aloud, a "that's horrible" trailing it. "What's it all mean?" she asks.

"It's so gappy," her father says. "You kind of have to fill in the blanks logically. Oscar and this Delia were married, obviously, and then Delia and this Littler fellow got together. It's just bits and pieces, this here, that there. And, of course—"

"A son," Cherie says, and her father nods.

Anna leaves the couch and whatever program she and Norm have sunk into and comes over. "What is this?" she asks.

"Stuff about Oscar Ray. You remember. That thing from grandma's house?" Cherie says.

"You're still in that?"

"Yeah."

"Why?" Anna asks. "What's it matter?"

Cherie shrugs. "Maybe it doesn't. But it's interesting."

Anna sits down. "Can I look at those?" she asks, pointing to the copies in front of Cherie, who hands them over.

"Here's what I don't get," Cherie says now, her attention back with her father. "This stuff is all well before and well after the date on that quit claim. And Great Falls. Nowhere close to Billings."

"There's a whole lot more, but it doesn't go anywhere. Delia Littler, dead in 1974. Oscar Ray, horse rustling arrest in 1937," Bill says. "Minor misdemeanors. Arrests. Trashy people, seems like, but nothing in sum."

"Horse rustling? Really?"

"Yeah," Bill says. "But look at this." He hands her a fresh sheet, another clipping, from the Billings paper, dated October 13, 1952.

Sought: Oscar Ray, by Mrs. Thomas Foley of Three Forks, who has important news regarding the missing man's son.

"Holy shit," Cherie says.

"What?" Anna asks. Cherie hands her the paper.

"Three Forks?" Anna says. "What's in Three Forks?"

"That's Ronald Ray, I'm guessing," Bill says.

Cherie nods.

"You figure Oscar and Delia Ray were divorcing in '39, so their boy was born sometime before that. If he's around, he'll be . . ."

"Sixty-three, at least," Cherie finishes.

"Right."

"Who's Ronald Ray?" Anna asks.

"Exactly the question," Bill says. "Everything dead-ends there, though. That's the last thing I found that mentions Oscar. Nothing on Ronald Ray. Not a word." He taps the paper in her hand. "That's all of it."

"Hon," Norm calls out from the couch. "You're missing it." Anna hands the stack back to her daughter, gets up, and leaves them to their ill-fitting pieces of the past.

Later, Anna and Norm retire to bed, a situation Cherie hasn't quite reconciled. On one hand, that her mother didn't go flitting off to Norm's place when he beckoned can be read as progress, if you hold it up to the light a certain way. On the other, Anna's bright idea was inviting him to live with them, with only a cursory pass at getting Cherie to sign off, more a case of *I've asked him and now I'm letting you know*. It was something short of a courtesy, for certain.

Cherie, still plowing through the pile of schoolwork but decidedly preoccupied, bundles into her coat and lets herself out, walking the front yard in the cold night. She calls her father.

"I want to thank you," she says, unlikely words that come easier now than she might have ever expected.

"You're welcome. It's not much."

"It's something."

"Yes."

"You know what I think?" she asks.

"What?"

"I think Larry Teasdale is a bunch of crap."

"Your mom's dad?"

"Yeah. Supposedly."

"Why?"

Cherie walks toward the street. "Because it's convenient. Larry knocks up grandma, Larry goes off to Korea, Larry dies there, Mom is born the following year. We're never to speak of it, because it's hurtful and shameful and because it makes Grandma feel so bad. We're not to talk to Larry's people—they're there, right there out of Billings, and you'd think they might want to know he had a daughter, but no, we don't say a word, because it would embarrass them. I don't think Larry had a thing to do with Grandma. I think she made it all up."

"OK."

"I think it's this Oscar Ray. I think that's who did it. And I think Mom has a half-brother out there somewhere, or did. That's what I think."

"It's a compelling theory," he says. "You're missing a lot of evidence, though."

"Leave it to a lawyer to say that."

"I'm just saying," he says. "I found everything I could find without, you know, putting someone on the payroll. I mean, at the end of the day, you've got a bunch of people you wouldn't want to meet—"

"Oh, I'd want to meet them," she says.

"—you wouldn't want to meet in polite company, and you've got a quit claim that was never executed. The rest is conjecture."

"I know," she says. "But I'm thinking there's at least one more thing I can do."

"What?"

"Go to Oregon. See where he's buried. Dig in the records over there. Find something. Maybe someone knows him. Knew him."

"Guy's been dead, what, thirty years?"

"Thirty-two," she says. "If that's him. I think it is. Had a Montana Social Security number. Has to be him."

"It's a long shot."

"Yeah." She hugs herself. Snow comes down, swirling and sticking to the sidewalks. Her frozen mouth catches on the words. "Will you go with me?"

"You sure? You want me to?"

"I want your Range Rover. I don't think my Honda has it in her."

"Ah," he says. "Now I see."

"Yes, Dad," she says. "I want you to come."

"OK," he says. "When?"

Anna Bowden

1953-2011

You came here because she didn't offer you any choice that you felt like amounted to a true exercise of free will. You went over to her apartment, right there on Main Street, up above a boutique, small place but tidy and cute. You thought you were there for dinner—it was nice, you thought, that the two of you still had dinner once a week, still kept the endpoints of your connection sparking, her place one week, yours the next—and she sprung it on you. Sat you down, said she had something important to say. Read from a piece of creased paper, her hands shaking a bit, so unlike her.

She told you she enjoys the time that you do get to spend together, that she knows it's not enough, what with her job and with yours, but it's special. She thanked you for her life and for her presence in yours. She reminded you of times past that were happy, Christmases, family vacations before her father and after, when the family was just the two of you. Remember Carlsbad Caverns? She did. Yellowstone, just outside your door? She did. You've given her a lifetime of memories, she said, and in many ways, a model to follow. She said she wished she was as good a cook as you are. Wished she had your head for numbers.

Then she told you how much the drinking hurts you, most important, but also how it hurts her. She reminded you that it's not that you drink every day—you don't; you never have—but that once the pouring begins, it doesn't stop until there's some intercessional. It doesn't stop until you get arrested for DUI, which you have been, or until you make a fool of yourself and others to such a degree that you're shocked straight for a while, as you also have been. But it never stops for good, she said, and that's because it hasn't been confronted in the only way that works.

She began crying. You cried, too. You hurt for her, and you hurt for yourself, in the shame she was digging up and presenting to you.

She reminded you of what your doctor last said, how you are really on a precipice now, it could go either way and soon. Keep drinking and die. Stop drinking and live. *I have stacks and stacks of charts on people who were deeper in it than you are, Anna, and they climbed out.* You don't have to be a bad statistic. You thanked her and you went home and poured two bottles of gin over the next day and a half.

You need to go to rehab, now, your daughter said. It's time. It's past time. She had it lined up. She said you could fly there that night, the two of you. She said there was one last part, a part that hurt her to say, but she had to: If you go right now, she'd walk the path with you, be there on the other side of a month when you'd come out, support you in what will be a fight for the rest of your life. But if you said no, she said, if you went home from here, she wouldn't be around when the next bender came. She wouldn't be there to pull you out of a bar or a restaurant, or out of some unknown man's bed. She wouldn't answer your call when you'd gotten yourself into some mess. She would let you go, because you'd already be gone, by your choice.

She left you no room for negotiation.

So you got on the plane with her, and you came here and you detoxed—goddamn, you thought you would die—and you talked and you listened, and you gained some insights, you really did, but much of the time, you felt as though they were talking not to you but to someone who really needed the help in a way you didn't. Don't. You can do this on your own, you're sure of it, and now you even have some more tools that you didn't have before. You have a better chance. It wasn't exactly what you need, this place, but it wasn't a waste, either. Cherie will be able to see that, right?

So you told them, you said thanks for everything, but this isn't for me. And they debated you a bit from a respectful emotional distance, said you're not really seeing the whole picture just sixteen days in. And while you appreciated that, you see enough of it. You've got it from here, you said.

And they said, well, it's not prison. You're free to go, if that's what you want. And that's what you want.

You huck the duffel bag over your shoulder, unlatch the door, step out into the night. February in Arizona is so much preferable to Montana, a light, warm breeze on your cheeks, not the stilled, suffocating air inside that you've been breathing lately. You need to get back home, but not right away. You consider the directions available to you, right and left, and you choose left, the brighter, gauzy lights against the night sky, beckoning, and you begin to walk.

25

Charley gets Nathan seated in the molded plastic chair and shoves him up tight to the long table, the edge of which aligns with the boy's clavicle. It'll have to do. No booster chairs or thick phone books in the press box, just the stares and the overdone witticisms of colleagues. Harper, from the *Times Herald*, comes with the gentlest of the mocking, saying, "Training your replacement there, Charley?" *Yeah, yeah, yeah.* Charley next fetches a boat of popcorn and a Coke and puts them in front of Nathan, who starts chomping happily. From his briefcase, Charley brings out a pad of paper and a few pens, different colors, for the boy, and a matching set for himself to chart the plays that will unfold on the field below them.

He was surprised and remains surprised that Electra had allowed it, the two of them to go off together for a whole Saturday, as tight a grip as she holds on her son most of the time—too tight sometimes, by Charley's reckoning, but he understands the impulse. He told her when he broached the possibility that they needed this, he and Nathan and even her, to get this mongrel dog of a family they were building to run on all of its legs. And he'd been clear that it would be a day that started early and ended late, and still she had said yes and didn't press too awfully hard to be made a part of it. On that count, it had been enough of a trick to get the Cowboys' PR guy to agree to one extra press pass for Nathan, let alone another for her. Not that he'd have wanted her along anyway. A bunch of sportswriters, almost entirely male, well-stocked in smartassery and cynicism, their frozen hearts might be moved by a little boy. A woman, though, a *girlfriend*, and the derision would have been too much. "Who are you, Stidham, Paul McCartney or something? Bringing your old lady out for the show?" Nope. No, thank you. No need for that nonsense.

"You ever watched a football game before?" Charley asks Nathan.

"I don't think so."

"You know how it's played?"

"No."

"It's OK. I'll explain it."

There's much to tell. The Cowboys are up 21-zip before the Redskins even put a measly three on the board. It's 28-3 at halftime, when Charley brings Nathan a hot dog from the midgame spread, then shows him how he's charted the plays and made notations on his own pad of paper, while Nathan's has houses and trees and bears that look like nervous cats. Clines, the beat writer from Charley's paper, leans over to the boy and says, "Cowboys look good. You must be a lucky charm, kid."

Charley explains the scoring, how a touchdown—Calvin Hill has two of those, Walt Garrison one, Craig Morton still another—is worth six points on its own, another point coming on a short kick afterward, and that the longer kicks by Toni Fritsch are worth three points. That confuses the issue for Nathan, who wonders why, and Charley leans on that wisdom he figures will get the boy through any number of future conundrums: "Just the way it is."

In the game's waning minutes, after a Fritsch kick seems to seal it up, they ride the elevator down—the two of them and a herd of sportswriters and radio and TV types—and they tumble out onto the field and post up on the sideline. It's here that the experience seems to get to Nathan, who stares in open-mouthed wonder at the environs he's landed in, the throaty roar of the partisans, the blurs on the field, the action on the sideline.

"There's a hole up there," he says, pointing to the roof, then he says it again at volume so Charley can hear him. Charley kneels and puts his mouth near the boy's ear and says, "Cowboys fans say that's so God can watch his favorite team."

Nathan looks at him in wonderment: "Really?"

"That's what they say."

Later, they're in the guts of the stadium, waiting for Morton to finish his remarks for the press. As the quarterback pushes through the scrum, he spots Nathan and removes a sweatband from his wrist and gives it to the boy, who clutches it like an amulet. They go back upstairs and Charley begins to type out his column. Nathan slumps in the chair next to him, idly working Morton's gift between his fingers. The day has made a hard turn toward six o'clock now, and Charley says, "Give me an hour and then we'll go." Nathan yawns.

My Pal Says … Maybe the Cowboys Can
By Charley Stidham

A rare Saturday game at the ol' football yard in Irving brought together the Dallas Cowboys and the Washington Redskins, and seeing as how we're 13 games into a 14-game season and I grow easily bored, I decided to bring my pal along to put some fresh eyes on the proceedings.

I'll not tell you who, precisely, my pal is—that's between him and me—but let me give you the short bio: My pal is a red-blooded American boy, younger than me (and, in all probability, younger than you), a smart kid, a recent refugee here from the wintry north. More important to the idea of a fresh perspective is this: Until Saturday, he'd never seen a football game in his life.

Well, he saw a whale of a game Saturday. Cowboys 34, Redskins 24, a margin entirely too close for the dominance the home team showed for most of the afternoon. I can't say Craig Morton, who completed only 7 of 17 passes for 61 yards, will exactly satisfy those clamoring for Roger Staubach to take over once he's healthy, but if the ultimate benchmark for a quarterback is wins—and brother, it should be, or what's the point?—then no one has much of a reasonable quibble with Morton. The Cowboys are 10-3 now, a fine record that would look even better were the Redskins not 11-2. They've split their season series, and it looks like both are playoff-bound. It's just a matter of the particulars now.

But first, back to my pal . . .

He has a few things to say about this game of football. First, he thinks it's a dumb word, football, that it should be runball or passball or catchball, rather like basketball or baseball, and now that he mentions it, I can't say I disagree. I told you he was smart.

Second, if God really was watching through the opening in the Texas Stadium roof, my pal hopes He tuned in a better program in the fourth quarter, when Billy Kilmer threw two touchdown passes and put the outcome in the kind of doubt the Cowboys never should have entertained.

Third, he thinks Cowboys fans are real swell people, if a bit loud, and he hopes their team will make them proud. If you ask me, that's right sporting of the lad, thinking about others first.

Finally, I asked him if he thought these Cowboys have it in them to win next week against the lowly New York Giants and make a playoff push. I gave him all the requisite information, that they would, in all likelihood, have to win two playoff games on the road just to make the Super Bowl, and those of you with even short memories know how disappointing that particular game turned out to be the last time around.

My pal said, and I quote, "Yeah, maybe. Can I have another Coke?"

It doesn't get any more definitive than that, folks.

So if you're inclined to see the world through my pal's eyes, you have a happy few weeks ahead of you. Me? I'm a veteran of these things, and perhaps even a bit cynical, and I have to say, my optimism on this front has abandoned me. The Cowboys were awfully good Saturday for an awfully big part of the game. And then, for a quarter, they were plain awful.

In stats class, I learned a concept: regression to the mean. That's a fancy way of saying that, eventually, you'll be what you are. I think the Cowboys are pretty good. Not great. And not the best. A win over Washington is better by far than a loss, but if you're expecting this team to bring home a championship, you might have felt some doubt creep in after it lost earlier this season to Washington and San Francisco, the two teams the Cowboys will have to crawl over to get there.

*It says here that the playoffs will end poorly for
these Cowboys. If the road to the Super Bowl goes
through Washington, as it just might, don't expect
the Redskins to wait until the fourth quarter to
make their move.*

Nathan sleeps in the backseat on the drive to the office, with Charley's typewriter case, covered by his doffed coat, acting as a pillow. It's only a short trip from the stadium to the exit they'd take were they going home, but they're not. They push on through the suburban tangle and turn south, toward downtown Fort Worth, the contours of the cityscape lit up for coming Christmastime and beckoning in the fallen night.

He'd called Electra before they left, to say they were off and that it would be a bit yet before they dragged home, to go ahead and have dinner without them and they'd catch a burger or something. She'd asked how it went, and he'd said he didn't know, that Nathan had seemed into it at times and somewhere northwest of boredom at others, and she'd said, well, that's the way of little boys, with their minds that sponge it up when they're interested and their eyes that follow any bright, shiny thing, ensuring that you can't hold them in any particular moment.

"I watched on TV," she'd said. "Thought I might see you. But no."

"That would have been unusual," he'd said.

"Well, thank you for taking him."

"Well, thank you for letting me."

His scanning eyes return again and again to the slumbering five-year-old in the rearview. Nathan wears Craig Morton's wristband on his own arm, where it hangs floppily, like a tube sock running for the border. What an astonishment the boy has been—the early hostilities, the outright defying of his mother, and that was a situation Charley just wasn't going to brook if there was to be any hope of a functional household, tossed together though it might be.

He had to give Lec credit there—when discipline was called for, she let him dispense it, let him make it known to the young man that dinners would be eaten and his mother would be obeyed, and if Nathan wanted to push things the other way, he could go upstairs and cry his eyes out to his four walls. Early on, Charley had been told "I hate you" more often than he's ever heard it from disconsolate fans after he's given UT a proper ripping.

It's been different, though, since the boy's father came, and that's its own bafflement. When Charley peeled himself off the sidewalk, he figured that for the end of the experiment. He'd as much as told Electra that he wasn't going to spend his time waiting for the next punch to be thrown, that she could let him drive up to Wyoming and defend himself properly or she could lower herself to the indignity of going to bed with something less than a man.

"Don't you get it?" she'd said. "You won. *We* won."

"Huh?"

"He accepted it. The only thing he had left to do was punch you. That's all he's got. He's acting out like the child he sometimes is."

"No child hits that hard. He has a rock for a right hand."

"Yeah," Lec had said. "And you'll never see another one. Don't you see? We beat him."

Charley's taking that on faith. The thing is, to his own surprise, he's come not to care what it takes now. He wanted nothing more, in the moment, than to chase that son of a bitch down and take his own shots, but that feeling passed, as anger often does. Whatever it requires now will be a small price for what he has, for what he and Electra and Nathan are and what they might yet become. He watches the boy stir and slowly come out of it. Nathan pushes himself up. The highway lights they pass beneath flicker across the boy's face. Charley thinks of what he said to her last night, that he doesn't want to be Dad, that there's a better job out there for him, if he can find his way to it. "He's got a dad," he'd said, holding tight to his hope that there's more of her within the boy than there is of the other half. "I just want to make my own way with him. I want him to love me. I'm trying to love him."

"Are we going home?" Nathan asks.

"Not yet," Charley says. "Can you stay awake?"

"Yeah."

"We'll be done soon."

Upstairs at the office, Charley drops off his books, the typewritten triplicates holding his column, typos and all, and makes the introductions all around the horseshoe rim of desk editors. He gives Nathan the names as they're known among each other: Bullet and Sturb and Wakesy and Gills and One-Eye Monte, on account of the patch, which Nathan, bless him, can't stop staring at, until Monte Muehler flips it up and shows him the palsied, closed-up socket below so they can get the gawking over with.

"I was born blind in one eye," Monte tells Nathan, and Bullet tosses in with, "Yeah, and he can't see out of the other one."

While Sturb works over Charley's column with a pen before typesetting, Charley takes Nathan upstairs to the vending machines and gets him a cold sandwich and another Coke, his fourth, which won't please Electra but might well keep the kid's eyes from blinking out. There are things yet to see.

After eating, they follow matters through the production of a morning newspaper, to the composing room where the type is set and the headline is fit and the words are cut into the page. Charley loops his arms around the boy's midriff and lifts him so he can see the layout.

"'My pal,'" Nathan reads the headline.

"Very good."

"Who's that?"

"You."

"*Me?*"

"You. You're my pal."

"Neat."

Next, it's downstairs, where the pressmen scurry around, placing the aluminum plates in order around the huge drums that will impress words and images onto newsprint. It's a cavernous room with a catwalk that Charley and Nathan stand upon, breathing in the musty air that doesn't circulate with any urgency. It's a Sunday paper they're making, one that will go all over the state, and Charley tells Nate that this edition, the bulldog, won't have all the best stuff that they'll see when the paper thumps their door come morning.

"It smells yucky," Nathan says.

"That's the ink."

"I don't like it."

"We won't stay long," Charley says. "But you'll want to see this."

He squats before the boy and takes him by the shoulders and turns him around.

"You have fun today?"

"Yeah," Nathan says.

"Can I ask you something?"

"OK."

"I was wondering if it would be all right with you if I married your mom."

"She's getting divorced."

That makes Charley laugh. "I know," he says. "I'm divorced, too. That's what makes it OK, because we're both available. But I'd really like to, if it's OK with you."

Nathan shrugs. "Sure."

"Thank you," Charley says.

"Can we go home?"

"Absolutely. Just watch this." Charley helps the boy step onto the catwalk railing, so he can get his eyes above the bar, and he holds a scruff of Nathan's shirt so he doesn't fall. An alarm bell goes off, quick and sharp, and Nathan cups his ears while Charley holds him steady. And then, slowly at first and steadily picking up the pace, the big cylinders roll, and the papers, folded and sectioned, come off, riding the conveyor belt in perfect formation.

For the entirety of Charley's working life, now chugging hard into its second decade, this ritual has been the demarcation between one day and the next. A fresh newspaper on the stoop, more reliable than the rising of the sun. He looks at the boy—someone else's genes, but now, effectively, his own son to mold—and he thinks of how he couldn't have seen it coming, this arrangement. He thinks of Holly, his ex, and the plans they'd spoken of tentatively that never got enacted, and those fallow years after, when he cozied up to solitude, not trusting himself with his own heart or anyone else's. And now, here's this wide-eyed, frazzle-haired, sleepy boy, and here's everything coming your way, Charley Stidham. What a world.

"You ready to go?" he asks.

Nathan yawns. "Yes."

26

November 2002 | Eastern Oregon

It's late morning on the high desert, Wednesday, day before Thanksgiving. Cherie sits in the bucket passenger seat, sunglasses on against the glare, and she's thankful for the small favor of rising southerly warmth. They'd awakened to frost on the windshield glass in Pasco, and that gave them at least some trepidation about what might be waiting for them in these final several hours, but things have toasted up nicely. Winter, still a month away but bearing down fast back home, is standing back where they are now.

Bill drives, as he's mostly done since they began slugging their way out of Montana and Idaho, through the high mountain passes packed with ice and snow, finally down from Spokane and into the irradiated bosom of southern Washington. He's been a trouper, she has to say, a willing participant in what seems little more hopeful than a goose chase. She'd given him the bad news that it would have to be Thanksgiving break or nothing for this wild notion of hers, that neither school nor her volunteering at the PD could withstand anything else, and he'd taken it with moxie: "I said I'd go, so let's go." And here they are.

"We're gonna end up eating turkey at a Chinese restaurant in Hermiston, I just know it," he teased her as they headed out, and she flung it back, saying, "That clinches it. I'm going vegetarian." They had a good laugh about that, but the levity is gone now, and an uneasy quiet has come in. Madras, where they're headed, is in their sights if not in their direct line of vision quite yet. Oscar J. Ray rests down there, Block 13, Lot 6, Space 6 at Mount Jefferson Memorial Park, and they aim to make the acquaintance of the man in his perished state. A newspaper office is there, too, the *Pioneer*, a two-horse news operation for a one-horse town, and they've told Cherie that they don't have the manpower to go digging around thirty-odd years ago, but she's welcome to bunker in with the archives if she can get there before closing time.

Cherie looks at the dashboard clock. It's not even eleven. They'll make it.

"Hey," Bill says.

"Hey yourself."

"Thanks for this. This time with you."

She tilts the sunglasses down her nose. "Thanks for the sweet ride."

"No, I mean it," he says. "You could have asked anybody. I'm glad it was me."

She nods, adjusts her glasses, becomes one with the road again. He's been funny, awkward, deferential the whole way. Insisted on separate rooms at the Holiday Inn in Pasco, an unnecessary extravagance, but he'd parried her insistence that they could double up. "It gets stuffy in the car," he'd said. "Take a break from your old man." Fair enough. She hadn't pressed the debate and had appreciated the solitude, a dinner at some ubiquitous American bistro, then a candy bar later from the mini-market at the front desk, a night of TV, a rare indulgence.

The fact is, she thinks, there weren't all that many candidates to be her traveling companion, certainly not as many as her father seems to assume. Her mom was out, for Norm reasons. Anna had damn near hit the roof with joy when she found out that they didn't have to throw together some staid family Thanksgiving around the dining room table, that she and Norm could decamp for a few days at Chico Hot Springs, just the two of them. That pairing continues to be a strange one, simultaneously representing Cherie's fear that her mother would lose herself entirely, again, inside a man and her balancing hope that maybe this would be the different one, as Norm really does seem basically decent, if irretrievably dorky. Whichever way it's going, it has turned their house into something inexplicably unwelcoming to Cherie. Not that she isn't perfectly entitled to bivouac there or eat the food or watch the television, though she rarely does much of that. It's just that she's become a third wheel, and it's difficult to figure, in the lookback, how that has happened. She'd stayed for Anna, and now the staying seems unnecessary. She wonders if maybe she can finally make a break toward her own independence. She hopes so.

Cherie shifts in seat and looks at her father, who's entirely locked in. She lets herself drift again. So who else might she have brought along on this interstate calliope? She thinks of Gunny. She's been deliciously distressed of late to realize that she often thinks of Gunny, sometimes in scandalous ways, and she's quite sure he doesn't think of her when she's not in the passenger seat of his cruiser. This is a guy who has a ring on a finger that tends to mean something and somebody, but she doesn't care. She thinks of Gunny and what this trip would be were he the one at the wheel, the two of them shooting down the blacktop that cuts through the semidesert of eastern Oregon. She might not be thinking of graveyards and newspaper offices and surely not of separate rooms, so for her purposes here, it's just as well that those thoughts stay firmly rooted in fantasyland. Mercy, though. She can warm herself up by rubbing those ideas together.

"There it is," he says, pointing toward the windshield and the town beyond, drawing her eyes back open. "Newspaper first?"

"Yep," she says.

Having done the earlier digging and having discovered when Oscar Julius Ray went spinning off to his cosmic destiny, Cherie finds it easy enough to zero in on a suitable range of dates to begin flipping through pages on the microfiche machine. She finds what she's looking for—JUNE 1-15, 1970—on a typewritten label affixed to a box. She blows the dust off the top of it, opens the box and pulls the black plastic canister out, draws the film roll from that, and threads it through the reader, as just-call-me-Mona up front had shown her how to do. She finds two artifacts in the few days after Oscar's June 6 death, a proper obituary (OSCAR J. RAY, 1905-1970) and a short news announcement (RAY SERVICES SET FOR FRIDAY). She presses the print button on the microfiche viewer, another act inspired by Mona's drive-by tutelage, and the page images spit out. Bill catches them and begins reading.

"Listen to this," he says. "'He is survived by his wife, Maybelle Brewster, and good friends.'"

"His wife?" Cherie asks.

"So it says."

"Maybe she's still around."

"Maybelle Brewster?" Mona says, her disembodied voice booming through the little office. "Nuh-uh."

Cherie stands and walks around to where Mona is, her father following.

"You know her?"

"Knew her, honey."

"So you knew Oscar?"

"Oscar who?"

Bill shakes the printouts at her. "Oscar Ray, her husband."

Mona laughs, a boomer, a knee-slapper, the kind sure to make anyone it's directed at feel plenty small for whatever they'd done to light the fuse on it.

"Husband? Oh, that's rich. Honey, listen. When I moved here in '79, Maybelle was wound up tight and put away. I never saw a man talk to her, even to say 'excuse me.' She wasn't approachable, is what I'm saying. Wrote me some dandy letters, though. Go back and look around in '82 or '83. You'll see them."

Bill pushes the obituary printout toward her. "Says she was married, right here."

Mona takes the sheet, gives it a quick read, hands it back. "Before my time," she says, as if to allow the possibility before she again closes the door on it. "But, nah. No way. Has to be a joke."

"What happened to her?" Cherie asks.

"Same thing that's gonna happen to me and you, eventually," Mona says. "She passed on. Gonna say it was '85. No, no, wait, no, it was '86, I remember, because that's the year that River Phoenix kid got famous. He was born here, you know."

"You don't say," Bill says.

"Yeah, people crawling all over town, Hollywood press, magazines, wanting to know about that kid, trying to tell the story about his upbringing. Unconventional, you could call it. Irritated Maybelle something fierce. People pecking around, asking questions. She didn't like it."

"I see," Cherie says. "Well—"

"She had a niece, Polly, Polly Mobley, who looked after her. Polly, she's gone, too, cancer, a year or two back. We're losing them quick. Can't keep up with it. Anyway, go see Tommy. He can tell you more, if there's anything to tell."

"Tommy?" Cherie asks.

"Tommy Mobley. Polly's husband. Nice guy. Colorful. How he stood those two women, I'll never know."

The address, pulled from the white pages, is the same as the one listed in Oscar Ray's obituary and the same as the one put down in Maybelle Brewster's death notice—which indeed does not mention any husband—nearly two decades on. And sure enough, just-call-me-Mona knows her local history, because Maybelle's survivors go in the record books as "niece Polly Mobley and her husband, Thomas, and assorted grand nieces and nephews." Cherie has been chasing Oscar Ray down the wind for months, and still the gusts carry him away.

It's a little gray box of a house, slung close to the ground, chimney belching smoke, a roofline scarcely pitching upward. Two small windows on the backside, facing the road, a larger one staring the other way at the small patch of lawn that got burned up in summer heat and shocked cold by nights in the desert. A man gets to the door before they do after they let themselves inside the fence.

"Help ya?"

"You're Tommy?" Cherie asks.

"If I ain't, somebody's been lying," he says.

"I wanted to ask you about Maybelle," Cherie says.

"And Oscar Ray," Bill tosses in.

"Especially Oscar Ray," she says.

"Well," Tommy says, "those'll be two ancient subjects. What brought this on?"

"It's a long story," Cherie says.

"I got time," Tommy says, turning back to the door. "Probably not as much as I hope, but some. Come on in."

Cherie starts to follow him, and her father tugs her coat. "Can we talk out here?" he asks.

"Nah," he says. "Fire's inside. Come on."

Cherie looks at her dad, gives him a clenched-mouth look of *don't foul this up for us now.* He shrugs, and they trundle inside on Tommy's heels.

Only Tommy's bottom legs and feet, swaddled in sweatpants and heavy woolen socks, are visible, the rest of him up through the ceiling and into the attic. He stands tippy-toed on the top step of an aluminum ladder, which Cherie and her dad hold steady.

"The thing was, Oscar was just a handyman, and not much of one by then," Tommy is saying, his voice muffled by the cavernous distance. "Too damn old. The old boy was a mile of rutted road."

A downward hand emerges, holding a leatherbound book. "Here, take this," he says, and Cherie does, kneeling and setting it at her feet, then rising and minding the ladder again. "There's one more up here, I'm pretty sure." He keeps rooting around.

"So, anyway, that spring, he's reroofing the house here, and he gets fearsome sick." Tommy now climbs down with another book, as dusty and neglected as the first. "Mice been shitting all over these damn things. Pardon my language. Here, give me that." He points to the first book, on the floor, and Cherie retrieves it and hands it over. He carries both heavily to his recliner, plops in, books on his lap, then slips the tubing from an oxygen tank into his nostrils and takes a hit.

"Sit down, sit down," he says, and Cherie and her father pile into the couch opposite him.

"Where was I?" he asks.

"Fearsome sick," Cherie says.

"Right. That spring. Just awful. I come in here one day and got an eyeful, he's lying back in that bedroom there, and I said, 'Maybelle, that man is gonna die.' Got so bad, she took him to the doctor, and that's a profound step for the likes of Maybelle, let me tell you. She'd rather have put an egg beater up her ass and played motorboat than go see the doc, for anything. Pardon my language."

"It's fine," Cherie says.

"Me and Polly, we were living about a mile down the road there, raising up some squirts, trying to stay a step ahead, you know? I really didn't see Oscar too much, but I sure enough remember how sick he got. Doctor told him it was the ticker. Nothing they could do, 'cept put him in bed and wait for the bomb to go off. Didn't take too long, as I recall."

"So they were married by then?" Bill asks.

"Well, no, not really."

"Explain," Cherie says.

Tommy shifts in his seat, takes two more hits of air, fiddles with his hands, grinding the bony fingers like he's trying to make them disappear. "I don't want to besmirch somebody my Polly loved."

"No judgment," Cherie says. "I won't whisper a word."

"Me, either," Bill says.

"The marriage was a sham," Tommy says now. "A put-on. A show. She only did it to get the Social Security. She said, 'That old fucker is eating my food, and I'll have to pay his doctor bill, too, and probably have to cough up the scratch to plant his bony ass.' Pardon my language. Or pardon hers, because that's exactly what she said, as I recollect. Maybelle, she just wanted the money, sad to say. Nice guy, from what I remember, but she was just picking the carcass clean."

"A Social Security death benefit is, what, like two hundred bucks," Bill says.

"Two hundred more than she had. Been times I'd have put my pecker in a light socket if it meant I could get two hundred clams. Pardon my language." He hands the books to Cherie. "Should be a picture of him in one of those somewhere. We took a few after the preacher came and hitched them. He'll be the one in bed, looking 'bout ready to croak."

The trip to the boneyard is a denouement in the fading day. A minor swirl of snow rides the air, the flakes darting like fireflies, illuminated by the lampposts flickering on in the dusk. Bill brings a flashlight as they find the plot and the row, but they don't find Oscar, not at first. Tommy Mobley wanders a couple of sections away, a coat over his sweatshirt, slippers on his feet, saying hello to his Polly. He bummed a ride when they mentioned one last errand, and why not, they figured. Nice enough guy, if you can pardon his language.

Cherie ends up on her stomach, digging through half-frozen mud under a juniper bush, which is where she finds the marker. She pushes back the bush, and her father uses a handkerchief to clean up the small square of marble, cut into with OSCAR J. RAY | 1905-1970. "We're probably the first people to see it since it went in," Bill says.

"A long way to come for this mess," Cherie says, standing herself up and trying to get the mud off her clothes, to no good effect.

"More than I thought we'd get," Bill says. "A lot more."

"Yeah, I guess. A picture of a half-dead old man. Not a lot of answers." Indeed, they'd pressed two questions, in particular, with Tommy on the drive over, and he'd had nothing to say to cast light on either of them. Did Oscar ever talk about a son? Did he ever mention someone back in Billings, Montana, an Opal Knudsen? Nope and nope. "Didn't even know he was from Montana," Tommy had said. "Can't say I knew the man below the surface." Cherie could relate on that point.

She sets to walking down the line of markers on the hilltop, and when her father starts to follow, she touches his cuff and says, "Give me a minute, all right?" He smiles and falls back, and she continues. Dark has come on, so early now, the days growing ever shorter for almost another month. She fixates on the fading outline of Mount Jefferson in the far distance, the lights of town sparkling nearer. She's cold. In her richest imagination, she'd pictured some new door to walk through here, but now she's gotten close, and it's just another wall. Having sunk the cost in time if not in actual dollars— her father has been buying the gas and the food and the lodging— she finds herself suddenly tired of the chase. For what? For whom? It's a mystery, yes, but one less compelling by the hour spent on trying to unravel it.

The search stops in this lonely spot, she decides, this living earth that covers a dead and forgotten man. A ghost he was when he became known to her, and a ghost he remains, just beyond her grasp no matter how strenuously she reaches. She can see that now, and she's humbled by the audacity of ever thinking it would go another way. Weeks ago, after her father brought the news clippings by, she'd fired up her laptop, gone to WhitePages.com, punched in the various searches—Ronald Ray, Ronnie Ray, R. Ray, etc.—and beheld the overwhelming possibilities. Hundreds of them, nationwide, and not a one of them in Mills, Wyoming, the only other scrap of a clue in the paper trail, which might have given her a foothold in a deeper search. That chance, it has evaporated on her.

Oscar Ray, dead. Opal Knudsen, dead. Ronald Ray, or whoever he is or was, a whisper in the world, this one or the next. As good as gone.

She turns around and walks back. Tommy stands with her father, the two of them looking at her for a cue.

"Let's go," she says.

27

August 2012 | Billings, Montana

Cherie stands aside, stretching herself flat to hold open the screen door and the heavier one behind it. The men, beckoned in, slip past her, turning themselves at an angle to clear the narrow entrance and emerge into the house. She closes the doors and ushers them through the kitchen to the table.

"Have a seat," she tells them, and they take her up on the bid. "I have coffee, juice, water."

"Coffee's good," Ronnie says. "Black."

"I'm trying to lay off," Nate says.

"That'll be a first," Ronnie says.

"Shut up."

She pours from the percolator and brings two cups to the table and takes her own chair, between the men. She reaches for a basket of muffins in the middle and makes the offers. Both wave her off.

Cherie has never considered herself any kind of savant when it comes to human behavior—fact is, she's continually astounded by just how shitty folks are capable of being to each other, and she's come to view that naivete as a weakness—but she knows tension when she feels it, and it's sparking off these two. She'd prefer some chitchat to ease into the thing, but she fears losing them if she doesn't get at it, and soon. She'd paced the house nervously until getting the text, unsure if it would come and contemplating her next step if it didn't. Chase them down to Texas, probably. That wouldn't have been creepy, right?

"Well—" she starts.

"Nate says you're a cop." Ronnie fixes her with a penetrating stare that's out of step with the recency of their acquaintance. It unnerves her.

"Yes," she says. "Correct."

"He in trouble?" At this, Nate begins agitating. She reaches out, an almost involuntary thing, and touches his arm.

"With me? No. No trouble."

"OK," Ronnie says. "But clearly, he's in trouble." He juts a finger, curled toward Nate's jawline, gone to an angry purplish. Whoever hit him got the full set of knuckles on it.

"We shouldn't have come," Nate says now, standing. She rises with him. "I'm sorry, ma'am, but he's just—"

"Hell, I already told you that," Ronnie says, slower to stand but making his way. "I don't know what the hell you were thinking, invading this nice young lady's—"

"I was thinking somebody wanted to do something nice and—"

"Please," she says. "Please. Just sit down. Please?" She lowers herself, as if to model what she wants from them. Haltingly, they give it to her, and she tries again.

"Look, I wasn't straight with you last night," she says to Nate. "Once you told me your dad's name, I wanted to meet him, and there was no good way to say it without saying all of it and—" She stops and tries to get a rope around her thoughts. A handful of things to say, all stuck at the exit of her spigot mouth. "Shit. And I had to be sure."

She pivots in her chair, toward Ronnie. "Hi, Mr. Ray," she says, extending a hand. "I'm Cherie Bowden." He looks at the proffered hand, baffled, then shakes it.

"Ronnie Ray," he says.

"I know."

"What can I do for you?"

"Nate Ray," Nate says, and she laughs, and he insists on a shake, too, and she obliges and says, "Yes, I know."

"I'll just sit here," Nate says.

"Mr. Ray," she says now to Ronnie, "I have a question for you."

"Shoot."

"Who's Oscar Ray?"

He goes from bemused to stricken with no transition between.

"What's your interest?" he asks. The words are meek, small, crumbling.

"What's your answer?" she says, as level and neutral as she can make herself be. "If you're who I think you are, I promise, I'll tell you everything, and you can tell me or not tell me anything you want."

"What's going on?" Nate asks.

"Mr. Ray?"

"He's my dad," Ronnie says.

Nate is on his feet again. "Who's this?"

"Sit down," Ronnie says, and Nate goes back to his chair, chastened. Ronnie looks at her. "Who are you?"

"I'm Opal Knudsen's granddaughter. That name mean anything to you?"

Now Ronnie stands. He pushes his chair in tight under the table, his hands shaky.

"Dad?"

Ronnie walks through the kitchen, into the living room. He stops there. He makes a quarter-turn. He cups the lower half of his face with a hand and squeezes it out. He takes a deep breath and lets it go.

"Dad?" Nate says again.

Softly now, Cherie says, "Give him a sec."

Ronnie goes to the couch fronting the western wall of the house and sinks into it, arms stretched on the back cushions, as if he is fortifying himself. Cherie and Nate stand and walk toward him.

"Needed a minute there," Ronnie says, looking at them.

Nate goes to the chair perpendicular to him and sits. "Dad, what's going on?"

"I should have asked you along yesterday," Ronnie says now, a glance to his son and then back again. "Goddammit, I knew it. Bob said as much, but I—" He stops, then pitches himself forward a bit, caught up in something that has drawn his attention.

"What?" Nate asks.

Ronnie reaches for it, the tin canister in the middle of the coffee table. "I know this," he says. He lifts the lid, and the notes plink out. He hums them, keeping the melody.

Cherie, lurking, moves closer, respectful and deferential in her steps. "I'd like to show you something else." Ronnie caps the canister, and it goes quiet. "If that's OK," she says.

Ronnie nods.

She goes to the mantelpiece and opens an intricately crafted wooden box that sits upon it. The box is stained a rich brown and lacquered and painted with roses, rather like a holder of keepsakes or secrets. She opens it, retrieving what she has stowed inside. She then walks to Ronnie and sits beside him. She lays a photograph on the table in front of him, torn in half into a vertical, a freckled teenage boy grinning back at them in black and white, a ghost hand on his shoulder.

"That's you, isn't it? And I'm guessing it's Oscar there in the missing half?"

Ronnie picks it up and holds it close to his failing eyes. He nods.

Nate, having migrated, sits on the other side of his father. "Can I?" he asks, reaching out. Ronnie gives him the photo.

Cherie puts down the next one. It's the same grinning boy, only this time, in full frame, a short, solid woman, dark hair pulled back in a tight ponytail, hangs off the right side of him. She looks not at the camera but adoringly at him.

"Opal," he says. "Is she still—"

"She's gone. Ten years now."

"Oh."

Nate reaches across and picks up the second photo. "Jesus, Dad, you were young."

"Sixteen," Ronnie says, and he begins weeping. Nate puts an arm across his shoulders. "Hey, hey."

"Mr. Ray," Cherie says, "I found these fairly recently in Opal's stuff, long after she'd passed. I'd forgotten about them, to tell you the truth. We—that is, my mom and I—packed up some of her things after she died, and that's when I found some papers that mentioned your dad, and I spent some time trying to find out what I could about him, and I—"

"I can't help you," Ronnie says. "No idea where he went. Didn't care. Told this one," he nods at Nate, "that I never knew my old man, that he ran off when I was little."

"You did?" Nate asks. "Why?"

"So I didn't have to speak of him. To keep the weight of him off me. Off you."

"Jesus."

"Oh, Mr. Ray, there's so much to tell," Cherie says. "I hope we have the time."

"Wait a sec," Ronnie says. "Your mom?"

"Yes, sir."

"Opal's daughter?"

"Yes, sir."

"When was she born?"

"Nineteen fifty-three." The date brings the inflection point she's been angling toward. She holds him in her gaze, looking for a crack, but she doesn't see one.

"What's her name?" Ronnie asks.

"Her name was Anna."

"Was?"

Cherie looks away, toward her clenching hands. "Mom died last year. That's what I was getting at. I found these photos when I was packing up her stuff. We'd always talked about going through Opal's things, but time, you know, it—"

"How'd she die?"

"Dad," Nate says, "be gentle."

"No, it's OK," Cherie says. "She killed herself. It was the alcohol that did it, though. She couldn't stop. I couldn't stop her. I tried, believe me. And eventually, she didn't want to stop, and—"

"What can you do, right?" Nate says.

"Right."

"Oh, god." Ronnie weeps again, and Nate, bewildered, is left to try soothing him.

"I've known your name for a long time, sir," she says, rubbing his shoulder. "Never had much hope of finding you, though. I've spent nearly ten years thinking Oscar Ray is my grandfather, and it's only in the last year or so, since Mom passed, that I've decided I might have been wrong about that." She taps the picture of Ronnie and Opal. "Because of that right there. Because of how she's looking at you in that picture."

Ronnie sniffles and swallows. "She didn't even know me then," he says. "But I liked Opal right from the start." He wipes across his nose and mouth with his arm. Cherie stands and leaves, gets a tissue from the bathroom, and brings it to him and sits down again.

"I *was* wrong, wasn't I?" she says. "About Oscar and Opal?"

Eyes closed, Ronnie nods.

"You were just a kid," she says.

"No," he says. "I knew what I was doing."

"Jesus," Nate says, as it all plows into him, like the car crash you don't see coming and don't recognize the severity of until you've shot through the window glass and are bleeding on the street.

"How you doing over there, Uncle Nate?" Cherie asks.

"Jesus," he says again. He's fallen back into the couch.

Cherie takes Ronnie by the hand and holds it tight between both of hers. He leans into her, disconsolate.

"There's a lot I know and a lot I don't," she says. "I was thinking—and what I couldn't say to Nate last night, because I was mostly sure but not a hundred percent, not until I saw you, and I was just hoping you guys would text me this morning and we could talk—anyway, what I was thinking is that maybe we can fill in the blanks together."

"Yeah," Ronnie says. "I think we should. I think it's time. There's a lot I should have said a long time ago."

"Well," she says, "why don't you go first?"

28

November 1952 | Billings, Montana

The first day Oscar is back from Miles City with a load of purloined lumber to redeem the one they'd missed out on in Billings, Ronnie and Opal make their time with each other on the sly, telling Oscar they're to make a run to downtown Billings and see the holiday display in the window at Hart-Albin, maybe buy some gifts for under the tree—maybe the tree itself, you never know, Thanksgiving is right on the doorstep, after all—and bring back something for dinner.

"Get the boy his own apron, if cooking's all he's good for," Oscar says, still inexplicably miffed about Ronnie's role in baking a pie, or perhaps in his general lack of suitability for small-time criminality. Either way, it's not terribly gracious, Ronnie thinks, after they shared a slice with him, a show of magnanimity in the face of what they were rightly keeping to themselves.

The two of them ride south in the faltering dusk, but they turn right up the hill before coming into Billings proper. They don't go downtown, don't shop, don't get a Christmas tree or a dinner. Opal's free hand finds his lap, her left holding the wheel steady, and her pickup ends up on two-track atop the rimrocks, parked out away from the other lovers who flock there in the nighttime like moths to a slice of light. Billings twinkles a couple of hundred feet below, its own little beckoning galaxy, but the discoveries for Ronnie and Opal are being made on other frontiers. After a go, and then another, they cinch up and straighten up and grin wildly on the drive back, lovers with a delicious secret.

Ronnie kisses her when they're on the other side of her door, and again in the kitchen, and he tries to move her to the bedroom, but hers is the cooler head that prevails. "He surely heard us pull up," she says, pointing to the barn. "Tomorrow."

Ronnie creeps into bunkhouse softly as he can, boots doffed and carried by hand once he's within the confines, the tube socks he wears making a run toward his ankles, a lightness to his step and his mood even as his insides agitate. He smells her on him, not surprising considering where he's been and what she's shown him, but it's a rising concern now, here in this place where she never lingers. He sniffs the air with vigor.

"Musta been some night," Oscar says from his spot in the darkness, startling him. "Gave up on you."

"Lots to see. Lost track of time."

"Obviously."

"Well, good night." Ronnie strips down. He pulls his wallet from his pants pocket, slips it under his pillow and covers that with his head as he goes prone. He closes his eyes.

"You happy here, kid?"

Ronnie blinks rapidly. "Yeah, sure. Why?"

"Just wondering."

"Sure. It's swell."

"Snow coming, radio says. 'Bout time. You had better be good with a shovel."

"I am."

"You'll get a chance to prove it."

It's hours, when Oscar is well into slumbering drift, before Ronnie lets his eyes close again. Sleep comes only after he's shuffled the vision he carries with him, about the nearer and farther shape of how life might go. The Army, the imagination of it, has sustained him, something he could picture in robust sharpness even as it sits out there, far away. Now, he's thinking other things, less certain things, more fanciful things. Could he have already wandered as far afield as he wants to go? Maybe. But there are problems with that line of imagination, too, notably the one sleeping a bed away. Ronnie shuts his eyes and brings on the darkness, and he sleeps fitfully.

Come morning—after the chickens are fed and the walks are shoveled and breakfast is eaten—Opal's big idea is that Ronnie can break away, just for an hour or so, and squire her down to the river. "It's nice down there," she says, "a nice walk, quiet, too," a drift he surely catches. "It's *ice* down there," he says, teasing her, and he tells her he'll try to pry himself loose.

Oscar raises no objections, just a bit of a flummoxed fuss. "Baking pies, going shopping," he says, shaking his head. "What that woman needs is another girl to run around with, not some callow boy." Ronnie hopes to whatever deity is convenient that he hasn't flushed vermillion and given himself away.

"Just being friendly," he says. "Nothing else to do, anyway."

"Tractor?" Oscar asks.

"Greased it up while you were gone."

"Coop repairs?"

"Those, too."

Oscar waves him off. "Well, go then. I hope she doesn't start fitting you for a bra."

It's far too cold for that, though she lets him cup a hand inside hers, after he's warmed it up on the small of her back. They're in the pickup and he's kissing her with a full helping of audacity, way better than Rock Hudson ever locked lips with Julie Adams, when she puts a hand on his chest and levers some distance between them.

"Do you think I'm bad?"

He reaches for her, but she leans back, away from him. "No," he says. "Why would you ask that?"

"I'd be in trouble if the law found us. Boy like you. Woman like me."

"Maybe not. Besides, they're not here."

"Neighbors would be yakking. Embarrassing."

"Ain't gonna happen," he says.

"But am I bad?"

"No. Farthest thing from it."

As if to show her the proof in his words, he takes her down again, his hands now practiced at loosening her clothes and his own, their mouths coming together inerrantly, a rhythm they've found that is theirs alone.

They're headed back to the house, calm yet riled, blood running high, those damned goofy grins, when she says, "I need to tell you something."

"OK."

"About a month after Oscar came out here, I got a visit from the revenuers," she says. She glances at him, then back at the icy road. "Knocked on the door, said I owed a couple hundred. Back taxes. Told me I had ten days. I don't know. I scrounged it up, most of it. Your dad, he give me forty-two dollars, the part I didn't have, and I thanked him, promised to pay him back. And I have, a little here, a little there, I gave him his money back."

"All right," Ronnie says.

"I feel so stupid." She pulls the pickup to the side of the road, sets it in neutral, leaves it running for warmth. She turns in the seat toward him. "Right before you came, he comes to me and says the revenuers wrote to him, found out what he did, told him it was illegal for him to pay my taxes. But he said we could put one over on them if he give me back that forty-two and I sell him that much interest in the farm."

"Oh."

"Does that sound right?"

"I—" Ronnie shrugs. "I don't know."

"You're hesitating."

"Am I?"

"He give me this paper, said he'd sign it, then I'd sign it, we pass the forty-two between us, done deal."

"You didn't sign it, did you?"

"No. I told him I needed to think. He says, 'Well, look, Opal, you're in big trouble with those tax boys. This'll fix it.' I asked for a little time. You showing up, it kind of distracted him."

"Good."

"I think he's a crook," she says. "I wasn't sure before, but the more I think about it . . . Ain't a straight arrow who traffics in copper tubing and lumber, is my thinking."

"Yeah."

"You think he's a crook, too, don't you?"

Ronnie nods.

"I'm stuck. I want him to go. But he can make trouble for me."

"I'm sorry." And sorry Ronnie is, both that she's in it and that he didn't put it together that she's been one of Oscar's marks right along. It's a hell of a jam-up, the kind that blasts apart some of the things he's been thinking about, underscoring the impossibility of shaking loose from the dreams he's already set. Frustration sits on him.

"Will you help me?" she asks.

"What?" Ronnie asks.

"Get him to go."

Ronnie gives it a pondering. The request is plaintive enough and justified enough, for certain, but in part, he wishes he could leave this behind without ever having been here, just back everything out to where he's there on the Foleys' farm and waiting for the next turn of life instead of knee-deep in this. And then he thinks of what he'd have missed had he stayed, or how different it might have been otherwise. She's made a faithful grope toward him, same as he has toward her. He owes her this, he figures, if he can deliver on it.

"I'll help," he says. "He's crafty, though. We're going to have to be smart about it. You understand."

Opal nods, and smiles, and comes across the bench seat again and plants one on him.

Back at the house, they leave things in the form of a tentative plan: They'll act like nothing is up, normal stuff, pleasant as punch, and Ronnie will try to get on his father's good side again with regard to the nighttime extralegalities, until there's something they can trade: Oscar's departure for Opal's not going to the sheriff with what she knows and what she can prove. It's a hell of a loose concept, they agree, with a hell of a lot of holes between conception and execution. It might just work.

It also might just incinerate in front of them.

"We gotta be careful with each other," he says. "No more foolin' around till he's gone."

"Agreed."

Ronnie gets out of the pickup and takes the long way around the house, leaving her to go in alone. At the barn, he slides the door open and calls out, "Dad?"

"In here."

He finds Oscar sitting on the wrong bunk, next to a suitcase that doesn't belong to him, packed and ready.

"What's this?" Ronnie asks.

"I think it's high time for you and the Army to meet each other," Oscar says.

"Why?"

"You know why. Not that I'm not proud of you and your swinging dick, but you're leaving peter tracks too close to where I eat."

"How did—"

"Suspected as much yesterday," Oscar says. "You know, kid, you can play with a puppy's pecker, and he'll come around the rest of his life and mount your leg, no grace at all. You're the puppy in this here metaphor. Plain as day you were popping her."

"But—"

"I was glassing you, up on that ridge, while you two were doing nasty things down there by the river. Was worried that you might see me, but you were balls deep in something else, weren't you?"

Ronnie stands himself up against his trembling. "You better think about the things I know."

"No, son," Oscar says, shaking his head. "You better think about what *I* know. You better think about what I can say about little miss in there. And then you better think about how this all goes away if you just get on a bus."

"I'm sixteen. The Army won't—"

"They will," Oscar says. "I'm your father. I say you're seventeen. Far as you know, you are. Why would I lie?"

"Fuck you," Ronnie says.

"You've reloaded already?" Oscar chuckles. "Ah, youth. No, son. Fuck you." He pushes himself up, lifts the suitcase by the handle, sets it on the floor, and pushes it across to Ronnie with his foot. "Take your things. Let's go."

Opal comes wheeling out of the house as they cut toward the pickup in formation, Ronnie in front, head down, carrying the suitcase, Oscar behind him a few paces. There are minor hysterics, a shattering sound in the noontime air but nothing that'll reach the ears of any far-flung neighbor. Nobody's coming to see this, to intercede.

"Where are you taking him?" she pitches, her voice shrill and shredded.

"Opal, hush. I'm taking him where he wants to go."

She looks at Ronnie, bereft. He can't formulate a thing to say. The grim math has already played out for him, as it'll soon do for her. Oscar holds every advantage.

"I'll call the sheriff," she says. "He'll stop you."

"For taking a drive with my son? I don't think so. Might stop you, though, if I start blabbing about what you've been doing, jezebel."

"Opal," Ronnie says. She looks at him again. He shrugs and shakes his head, wide-eyed.

She falls to the snow, weeping, put there by every implication and every idea she might have had that's been thwarted before she can act on them.

"That's a good girl," Oscar says. "I'll be home soon."

Things go as Oscar suggested they would, a quick-strike battery of assessments, some basic questions, straight-up acceptance. *The U.S. Army needs good, solid men in times like these, son, and you look like a fine addition. Nice of your old dad to see you off like this. So what'll it be, soldier? Infantry? Fine, fine. Here's your bus ticket. They'll be expecting you at Fort Sill in a few days.*

Afterward, they walk the blocks to the downtown station, cutting between the buildings and the heaping trash bins in frozen alleyways. "Don't look so glum," Oscar tells him. "No other way it could have gone." Ronnie trudges on, silent. This life comes with a hell of swing, he thinks, everything you want in no way you ever wanted it. He thinks of Opal and the tangle she's in, and he ponders the narrow paths she has out of it. It's a mess partly of her making, and partly his, too, and that's where the sorrow lines up for him. They didn't have a chance.

Oscar puts a hand on him, stopping him, turns him around so they're facing each other. "It's right there," he says, nodding at the building they're behind. Exhaust from the idling buses spills in swirls onto the street. "Gonna say so long now." Oscar rears back, a loaded right hand, and he lets it go, hard and flush, then he grabs his boy by the jacket and guides him down so he doesn't hit the concrete at a homicidal speed. Once Ronnie is on his back, Oscar rolls him over and gets at his pockets, lifting the wallet, which he opens to count his good fortune. He removes a handful of bills and drops the wallet atop Ronnie's fallen form. "The cost of getting in my way," he says, and he's out of there, and Ronnie rolls onto his belly, face down on the ice, trying to gather himself and the rest of what's been thrown away.

Brandon Ray

1987-

You find your father there in a dark corner of his favorite North Side Mexican restaurant, one you think has grown a little bleak around the edges, frankly—there are nicer places downtown, for sure—but he'd called and plaintively asked for your time and seemed meek and apologetic in the asking, so you hadn't fought him on the venue. You'd shown up and found his truck in the parking lot, easy enough to see at four p.m. before the dinner rush, and you'd come in to find him sipping from a longneck. He scrambles up when he sees you.

It's the wrong foot, something for which the two of you seem to have a particular talent, but you note that he seems to be starting early on the drinking today. It's a facile line more than anything. If past is prologue, he started hours ago.

"Thanks for coming," he says, taking his seat again and beckoning you to yours. "Appreciate it."

You nod. You weren't sure you would. Right up until you actually did hop I-35, coming home from another day of hauling tenth-graders at Southwest High through a block of English lit, you weren't sure you would. And now you're here and don't know how long you'll be staying. Depends on what's on his head and how he manages to churn it into words.

A server swings around. You ask for water. He asks for another bottle of beer.

"First," he says after she's gone, "again, I'm sorry. Please tell Kelly I'm sorry. Please tell her that."

You need to tell her that, you say, and he tosses up his first protest—you figure now that you're in it, you have tolerance for one more before you're gone—and says he tried and that she's not meeting him in the middle to receive it, and you say, look, man, you don't get it. You did what you did. It was a horrible thing, a traumatic thing, and it's on you to cover the distance to where she is. It's on you to make being sorry mean something to her. You tell him that he's not a stupid man—he just does stupid things—and the answers here aren't so complicated if he doesn't insist on making them so.

"I'm trying," he says.

So you bypass the old Yoda logic that there is no trying, there is only doing, and you tell him instead the hell of the entire thing, that it was only out of an abundance of care that she'd gone out there at all, that she'd been on an errand to see to his wellbeing, not to put her own in jeopardy. And he nods and says, "I know—I was out of my mind," and maybe that's the first thing with which you're not inclined to take issue.

You pity him, that's the thing, and you suppose that's the reason he can still bring you here, where you don't want to be, with a soft request, why he can move you to acts that, prompted by anyone else, you'd reject. Bail money. Rides home at two a.m. *Enabling.* You know you do.

You look at him and you wonder where it went into a skid, even as you realize that it wasn't a singular moment but a pileup of many. You're twenty-five now and it's been most of that life since your mother plucked herself and you out of the downward swirl of job loss and local transience and days and nights when he couldn't be persuaded or moved out of his own tumbledown. It had been good—a little suburban house in North Richland Hills and a good job for him at Hudiburg Chevrolet—and then it had been a shambles, and the two of you, you were out of there. A few years with him. Long enough to cement some memories. Many more years gone. Long enough to try to outrun them. Long enough to end up in the house of another man, a reliable one, someone who wrenched your head open and poured notions into it. You've lived your life in the gravity of two older men, both of whom love you, both of whom you love—one natural as can be, even though he's one who was chosen, and the other inexplicable, even though you pump his blood. It boggles you.

"Tell me what to do, and I'll do it," he says, and you say, no, that's not how this one works. But it does occur to you that now is the time to put the stakes on the table, so he can see what's in the lurch. It feels like a whipsaw, the revelation, but he'll just have to deal with that.

We're pregnant, you say. Haven't even told mom yet. It's privileged information you're giving him, the kind that has a deadline attached.

Dad, you tell him, I love you. But if you don't make this right, you'll never meet your grandchild.

You stand up and you leave him there, weeping.

29

December 1972 | Euless, Texas

Electra and her son hustle down the sidewalk, cutting tracks in the light dusting, a nothing of a snow where they've come from but a freakout for the Texans they've landed among. It has been skidouts in the school parking lot, kids yanked from their classes early on the last day before Christmas break, everybody in a rush to get things buttoned up, stressed-out calls of "see you next year" across fast-emptying hallways. She'd had a devil of a time finding Christopher and Nathan in the scrum. "Come on, come on, let's go," she'd urged them, and now that they've spun their bonus boy into the waiting arms of his mother, they're clopping along to get out of the cold sinking in below the skin. She'd called Charley after the lunch rush to ask if he might fetch them, but he hadn't answered, no real surprise. After seeing the jam-up, she's glad it went this way.

Up on the porch, she tugs the handle, but the door doesn't give. Locked. She makes a hammer of her gloved fist and pounds away.

"It's cold," Nathan says.

"I know, honey."

"*Whooooo eeeeeees eeeeeeeet?*" from the other side comes Charley's cartoon voice, the one he uses to amuse Nathan at breakfast.

"Come on, Charley."

"*Juuuuust a seeeeeeeecond.*"

Another rap on the door from Electra. "Not funny."

She leans on the door in the same instant it gives way, and she stumbles in, with Nathan zipping behind her, and she sees them, all of them, the most wonderful assemblage of them she could have imagined, had she dared to wish for such a gathering.

"Grandma and Grandpa!" Nathan yells, finding the words before she does, and he darts through to the living room and hugs the legs of Sid and Suzanne Griffey, and yes, it's really them, but it's also Sally and Terry Briggs, Charley's sister and brother-in-law. Electra stands in slack-jawed awe, and Charley steps to her and cups her face in his hands. "Surprise, sweetheart," he says, and the tears break loose and she leans into him and she says, "I'm a sight."

"You're beautiful. What are you talking about?"

It's a group hug now, everyone crowding in, embraces for Electra and kisses for Nathan, whether he wants them or not, and murmurs and *I love yous*, and at last Charley breaks it up and says, "Hold on, hold on, everybody. Just hold on." When he has a semblance of order, he says, "We need music. Nathan, could you do the honors, maybe a little Nat King Cole instead of the Beatles?" The boy makes a break for the stereo cabinet and Charley's impressive stack of LPs, which the two of them have been sampling lately.

"And we need wine," Charley says. He bows and scrapes before himself. "Charley, would you please? Why, yes, yes, it would be my pleasure." He heads for the kitchen, and Electra follows him.

"You are a continual surprise, Mister Stidham," she says when they're alone, and at that he offers her a devilish wink. "When did you think of this?"

"Would you believe October?" he asks.

"You did *not.*"

"I did. I thought of it in October. I just didn't do anything about it until last Tuesday." That breaks her into the widest grin. "Now, honey bear, you carry the bottle and I'll tote the glasses. How's that?"

Sid Griffey thinks there's something Charley Stidham ought to know, if he's as serious as he says he is about this business of football.

"Oh, I'm plenty serious about football," Charley assures him as they stand off to the side of the festivities and get down to it, man to man, now that they've made proper acquaintance and aren't just voices over a phone line. "Right up until baseball season, I'm all about it."

"The 49ers are gonna kick their butts," Sid says, emphasizing his certainty with a sloshed drink.

"The Cowboys, you're saying."

"That's what I'm saying."

Charley crosses his arms and purses his lips and nods politely, acknowledging the possibility. "Certainly did a few weeks ago."

"At Candlestick, it'll be a romp," Sid says. "That's my team."

"We'll see," Charley says.

"I'm telling you."

"Yes," Charley says, "I understand. But here's the deal: It makes no difference to me. I just want a good story. And some good seafood."

"You're coming out for it?"

"Yep, absolutely."

"Well, come see us in Monterey. I'll take you out fishing."

"I'd like that."

"You a fisherman?"

"No, sir."

"Well, I'll teach you. Ronnie, he loved to fish. Didn't see as much of him as we'd like, but . . ." Sid stops himself. "Shit, I'm sorry."

"No trouble," Charley says.

"You don't want to hear about that."

"No trouble."

"OK." Sid eyeballs him. "You're a good guy."

"Thanks."

"We weren't sure. But you're a good guy."

"I appreciate that," Charley says. "I wasn't sure about you, either, but you're a good guy, too. Makes us even, right?"

From across the living room, the women consider them. Once the wine was poured, Electra dashed upstairs and changed out of her dowdy, flour-dusted work clothes and into her favorite dress. She feels more in the moment now, less bowled over by the spectacle.

"Daddy likes him," Suzanne says. "I can tell."

"You can?"

"Look at him there, the puffed-up chest. He's showing off." Sid is making a particularly dramatic point, a whole hand's worth of fingers turned on Charley and pressed into gesticulating duty. Charley nods repeatedly with a proportional fervor.

"I like him, too," Electra says. "I love him."

Suzanne smiles. "He surprised us, inviting us out. Knowing how we felt."

"He's surprising. In good ways."

"Yes," Suzanne says. "I can see that."

"Mom, he's the best man I know. He's kind and gentle. He's so good to Nathan."

"Nathan! The boy is a weed, he's grown so much. Looks like we're coming to Texas regularly."

"Looks like," Electra says. "This is where we'll be."

Suzanne pulls her daughter into an embrace and holds on.

The party winds down. Nathan has shirked his disc jockey duties, having run through Cole and Como and Crosby and moved on to *Rubber Soul.* He now snoozes on one couch pillow to the tones of

"Norwegian Wood" while the Briggses hold down the other two cushions. Charley goes to the landing with his wine glass and clinks it with a spoon until the chatter subsides.

"Nathan. Nathan!"

The boy wakes. "Huh?"

"Could you shut that off and come up here with me, please? Electra, you, too."

"Now," Charley says, once they've joined him, "a couple of things. First, thank you all so much for coming. We're having cold cereal for breakfast, so enjoy the hospitality while you can." That draws the laughs he's seeking, and he goes on. "We have two more things for your consideration tonight, the first being a comedy routine from our own Nathan Ray."

Applause comes, and Nathan steps up. Charley kneels beside him and whispers. "Like we practiced. Remember?" Nathan nods.

"Grandpa," the boy says. "Knock, knock."

"Who's there?" Sid asks.

"Strawberry."

"Strawberry who?"

"Knock, knock."

"Who's there?"

"Strawberry."

"Strawberry who?"

"Knock, knock."

"Who's *there*, Nathan?"

"Orange."

"Orange who?"

"Orange you glad I didn't say strawberry again?"

Laughter and claps, and the boy is well pleased, then Charley steps in and says, "Wait, wait, one more. Go ahead, Nathan."

The boy clears his throat and says, "Did everybody hear the one about the lady who got together with the guy who carries a typewriter everywhere he goes?"

"No," they all say.

Nathan grins. "She met Mr. Write."

Charley, having taken a step back and gone to a knee, says, "Get it?" Electra turns and sees the ring he's holding out to her, and her hands fly to her face, covering her nose and mouth. "What do you say, Lec?" Charley says. "Want to string together some paragraphs?"

30

Thanksgiving 2002 | Outside Bozeman, Montana

It's taken most of the two-day drive home for Cherie to spill what's in her head and in her heart. She's needed the time spent with her father, the hours together she's been resisting since he left them, to come around to the notion that maybe they're not so different. It's been a slow draining of two things she's been holding tight, the desire to unravel Oscar Ray and the insistence on a grudge against her father. She wants to let both go now.

"Why'd you leave?" she asks him, having decided at last to embrace the inherent bluntness because her various conceptions of how to ease into the question seemed equally impotent.

He glances sideways at her.

"Why'd you stay?" he asks. "I suspect it's the same reason."

"Don't be cryptic."

"I'm not—" He stops himself, abandons the impulse toward defensiveness. "It wasn't going to change." She cringes at that, and

| 298 |

he adjusts his heading, saying, "No, that's not exactly what I mean. I hoped it would change, and I still hope for it. What I decided—rightly, I think—is that changing or not changing wasn't going to be affected one way or another if I stayed. Quite the opposite, I'd begun to think."

"And I was, what?" She says it with equanimity, no tilt to the words, a far cry from where she's been on this thing for going on five years now. For the first time she can think of, she wants to hear him out.

"Mature enough to handle it, I guess," he says, and she cringes again, wholly unsatisfying as it is as an answer and a rationale. "I figured, you know, I'm here, I'm right here in Bozeman. If you needed me, I'm here. That's what I was thinking. The mistake I made, and it was a big one, is that I wasn't clear with you. I didn't invite you to come to me."

"I gave up on you," she says.

"I know."

"You gave up on her. Felt like you gave up on us."

"I know it seems like it."

"You did," she says. "But maybe I understand why a little more now, the way things have gone."

She looks out the passenger-side window. The valley has gone dark. It's pretty and lonely and stark, the lights from distant farmhouses little pinpricks in her vision. She misses nighttime driving that isn't attached to some larger activity, like holding the line in the Bozeman city limits. Just get in the car, disappear, the shroud of darkness pulled around you as you go.

"I was sorry you said no to Annapolis," he says. "Was hoping you'd run toward it and away from here."

"I couldn't."

"You could have, though."

"No," she says. "I couldn't. I wasn't going to."

He clams up, and she's glad for it. They'll never get to the same vantage point on this question, so why go crashing heads? Too much of that will ruin what has been time she's glad to have had with him, if not entirely for the tangible results—a picture of wiry-haired Oscar Ray almost all the way to dead—than for the prospect of future times of near normality. She wouldn't have lain odds that would ever come their way. The surprises of time, and all that. Who knew?

Bozeman makes a steady reveal of itself, the outer bedroom communities first, the thickening traffic, even on the holiday, then the lighted expanse of the city and the exurbs. They've missed what she harbors in memory, the football, the Lions and then the Cowboys and then the food, but the absence she feels is not for her own holiday comforts but for Opal and her first Thanksgiving in stardust. How her grandmother inexplicably loved the Cowboys, the star on the helmet and the hole in the roof and the dancing, jiggling cheerleaders on the sideline. The whole damned spectacle. For the first time, Cherie really, really misses her, and now, with the knowledge gained since Opal died, she's left to wonder what depths were in her that went unnoticed. She wonders if Oscar was good to her. She hopes he was, whatever the circumstance that took them apart and sent him west. She feels a weakening in her bearing, brought on by what she can ask and not answer, and she sets her head against the window glass and waits for it to leave.

God, how Bozeman stretches out, she thinks, becoming ever more the pejorative Bozemangeles that Gunny and the others frequently and derisively call it. It's a city that flexes outward, increasingly straining budgets and services and neighborliness as the cashed-out folks from the coasts crowd in, unwanted and yet unable to be repelled in their riches. The place is changing, she thinks, and not for the better. She's found it easy, in her volunteerism, to see the cracks and the crumbles and the problems that seemingly can't be solved. It's harder and more worthwhile, she's found, to insist on loving it. She's trying. She'll keep trying, she reckons.

Bill pulls into the driveway and sets the car in park. "Here," he says. "I had fun."

"Yeah, me, too."

"Can I say something?"

"Of course."

He turns toward her and offers all his attention. She grants him the same.

"I'm proud of you," he says. "I always have been, and it's my fault that I didn't say so enough."

"I didn't really let—"

"Hold on," he says. "Please?"

"Sorry."

"I just want to say that the thing I've figured out, if I've figured out anything, is that it's easy to lose yourself. Don't lose yourself, Cher. At some point, you have to figure out where others end and you begin. Find that place and live there. You understand?"

"I think so."

"OK. I don't want to be cryptic, as you say." He smiles at her, bringing the line in for a soft landing.

"I'll let you know if you are," she says, and she gives him a hug, then bounds out of the car, pulls her duffel from the backseat, and heads for the door, fishing her keys from her pocket.

She finds the place a mess, papers strewn and plates smashed and the recliner gone. She drops her bag at the door, and she runs to the main bedroom, frantic, and finds it in similar distress. She throws on lights, all over the house, and checks her own bedroom, and it's free from the chaos, and she checks the hall bathroom, which is empty, and finally she goes back to the master and the closet, and that's where Anna sits, naked, her knees drawn up to her chin and enfolded by her arms, her glassed-over eyes staring.

"Mom."

"Norm left."

"Oh, Mom."

"He doesn't want me." Anna sinks her head downward into her knees, weeping. Cherie goes to her, smells the stink of what she's dropped herself back into, wraps her up, and Anna comes apart in her arms.

"He doesn't want me," she says again, and Cherie tries to shush her, but there's no stopping it now, the old pain renewed, coming out of the familiar places, the despair that walks the perimeter like a black dog, guarding what it has claimed, snarling at her mother, snapping at anyone who dares come near her. It has its teeth into her now, holding her, holding off others, owning her. Cherie puts her head into her mother's shoulder and she tries to hang on, because here it all comes again, and she's so tired, and she has been for such a long time.

31

November 1952 | Billings, Montana

Ronnie pushes the twenty into the hand of the cabdriver, insistent. "Take it. I appreciate the ride." He had the bill tucked into another compartment in the wallet, a sad confirmation of his wisdom in coming to expect the worst from his father. It had taken some talking to get the guy to drive out this far, but maybe directness and desperation had their persuasive qualities. The guy has gotten him where he needs to be. *Take the money, bub, it's yours.*

He leaves the car and goes at the house at an angle, crouching low, until he's worked his way around back and to the kitchen window. He brings his eyes level with the eave and peers in.

Opal sits, face red and tracked by tears. Oscar stands behind, her long hair wrapped up in his fist and pulled back tight. Ronnie ducks down. He smells the fear, his and hers, like aluminum sweeping through his nostrils and out his breathing mouth.

He crouches again and cuts back against the house to the fence line, then works his way down from there to the barn and goes in. Every sound—every stepped-on blade of frozen grass, the creak of the barn door, his boots on the floorboards—comes across amplified. He hears his beating heart in his ears, feels the weight in his movements, tastes the tack in his mouth. In the darkness, he relies on repetition and memory, finds the bureau drawers, slips his hand behind them and probes around until he has the cold double barrel of the shotgun. He goes to his stomach for a deeper reach in search of the shells. He can't bluff this one. He needs them. Finally, on his last strain, he gets fingers on the box, barely enough for a grip, and he inches it to him as the terror—at what he might have to do, at the possibility that Oscar's coming and the jig is about to be up, at what's happening to her in there—washes across him in waves.

He bounces up, loads both barrels, puts extra shells in his shirt pocket, and he gets out of there with the advantage, perhaps, finally edging over to his side. He ducks low, the gun in both hands in front of him, and again he sticks to the fence. It's a hard angle from the kitchen window—to be seen, you'd have to have somebody leaning hard against the glass and making a point of looking, and Ronnie is counting on preoccupation to hold Oscar in abeyance. He gets one chance at this, he knows, and some of the determining factors don't ride with him.

He's at the back door now, the last barrier aside from the question of whether he has the requisite guts. He draws in a deep breath and rears back for a kick. *Opal, she never locks anything. Please let that be so.*

Ronnie's aim is true. His foot lands near the mechanism, the door splinters open, and he's in.

32

August 2012 | Billings, Montana

"I told him to let her go. Even a disagreeable man can become agreeable when he's got two barrels on him. I moved him into the main room there, hands up, and Opal, she just went to pieces at first, on the floor, crying, and I say to her, I say, 'Opal, I need your help here.' He's sitting on the couch, hands still up, watching me, and I'm watching him, and your grandmother, she was strong, she got herself together. I asked her, I said, 'Well, what do we do with him?' She goes, 'Kill him.' I was thinking, you know, that's probably what it's come to. Fornication and real estate shenanigans, and there's where we were."

Nate rubs his eyes. Cherie sits silent with it, processing. "Jesus, Dad," Nate says. "Did Mom know about this?"

"Nobody knows about this."

Ronnie reaches out and spreads the artifacts idly, then stacks them back up. He thinks it's like seeing your life on replay, only you don't quite remember the order of everything, and you wonder if that's really you or somebody else who breathed other air in other times. He'd flushed with memory of Dick Littler's passing when she'd shown him the obituary photostat—no sad occasion, that—and remembered how Electra had urged him to go, to make right anything that could be made right with his mother, to stare down into that hole if he had to and let Dick go. None of that had taken, really, except ensuring that those scant connections with Linda and the family she was building up in Montana would stay live. Years at a time would go by, his wires touching hers but not sending out transmissions, but the link was there, at least. More than he had any right to expect.

Ronnie shrugs. "Of course, you know we didn't." He pulls the photograph of his old man, eighteen years after he last saw him, just about food for worms, the grim folks around him in black and white, the one Cherie has pointed out as Maybelle, his for-show wife. He thinks it fitting somehow that Oscar spent his final breaths getting rolled for the last dollars he'd ever churn. What did Nate call it? *Poetry.* Sure enough.

"So what happened?" Cherie prods. She's been quiet, mostly, taking it in. It's a lot, whether you get it all at once or you bottle it up and carry it with you from year to year. You get older with each new day that comes around, and it stays where it is, forever young. Ronnie has been thinking about that a lot, how his seventy-six years can become sixteen or three or any of the numbers between if he lets a memory settle in. It's been keeping him up nights.

"I cut him a deal," Ronnie says. "Told him he could give me my money, get in his pickup and go, tonight, and never come back around, or I could take him out in the yard right then and turn him into fertilizer for sugar beets. Not much of a choice, I have to say, but he took the right option. So he lit out, and I lay down with Opal, and the next morning, I told her to keep that gun loaded and at the ready for a while, just in case. And she drove me downtown and I got on my bus and I showed up late for basic, and boy, did they ever have the red ass about that."

"You never saw her again? Never called?" Cherie asks. The questions don't strike Ronnie as judgmental—not that he'd blame her if they were—but rather just searching, contextual, something she wants to understand. This stack of paper, these photographs, these things she's come to know and has been spilling to him, they show she's been looking for understanding for a long time. He's been holding it all away from those he's loved for much longer than that. He's let Montana recede as far away from him as he can, even the things he's been curious about, for fear that they'd taint others. Opal, for certain. The Foleys. He'd come to view that part of his life as an anthill—you can't get a good look without taking the top of it off and sending everything to scurrying. Better not to look at all, he'd figured.

"Opal and me might have had a season, instead of a week, but I was gone come springtime, whatever happened."

"Yeah, but—"

"I thought of her, sure, hoped she was OK, expected she would be. Oscar, he was a coward. I've seen it twice, and I figured he'd cut his losses and be glad to still be breathing. But I come back from the Army, I've got a wife, later on a kid, wasn't any reason to go opening those doors. At least, no reason I knew of."

"I was about to say, grandpa . . ."

"Holy shit," Nate says. "*Grandpa.*"

"Can I have that?" Ronnie asks, pointing at a photo atop the stack. It's Anna, mid-1990s, head tossed back and winsome, a Christmas tree sparkling in the background like hope renewed. Cherie had shown it to him as representative of the best of her, one of those moments when she dug in with the world and found happiness in its embrace.

Cherie gives it to him. He holds it gently. "I had no idea," he says.

"You couldn't have," she says. "I think you would have liked her. Loved her. I did."

Nathan Ray

1967-

It happens fast. The decision is a lightning strike in your hippocampus. You're four hours into the drive back home and you tell your father you're leaving the interstate just north of Casper and you're going where you should have gone a long time ago and you have some things to say that you should have said a long time ago. You tell him he needs to listen to you and hear them now. And that's just how it is, because you're tired, tired of all of it, and after what went on back there in Billings, you figure now's the time.

So you park the truck in front of the house in Mills that seems impossibly small here in front of your eyes, cast as it is against the predomination of your memories and your dreams, and you tell him, straight up and in full, what it means to you that she took you from this place and showed you something else. Something better. And, yeah, it didn't last, but in the long view, nothing lasts. At least you had it for a time. And, no, you say, you don't blame him, not anymore, but if he gets to reckon with his memories and come out clean on the other side, good for him, but you're going to reckon with yours and he's going to have to sit there and listen to it and take it and accept the conclusions you've reached.

You tell him he had no right to pull you back from what happened. She was gone, yes, and he was the other half of you, also yes, but you should have had a say. *You should have had a goddamned say.* You were a boy, and she did what was best for you, and he undid it after she was gone. And, yes, dammit, you own every decision that belonged to you thereafter, and no, you can't blame him for where you've ended up—that's all on you, with the chance of turning around the reversible parts still in front of you as long as you're drawing breath, as long as you're around to think about your son and what's coming for him, to think about this family you never knew you had, to get the text message from Rhonda that came that morning, telling you *the version of the guy I met who's clean, who's honest, that's somebody I'd like to see again.* Hope abides, does it not? Maybe you can find it, if you bear down and you try. It's been so long since you hoped or you tried, and here you are. It doesn't work, not hoping. Giving up. That's the end, and you're not there yet.

You tell him you all must do better, that he must do better, that it's not just you and him anymore. There's a daughter gone, a sister gone—you didn't even know her, but still you'll mourn for her—and there's Cherie, who's a granddaughter and a niece, and Brandon, who's a son and a grandson, and Brandon's own child on the way, and they're all counting on the two of you. We must do better, Dad, you tell him.

It's when he says "I did what I thought was best" that you leave the pickup and start running, because isn't that just the whole problem bundled up in a first-person excuse? We're all doing what we think is best, but we make our decisions in a vacuum, in a limited view, our own self-interest at the front of the pecking line, and we wonder where all the subsequent damage comes from. It's human vanity, and it's a wrecking ball.

You run across Poison Spider Road and you slip through the security fence and you go to the base of the tower and you start climbing, hand over hand, boot heels against the rungs below you, you don't look down, you should never look down or it's not happening. Halfway up, your bad knee gives, and you catch yourself, hanging there, one hand on the rung above and one boot on the one below, and you gather yourself, and your thought is so damned prosaic: You want to be around long enough to fight with those VA bastards about your damn knee, so you keep going. All the while, he's down there, having gotten in your truck and driven over, and he's honking and yelling. "I'm sorry," he yells. It's what you've wanted to hear, and it's right on time and entirely too late.

You crest the tower and pull yourself up and you stand atop it, and you take it all in. Mountains west, a shimmer in the afternoon heat. The neighborhood you once knew to the east. You can see the pitched roof of your old house, the backyard where you used to play, the front yard where your mother tended to her roses, Richard Miles' house two doors down from there. You remember all of that.

He's inside the fence, calling to you, telling you not to jump. He doesn't get it. You're not going to jump. You think of the gun, under the bed, in the old travel trailer if your son hasn't scrapped it yet. You think of the plans you'd made for it when you got home—lying there in that alley, you'd decided how it would be, that you'd drive the trailer onto some lonely road somewhere and finish what you started so long ago. And then you think of how you've reconsidered, just today, and how if you'd *really* been of a mind to do that, you'd have done it after you put that gun in the face of your daughter-in-law, in a stupor, out of your mind, when all she did was drive out to check on you. *Cared* about you. You think of how you chased her off, her thick fear moving her more than your addled voice and waving gun did, and you think of how there hasn't been an apology sufficient to cover it because you can't shake the shame. You think of what it's cost you, and you think, if you were ever going to do it, you'd have done it then.

You pull your phone out of your pocket and you call your son, and when he answers, you tell him what you see. You tell him you're looking due south and you can see him from where you stand, there below windblown Wyoming and colorful Colorado and the wedge of New Mexico, past the mountains and beyond the long, lonely miles. You can see him across the Llano Estacado and the cityscapes and the pillowed plains. You can see the boy, and the man, and the father to come, and have you ever told him how proud you are and that you love him? You should tell him every day, those things. You see him now, and you say you're sorry, and you need help, and can he help you? Could he help you? Please, will he help you?

And he says, "Dad, yes, I'll help, just please, please come home."

Acknowledgments

Northward Dreams wouldn't be if not for the lifetime of memories and lived experiences I've been granted. It is, undeniably, a work of fiction, but that work has been informed by the people I've known, the places I've lived, the things I've seen and done, and the inscrutable factors in each that have preoccupied me. In short, I'm grateful for everything, even those things I profoundly regret. Maybe those things most of all.

More practically, the following people deserve thanks for their contributions:

Nalini Akolekar, my wonderful agent, who advocates for my stories and is a seemingly endless well of perspective and encouragement. This one was tougher than most.

My beta readers, in particular Courtney Shultz and Kathi Fitzgerald, who delivered encouragement and actionable feedback. The story is better for your contributions. My life is better for your friendship.

Michael Gilluly helped me with the police stuff, a small part of the story but something I didn't want to get wrong. Appreciate you, my friend.

Monte L. Hurlbert for that wonderful painting that graces the cover pages. His bio says he's been "an artist, a con artist, a boxer, a fisherman and a horse skinner." To that, I add friend.

The colleagues and friends who've offered endorsements of this book in particular and/or the sustenance of fellowship in my daily life: Malcolm Brooks, Giano Cromley, Jonathan Evison, Carrie La Seur, Caroline Patterson, Richard and Kristina Ford, Cheryl Unruh, Margo Turley, Dina Brophy, Scott McMillion, Bob Kimpton, Craig Huisenga, Corby Skinner, Jim Thomsen, Dan Gray, Maggie Anderson, Duella Hull, Amy Smith, Cass Sullivan, Mark and Tam Miller. The list goes on, as does my gratitude.

Independent bookstores everywhere, and in particular This House of Books in the town where I live. Long may you stand.

My family, whole scads of them, Lancasters and Clineses and Conniffs and Lorellos and Mottolas and Vandivers. Love to all, every last one of you.

Finally, to Elisa. My best friend and companion.